Confessions of a Swedish Mediocrity

Karin Oswald

©Cover photo by Weronica Fremenius

© Karin Oswald 2016
Förlag: BoD – Books on Demand, Stockholm, Sverige
Tryck: BoD – Books on Demand, Norderstedt, Tyskland
ISBN: 978-91-7699-300-2

Everything started with a plastic knight figurine.

My friend Pontus had his own play room, filled with building bricks, train track, car garage and all things that were every boy´s dream. Our favourite was the castle with all the knights. We could play with them for hours. Almost every weekend that autumn in fourth grade I went home to Pontus, and if we promised to do our homework before we started playing, and if I promised to come home for dinner, I could follow him home on school days too. Often, that's what messed things up. Dinner was always served at five thirty at my place. A nice watch with dark blue watchband decorated my wrist, but who can keep track of time when there are evil knights to defeat and a castle to defend? Not us. The price I had to pay was coming home late, time after time. Often it was so dark that Pontus' mother had to follow me home. Not that it was far, but I was terrified of the dark.
This particular day, Pontus' mother wasn't at home. It was way past 6PM and it was pitch black outside.
-Can I borrow your phone? I asked with a small voice.
I could, of course. Fingers trembling, I dialled my home number and heard my older sister Amanda's annoyed voice. No, she really didn't want to come and meet me! It was time for me to Accept Responsibility and Consequences! I should be grateful if there was any food left for me when I got home! *Click. *
Pontus and I looked at each other.
-You could sleep here, he suggested lamely, fully aware of that we never were allowed to have a sleepover on a school day. He was just as afraid of the dark as I was, even if he didn't want to admit it, so for him to follow me home was not an option.
Tears were burning behind my eyelids. I would never be late again! Never ever!

That's when Pontus got his idea, that has stayed with us over the years. With a dramatic gesture, he grabbed a knight figurine in armour.
-This, he explained solemnly, is Knight Pont-du-John! He is asking you to Challenge Your Fear! Defeat the Darkness, and Knight Pont-du-John will stay with you and protect you from this day into eternity!
Almost hypnotized, I reached for the figurine. A challenge! That was nothing to sneer at.
Pontus helped me put on my jacket, as if it was a suit of armour. In the doorway, he saluted me. It felt as if I was going on a real adventure, on a Quest!
I was afraid, but I made it home! Breathless and proud I called Pontus before I took my coat off.
-I did it! I made it!
-I knew it! Please, keep Knight Pont-du-John for Time and Eternity, you brave Knight Johan!
Devoutly, I beheld my new talisman and made a space for him on the top shelf in my wardrobe, out of reach from my little sister, who might find him irresistible, and inevitably would put him in her mouth and suffocate. That's no destiny for a knight!

From that day on, this inspiring plastic knight helped us both whenever one of us could use a little extra encouragement, stood at a crossroad in life or if we simply wanted to challenge each other, for fun or in more serious matters. Pont-du-John was the one who made Pontus learn to ride a monocycle, and who gave me courage to go on a language course abroad with Lisa after ninth grade. And now, he's the reason why I'm writing this book.
-Everybody's lives are interesting, claimed Camilla, Pontus' girlfriend, with the same conviction that she always had when she talked about something that was important to her at the moment.

We had enjoyed a three-course dinner at their place and had reached dessert, a lovely apple pie with homemade custard, when she started talking about the writing class she was taking on Wednesday evenings.
-It's all about how you're telling the story, not necessarily what you're writing about! A boring author could make a most exciting life story seem like a desert, while a skilled actor may make the telephone book sound interesting. A life story that might seem mediocre and dull can completely capture you if it's told in the right way!
-Like mine, I commented dryly and cut another piece of the pie.
Camilla nodded with a broad smile.
-Exactly!
Pontus was loyal enough to protest.
-You're no mediocrity, Johan!
-Right. I get up, I go to work, I go to bed. I would like to see who could make an interesting story about that!
Camilla is a nice girl, but she's not very sensitive. She went on:
-But that's the point! You're actually the most mediocre person I know, what if your life still could be interesting to read about? It's no big feat to write an intriguing story about Ingrid Bergman or Raoul Wallenberg, people who have done something with their lives, but you? You don't do anything! Your life would be a challenge to narrate!
I shrugged. No need for comments, that's the way it is. Neither tall nor short, neither dark nor light hair, neither stupid nor smart, the image of Average, with no wish for being anything else than what I am. As my ex threw in my face once, I have no ambitions whatsoever.
Pontus suddenly got a glimpse in his eyes.
-I challenge you!
-Say what?

With a shrewd smile he got up and searched in one of the kitchen cupboards. I had made him keep an old chipped cup that had belonged to his grandmother, since it had the exact volume of a "coffee cup", a common measurement in old recipes. In this very cup, Pont-du-John stood at attention.
-I challenge you to write The Story Of Your Life! Confessions of a Mediocrity!

So, that's what I'm doing now. It took some time to convince me, though. I really don't want people to read about me, but since that was the point, to see if my life could be interesting, Pontus told me to write in English. That would place some distance between me and the people who might read my story.
My English is quite good, in the sense that I can read in English without having to look up words, because the context explains them enough, and I choose English subtitles when I watch a DVD in that language. Most Swedes my age have a decent passive vocabulary. But it's a whole different matter to write. In some ways, you could compare it to looking at a painting. You might not understand the technique, but you can see that it's different shades of yellow, purple, green, whatever, and you can describe it very well. ”This yellow is more mustard than lemon, and this pink has a salmon hue.” But when you have to paint yourself, you stand there with just the basic colours, having no idea whatsoever how to mix them to get the exact nuance you are searching for. That's what it feels like when I try to write in this foreign language. How can I describe the look on Pontus' face when he challenged me? Or how my voice sounded when I called Amanda that day? Now, that is a challenge! And don't even get me started in how on earth I will be able to interpret the way Lisa talks. She has a very academic

language, that sometimes can be difficult to understand even in Swedish. But I'll give it a go. With the dictionary in one hand, I will try to get through this. Even if I have to stop every minute to look up a word. I would understand the word "unicycle" or "monocycle" if I came by it in a text, but they weren't in my active vocabulary. Also, my use of grammar, the word order and prepositions would make Lisa's mother faint if she saw. But hey, there are enough books in correct English in this world. Let this be the first in Swenglish! You can understand what I'm trying to tell you, right? Everything doesn't have to be perfect. I will use the spell checking program before I print it (if I ever do, this might be the shortest book in history, or I will chicken out if it ever gets finished), and see if my friends Peter and Lydia in Hastings might give me a hand with the grammar, but as for the rest, well, if you're good at English, feel free to smile at me, if you're not, then I'm sure you will forgive me and recognize my struggle.

To begin with, I want to tell you that I won't sound authentic when I describe my own lines. The thing is, I stammer. "A stammerer" some people call us, but that's not who I am, it's just something I do. Always have, as far as I know. Apparently, there are different ways to stammer, and all of them have to do with that the muscles for some reasons don't cooperate properly with the brain. One of the problems of stammering is that it's difficult to start formulating your speech, so that you stay silent for a lot longer than is socially acceptable. Another is that some consonants become much longer, because your mouth get stuck. Sometimes, beginning a phrase, one word is repeated several times before you get started. In my case, I get totally silent in pressed situations, and almost always I get stuck on the words that start with a plosive, that is, d t k g p b. Pretty impractical when your best friend and his girlfriend are called Pontus and Camilla. You can see that it would be quite an onerous read if I wrote P-p-pontus. Why the muscles won't obey, nobody really knows, and there's a lot of research going on. My favourite theory is that the person who stammer uses the left and the right half of the brain simultaneously, and that gives birth to a clash of some kind. Freud, of course, would say that I have unresolved issues with my mom. Actually I do, but they are of a later date so I don't think I can hold my speech problem against her. I don't want to hold it against anyone or anything. Something is wrong, nothing different from having diabetes or scoliosis. It happens.

There are some exceptions, though, where my speech flows: Singing, whispering and speaking English. When I sing, I focus on other things and the brain gets tricked, I think. Whispering... Well, have you seen the movie "A Fish Called Wanda"? One of the characters have a really bad stutter, but when the femme fatale kisses him to get him relaxed enough to reveal the complicated name of a hotel where some diamonds are hidden, the words flow from his lips like a soft stream. My ex wanted to try that on me, after watching the film. To be honest, it felt a little bit humiliating, but one thing I have to give to her, she's an excellent kisser. That's what I miss the most. Anyway. She kissed me into liquid and I could say "packa pappas kappsäck" three times in a row without any problems. To pack daddy's trunk, an articulatory exercise that usually turns into "packa kappas packsäck", if you are able to get over the initial P. She laughed and said that she had cured me, which was quite hurtful, indicating that I'm sick, so that was the only time it worked with her. But I whisper a lot at my job, and then the sounds obey me. As for the

English, I really don't know. Maybe it's because the mouth is formed slightly different?

I've read a lot about stammering. I prefer that word to stutter, because it's closer to the Swedish word, "stamma". It's called "the top of an iceberg", meaning that there is a lot going on underneath it. If it is to be treated, you have to keep a holistic point of view, where you treat the whole personality. Communication, behaviour, everything. Ninety percent lies beneath the surface, and the stutter is the only obvious part. Camilla has tried to get me interested in CBT. Thanks, but no thanks. There have been enough useless sessions with speech therapists of all kinds. If anyone else has a problem with the way I speak, let them analyze themselves and leave me alone.

Here comes my first confession: I hide behind the stutter. It conceals my shyness. To be shy isn't something that is accepted in our society today. Even toddlers in preschool are pushed to assert themselves, to be more on-going. There's an expression in Swedish, "ta plats", directly translated to "claim space", meaning that you should be loud and pushy and steal the other kid's toys and... well, not meaning exactly all that, but there's a fine line between claiming space and being a pushover. To have a loud voice is considered good, to be too loud is considered a problem. So is being too quiet. There's a Swedish word called "lagom", meaning not too much, not too little. Google Translate suggests the word "moderate", but lagom is so much more than just a word. It's our nation's whole philosophy. You can become popular by crossing conventional lines, but you have to cross them lagom. Not too much.

In Sweden, there are nine mandatory grades in school. You start first grade the year you turn seven. Before that, we have the optinal preschool. When I was a kid, the

normality was that the mother stayed at home with the children until preschool. If she couldn't do that, they were sent to daycare. Today, the daycare is also called preschool and most children start when they're around a year and a half. The year before grade one is called grade zero, or preschool-class. My mother would never have left us to daycare, because what would people say if she did? It would be a disgrace, leaving your darlings to strangers! Had I been born today, she would have put me in preschool when I was eighteen months, because what would people say if she didn't? The trend changes.
We call the first three years "lowstage", grade four to six "middlestage" and seven to nine "highstage". I'll stick to those terms, because every nation has its own system. High school can mean Junior High in one nation and College in another.

The preschool teachers were worried about me, and had serious talks with my parents. "Johan needs to claim more space". I wanted to shout to them: "But I have my space! Here under the table, here is my space!" I loved being left alone with a book or a puzzle. The worst time of the day was the morning gathering, when we sat in a circle on the floor. Mondays were the worst. All the other kids – so it felt, but probably there were more amongst them like me who didn't want or didn't get the chance to speak – just boiled over with all their stories about the weekend, all at the same time, no matter if anyone listened or not.
The ones who listen, why can't they be accepted for their individuality?
My mother was concerned. Amanda had never caused any problems, she was so easy-going, were they to have a Problem Child? She didn't want that at all! And then there was the stammering. What was she going to do about that? Nothing, she was told. Many children had

speech issues, especially boys, and most of the time they
grew out of it. Just wait and see.
With me, it didn't. I'm one of that one percentage who
are adult stammers. And as I said, I use it as a shield. Of
course I'm so quiet when my words betray me! To be shy
is not okay. To have a disability that makes you shy, well,
it's not as acceptable to accuse someone for that. Some
probably say that it's connected, that I stammer because
I'm shy, but please, separate it? Shyness is a part of my
personality, the stutter is a part of my body. I wouldn't be
any different if that disappeared, I'm quite sure.

Amanda is three years older than me. She always had lots
of integrity. Instead of reading under a table, begging to
be alone with your body language and silence, she sat
reading in the sofa, using words to avoid the preschool
activities she didn't find interesting. Same wish as mine,
same but very different because she didn't radiate shyness
and that gave her a free pass.
I think we were quite an ordinary family until I started
school when I was seven. My father still works with the
local newspaper as a sort of handy man. Mother is a
hairdresser, and worked in a fancy salon with weddings
and posh parties as their speciality. She subscribed to all
the fashion magazines and loved to arrange fashion shows,
preferably with me and Amanda as models. Guess if I
appreciated that. Not. Once she managed to bribe me
into setting my foot on that intimidating runway in an
awful sailor suite, by promising me a toy boat. Like a
rabbit caught in the headlights I stood there, paralyzed.
Never in her entire life had she been more embarrassed,
she hissed at me when she lifted me up and carried me
backstage. What would people say!
That was her mantra. What would people say?
I always wondered who those ”people” were. Still do.

As a grown-up, I can understand her better and forgive her behaviour. I can't make excuses for it, but forgive. You see, my mother is also a mediocrity, but unlike me, she's not settled with that. She strives to be perfect. The one thing she could control was the surface, so the surface became the most important thing to her. The house had to be spotless, because someone might come on an unexpected visit and what would they say if they found a mess! Amanda and I always had to be clean and neat, because people might have low opinions of her motherhood if we weren't. She didn't mean to be nasty to me at that fashion show. To yell at me became like a safety valve, someone else to blame when the beautiful facade broke. Through my waking nights I've managed to comfort my five-year-self retroactively. I wish I could go back and explain to the nervous mother that those people probably would like her even more if she wasn't so desperately perfect.

Soon after I started first grade, I overheard a conversation between my parents that clearly wasn't for my ears. It was late in the evening, I went to get a glass of water because I couldn't sleep.
-Is this such a bad thing? I heard my father say in his soft voice.
-At my age! I'm forty-two! What would people say?
-Congratulations, I guess. It's a child! A miracle of life!
-But I don't want any more miracles! mother sobbed. I... I want to... make it go away!
The silence suddenly felt heavy.
I didn't understand what they were talking about. That my mom was having another child I could figure out, but to make it go away? Was that possible? Could she make me and Amanda go away too?

My dad loves children. When the doorbell rang, it wasn't
for me or my sister, it was him the children in the
neighbourhood wanted to play with. Could your dad
please come out and play some football? Indeed he could!
He built snow fortresses, made enormous piles of leaves
to jump in, taught everyone to play with marbles and
embarrassed my mother by playing horse on the bike lane.
He wouldn't want us to disappear, would he?
People. Dad knew that it was the heaviest weapon he
could use. It was quite ugly, but I guess he didn't feel like
playing fair.
-Well, if you aborted this child, that would really give
people something to talk about!
Mom started to cry.
I sneaked out and crawled under Amanda's bed and
couldn't sleep for a long time.
A few weeks later my beaming father told us that we were
having a sibling. Mom smiled faintly. Amanda was
thrilled!
-A baby sister! Oh, please, tell me that I will have a little
sister to play with?
She was ten, so she didn't mean play together with, but, as
she said, play with. Like a living doll, I guess.
Dad laughed.
-We'll see. But little brothers aren't too bad either, right?
Amanda snorted.
-Little brothers are a nuisance!
I didn't say anything.
-What's the matter, Johan? Aren't you happy about this?
My voice didn't hold.
-Hey, lad? Does it feel strange? We won't love you any
less, you understand that, don't you? It might be a little
chaotic for a while, having a baby around, but it will be
fun too.
The lump in my chest threatened to explode.

-Are you going to make it go away? I whispered.
Dad became serious, exchanging a look with my mother
who gasped.
-Go away? Nonsense, of course we won't! Whatever gave
you that idea?
-You said so. Mom said so.
Amanda seemed a bit worried as well.
-What are you talking about?
Dad tried to put the pieces of the puzzle together.
-Did you hear us the other night, son?
I nodded, feeling miserable.
Mom sat down on the nearest chair and hid her face in
her hands. Apparently, this was dad's mess to clean up. He
put an arm around my shoulders.
-To be honest, this little sibling of yours came as a
surprise for both me and mommy. When you're
surprised, you sometimes say things you don't mean. This
baby is just as welcome as both of you were. I'm sorry that
you overheard us, Johan. I understand that you got scared,
but mom didn't mean it, she was just taken by surprise
and overreacted. Can you understand that?
Not really, but it sounded reassuring so I nodded and let
it be.

The next conversation with my father was more serious.
-There's a very big chance that your little sister will have
something called Down syndrome. Do you know what
that is?
Amanda nodded.
-Some of the children in the special program at our
school have it. They're retarded. But they seem very sweet
and kind!
Dad hugged her thankfully.
-Yes... I think everything will be all right. But mom is a
bit sad. I think you will have to start practicing being

older siblings, and help out a little more here at home. Of course you will get a higher allowance. Is that ok with you?
My big, strong daddy who knew everything pleaded to his children. I felt both sorry for him and a bit scared at the same time.
Amanda, always the strong one, nodded and straightened her back.
-We'll be good, daddy! Just wait and see!

So, now you know why Amanda successively took over the household, and why my speech problems got sidelined. Dad had his hands filled with my mourning mother during that time, so he just dismissed the letters from school. Did they want me to see a speech therapist? Suit yourselves, if this is a problem for you, then it's up to you to solve it, we have more alarming things on our mind right now.
The first speech therapist they sent me to was a strange lady with ideas taken from books that embraced the theory that the reason for the defect was anxiety. We were to relaaax! Lie together on a shaggy rug and listen to Whale Songs and take deeep caaalm breaths. I was too young to object. The rug looked like a living creature, filled with dust and crumbles with an odour that I didn't want to analyze. Every Wednesday morning I was supposed to go there, and if I hadn't been anxious before, this surely made me! Once she burned incense, but then I couldn't breathe and had to go to the school nurse instead.
The next expert was of the opinion that I had learned everything wrong from the beginning, that we needed to go back to the original sounds. Mmmommy. Dddaddy. Lllook! With tears of humiliation burning behind my eyelids, I had to sit there and talk like a baby. I only went

there once, refusing to return. My classmates didn't care
that I talked funny, I didn't care either, so I couldn't see
what the problem was. Why couldn't they just leave me
alone?

It wasn't until I started highstage that I regretted skipping
these sessions. When the girls suddenly got pretty and
interesting, when you wanted to seem a bit urbane and
nonchalant. Maybe the baby talk could have worked?
Maybe there was another kind of therapy in highstage
that suited me better?

And, for the first time, highstage was when they started to
make fun of me. The first six grades I'd been spared, but
when we started seventh, we had to go to a bigger school
with new constellations. You probably know how it is.
Many feel the need to compete and in one way or the
other stand out in the new crowd. This could be expressed
in many ways. By dressing outrageously, dye your hair, be
too loud (but still lagom too loud!) or cover every skin cell
in your face with makeup. One classic way to show how
cool you are is to pick on somebody else. Naturally, I
immediately fell right in the line of fire. A group with
leather jackets, black makeup and spikes loved to tease
me. It wasn't for much longer than a few weeks, but I can
promise you, those were the longest weeks in my life! The
regrets escalated. All the guilt. Inferiority. If Lisa hadn't
stepped into my life then, I'm not sure what would have
become of me. I thank my destiny that I never have to
know.

Writing this, a Calvin & Hobbes-strip comes to my mind.
Six year old Calvin is writing his autobiography, spiced
with episodes that are imaginary.
-Why imaginary, his toy tiger Hobbes wants to know.
-Because in my book, I have a flame thrower!

If I'd been writing a fictional autobiography, I would have used catchier names than Johan, Pontus and Lisa, and I would have created one of these friend groups that maybe only exists in fantasy. You know, a group of characters that are different but still complement each other and stick together through thick and thin (in Sweden we say in wet and dry), regardless of heartbreaking ex-relations, lies and betrayals. Or I would have described us as the Three Musketeers, one for all, all for one!

The truth is, that my two best friends don't really like each other much. Lisa thinks that Pontus is a big goof, that laughs too much and is way too insecure. And he is. Pontus thinks that Lisa is loud and pushy and a know-it-all. And she is. Forgive me, my dearest friends, but you are both right and I like you just as you are. You surely have good taste, since you want to be my friends, how could I not appreciate you for that?

Seriously, I believe that every being have their own value. Nobody is worth more than anyone else. More or less easy to replace, sure, but with the same human dignity. Nobody should have a low self esteem. Yet we keep on comparing us to each other, measuring ourselves, wanting to claim a space on some kind of ladder. Better than him. Worse than her. Can we please stop doing that?

Look around you. Have you got anyone who cares for you? Anyone at all?

If you do, then you don't only have your own value, but you're valuable to someone else.

To belittle yourself is to be rude to the people who appreciate you.

I might call myself a mediocrity, but I do have friends. That makes me a valuable mediocrity!

It didn't sound very difficult when Pontus and Camilla
suggested that I should write about my life. Partly because
I didn't think there was much to write about, but also
because I thought that it would be to just write? From the
beginning to the present?
Only a couple of pages into the story I feel that the more I
write, the more I remember and the threads in the story
are hanging loose like on a lace pillow. "You need to find
a storyline and keep to it", Camilla would growl at me.
"It's impossible to read when you skip back and forth all
the time!"
Well, excuse me, I've never written a book before. Be
patient with me, please?

Back to my baby sister.
Sara was born a beautiful spring day, with a planned
caesarean because there was something wrong with her
heart. At first they didn't know how serious it was, but it
only took a few hours before she was rushed to
Gothenburg to have surgery. We have an excellent
hospital here in Uppsala, one of the biggest in Sweden,
but we don't specialize in tiny baby hearts.
Mom had been depressed ever since she found out that
the child she carried had a defect, and my father has much
later confessed to me that he was scared that she would
suffer from psychosis. But Sara's heart condition snapped
her out of that. She straightened her back, seemed to
grow several inches and declared:
-Sara will get well. I'll make sure of it!
So she went with her baby to Gothenburg and fought like
a lioness at her side. She devoted her whole life to Sara.
Maybe the beginning of my story gave you a stern
impression of Amanda, when she didn't want to come and
meet me in the dark. When she alone had cooked dinner
for herself, me and our father and had highstage

homework to attend to and was fed up with me not
checking my watch, when mom once more was in one of
the neverending visits to the hospital with Sara. Yes, she
can be quite stern, but nobody has a bigger heart than she.
When mom and our newborn baby sister was in a foreign
town, isolated from friends and family, Amanda went to
the salon and asked the owner to help her show how
much everyone missed our mother. The owner's heart
melted, and a big package was sent to the hospital with
cute little baby clothes and beautiful cards from both
customers and colleagues. We're thinking about you both!
We miss you! We long to meet your little princess! You
are so strong! Keep on fighting!
That, dearest mom, is what people say when someone's
perfect surface crackles. I wish you would have
understood that earlier, but I'm glad you finally found
out.

Sara spent her first years more in than out of hospital.
The first heart surgery was followed by a second, her guts
were tangled, and she had a cleft palate which meant that
she had to be fed through a tube in her nose to avoid
getting food in her lungs. In the beginning it felt surreal.
We hadn't got a baby, we had got... well, almost like a
kind of living Tamagotchi. At the right moment we had
to press the right buttons, give the exact amount of
nourishment at the exact right time, weigh, measure,
check the oxygen in her blood, check the pulse...
Everything focused on pure survival, and we didn't get
very much in return – until she learned how to smile!
I've never seen anyone smile like Sara! As soon as she
spotted someone she recognised, it was like the smile
started in her toes and worked its way up through the
whole body until it finally exploded as a cascade of lifejoy
and love through her eyes. The smile was our reward for

everything that felt heavy around her. If anyone sees a
child with a severe handicap and feel sorry for the child or
the family, and maybe secretly thinks that it would have
been better if he or she never had been born, I can only
shake my head at their ignorance. They don't understand.
Love is the strongest power I've ever come across. The
heart doesn't ask for usefulness. I won't deny that we took
turns crying over backlashes, crying from helplessness and
fatigue after seemingly endless waking nights, but
eventually, the morning always came. Even in the darkest
night we loved Sara and she loved us. It was as simple as
that. A simple core in a complicated and dense shell.
She became the centre of our lives, the one everyone
asked about, the first we looked for when we came home
from school. The house was depressingly empty and quiet
during the periods when she was in hospital, and so full of
life – and chaos, I won't deny - when she was at home.
Eventually, most of her defects were corrected and she
developed as normally as she could, considering the
circumstances. We learned to understand her speech. O-a
for Johan, A-na for Amanda, A-ma and A-pa. I teased her:
-I bet you also stammer, you just cheat and skip all the
silly consonants!
She laughed, not understanding the joke, but she could
hear the joke-tone in my voice and that was enough to
make her laugh!

Sara liked everyone, but I think she loved Pontus the
most.
We had known each other since first grade and were in
the same class until highstage. He had to take first grade
twice and was born in January, so he had always looked
and also been older than everyone else in our class. When
I was a kid, I figured he had everything. I've already told
you about his play room. Their house was big, an old-

fashioned stone house with spacious rooms and miles to the ceiling. He lived there with his mom and aunt, and every year he wrote "dog" or "sibling", whichever was easiest to get, on his Christmas wish list. Every year his mother was sad and tried to explain that it was impossible. His aunt was allergic and siblings... No. I never heard a word about Pontus' father. Ever. When I look at the situation with my grown-up glasses, I understand that his life might not have been as perfect as I thought then. Tons of toys are a poor substitute for a puppy or a sibling. Pontus is tall, clumsy, overweight and just as Lisa says, he laughs too much and is far too eager to please. For a while, he was popular and everyone wanted to play at his house, simply because he gave his toys away. He could do that with no regret, because he always got new ones if he asked for them. When his aunt found out that he bought his friends, the party was over for the freeloaders. That day he came to my house and cried. It was the first time he had been over since Sara was born. Mom was so worried about infections that she didn't want any strangers near the baby, and I appreciated a break from everything so I enjoyed going home to Pontus. Also, I think this thing with feeding her through the nose and all made him a bit nervous, he had never asked if he could come over. But now, one of the last days of Christmas break in second grade, after having given away all his Christmas gifts, he stood crying at our doorstep, and my mother didn't have the heart to tell him to go away.
-My aunt says that nobody is allowed to come and play with me anymore, he snivelled. Nobody except you because you never take things from me.
I won't deny my envy of his playroom, but even if he had offered me toys I would have said no. With Sara in the house, there were no more small things lying around. She couldn't move on her own, but who knew when she

suddenly would be able to crawl and put things in her mouth and suffocate. Haven't we had enough time at the hospital? Did I want us to rush to the ER with her, on top of everything else? No, of course not, books are good enough for me. Duplo? No thanks, please, that's where my dignity steps in! I'll go home to Pontus instead.
Feeling awkward, I didn't know how to comfort my friend. He always lent so much neat stuff to me, and I had nothing to give back to him to make him feel better. Unless...
-Come!
Mom was busy in the kitchen, so dad must have the Saracheck as we used to call it. He wasn't as anxious as mom, so we sneaked into my parents' bedroom where Sara was taking her afternoon nap.
-I'm not sure if I...
-Don't worry! Just come with me?
Dad smiled at us.
-Have you come to say hi to Sara? Great! She just woke up.
I explained what all the tubes and cords and devices were and how they all worked, and felt quite proud, knowing so much about important and complicated things.
-This is a pulse oximeter, where you check the oxygen in her blood. And the pulse. If the oxygen is under eighty-five, we need to give her some extra. See this tube? It's full of oxygen! If our house catches fire, the firemen have to be told that we have this, because it could be very dangerous!
Pontus nodded, full of awe before my knowledge.
Sara beheld him with her oblique, omniscient eyes. As I said, she likes almost everyone, but not without a thorough review.
-Say "buh" to her, I whispered to Pontus.
-What?

-Scare her, just a tiny bit. She likes that. Promise!
Pontus didn't know what to make of this, I could tell. He
looked at the little goblin in the crib, and tried a:
-Buh to you!
In that moment, a mutual love relationship was born.

In Sara's eyes, Pontus was nothing but perfect. In fourth
grade, he was so tall and, well, bearish that he needed to
get an ID-card because the drivers wouldn't let him buy a
child ticket on the bus.
-Us biii! Sarah yelled raptly.
-You bet, sweetpea! Pontus is biiig!
My clumsy friend laughed and lifted her up, high into the
air, and forgot all the taunting words that had been
thrown after him all day.
-Pontus is big and strong and will protect his little
princess for time and eternity!
-Yeeey!
A Beatles song always comes to my mind when I think of
Sara and Pontus together.
Love, love me do.
You know I love you.

Mom stopped working in the salon to take care of Sara.
Amanda's idea with the greetings, however, had touched
many. Children with special needs often get a special
place in people's hearts. Every little progress becomes
huge, and is in a totally different league. When they
talked about children and grandchildren in the staff room,
there was this unpleasant element of competing. I noticed
that when I was visiting before Sara was born. Oh, hasn't
little Petter learned to walk until now? Johan was up and
running when he was nine months! Amanda could indeed
read when she was four. Mom was the worst of them all,
you know, the perfect surface. But with Sara, she could

finally let her defences down. Nobody had ever expected
her to ever be able to sit up without support, but look at
this! She can do it! Look at what she can do! With all the
wishing wells safely kept in her heart, my mother started
to change. She was torn between anxiety and a wish to
keep Sara safe from infections and strangers, and the
desire to share all the miracles. So, with a mosquito net
over the pram, as a symbolic fence against all microscopic
bacteria, she often went to visit the salon. Both customers
and staff fell in love with my sister. After a few years,
when she wasn't so fragile anymore, they asked if mom
please would consider coming back to work for them
occasionally? Maybe a Saturday now and then? They truly
missed her, and she was so good with bridal hairdos!
The deal was settled. Everyone would love to see Sara
too, so we took turns in keeping watch over her at the
salon, both me, Amanda and dad. I wasn't very amused, I
admit. There are definitely more interesting places to be
for a nine year old boy on a Saturday.
This was wonderful for my mom. She flourished, dad fell
in love with her again and everything was idyllic. This is
one of the issues I'm trying to process during the nights.
I've come so far that I can understand her. After the long
period of depression, worries and sadness, she deserved to
feel good. But it would have been nice to get just a tiny bit
of her time and attention. Just a little.

Now is the time to introduce Lisa properly.
We have a wonderful word in Swedish – allrakäraste.
It's translated to ”dearest”, but it is so much stronger, it's
not the kind of ”dear” or ”love” as I was shocked to hear
people use in everyday conversation when I went to
England. I was almost afraid that the old lady in the
corner shop where we bought our daily bag of crisps had

fallen in love with me. No, allrakäraste is what you call the person you love the most.

My allrakäraste Lisa! My life saviour, my helium filled anchor, my motor.

She hit the hardest when we played rounders, she ran the fastest, climbed the highest, talked the loudest, dared everything and always talked back to the teachers if she didn't agree. She sneered at the girl´s silly games, like the quacking in the changing rooms to the pool, iiih, the boys are peeking in the tiny gap under the door! Put a towel there! Oh no, they're trying to take the towel! Well, you silly fools, what did you expect? You're so full of nonsense! Lie down on the floor yourselves and see how revealing that little gap is! A small glimpse of tiles, oh no! Boy tiles!

She also resented the boys-chase-girls-games. If anyone tried to chase her, and caught her just because she didn't run, she would ask: ”Now what?”, leaving them confused. Lisa wasn't very popular. She wasn't lagom.

Party in the fourth grade. I hated parties. Still do. Sometimes I wake up from a nightmare where Pontus is getting married, wanting me as his best man. Nowhere to hide. But Pontus really wanted to go to this party. He had spent hours in the bathroom, water combed his hair, put on aftershave which he sadly needed since he had to shave even then. Please, he didn't want to go alone, please come?

-Pont-du-John is challenging you to Dare To Go Alone, I tried and climbed up to the highest shelf in my wardrobe where I kept him, far away from Sara who considered everything to be edible.

Pontus looked like a sad St Bernard dog, big eyes and his head hanging down.

Amada meddled.

-Of course you're going to this class party! Don't be a
sissy. You never do anything, you just sit here at home or
at Pontus' place. You need to get out once in awhile, you
know!
-I bought your favourite crisps, Pontus said, mildly
hopeful when Amanda backed him up.
-Come on! I'll let you borrow my vest!
Amanda's vest... She never let anyone borrow that! It was
a fringed leather patchwork vest, the most amazing piece
of clothing that I had ever seen. I started to falter.
Authoritatively, Pontus held the figurine before me.
-The Knight challenges you to accompany your brother
in arms to face the enemy, where we will infiltrate and
expose their evil plans! It takes courage and cleverness!
Are you brave enough, soldier?
-I'll come and meet you, Amanda filled in benevolently.
The thing was, I was quite proud of Amanda. Still am.
Amanda was cool, in her own non-mainstream way. And
she was in highstage! To borrow her vest, and to be
picked up by her, that would probably give me some
points in the invisible, never resting coolness protocol.
-Eight, I muttered reluctantly, capitulating. Not a minute
later!
-Not a minute later, I give you my word of honour!

If I die and go to hell, a school class party will be one of
the levels in Dante's individually adapted inferno. To
splash it with a bit of Tabasco, there will be Truth or
Dare. And the bottle will point at me.
For a few seconds, people looked expectantly at me before
Pontus took mercy upon me and without a word spinned
the damned bottle again. You see, stammering can be very
practical sometimes! Nobody expected me to give an
answer in a pressed situation like that.
The bottle pointed at Lisa.

-Truth or Dare! the choir echoed.
-You have to pay dearly for my secrets! I will take the consequences of my right to remain silent about my innermost thoughts!
Overdramatic, is a word that Pontus also has used to describe her. And she is.
There is, or was, I'm not sure kids do this anymore, this expression called "ask chance". I never quite understood the rules. I think it was supposed to let you know if the person you asked for a chance might be interested in having a relationship with you. Whatever that meant when you were eleven. When the bottle pointed at Lisa and she chose Dare, someone exclaimed:
-Ask chance on somebody!
With an air of boredom, Lisa swept her eyes over us.
-Åsa, do I have a chance on you?
-Nooo, that's cheating! You have to ask some guy, not a girl!
-Why? Isn't this a free community? Or is your mind clouded by prejudices?
-Cut it out, Åsa snarled, not at all amused.
-Sure, if you want to stay rigid and are unable to think outside the hetero standard... Johan? Do I have a chaaance on you?
The mannered tone hurt me. Instead of hiding inside my shell, as I would normally do, something poured over inside me. First there was this stupid party that I didn't want to go to. Then there was this stupid game that I didn't want to play, and above that, I was to be scorned?
-YES! I shouted and startled all my classmates. So now we're a couple, like it or not!
Then I ran into the boy's bathroom and locked the door. Pontus came after me.
-I'll keep guard, he said reassuringly and giggled: The others have to pee in the girl's loo!

Amanda never found out what had happened when she came at eight sharp, and she was wise enough to not ask when she saw my face. My eyes, that use to be bluegreyish, were probably black. Pontus talked rushed and loudly about nothing on the way home. When we had left him at his house, it was dead silent.

When we came home, I went straight to my room and shut the door. I was torn between a wish to be alone, and a wish that someone would come in and check on me so that I could yell at them to leave me alone. And the wish for a hug.
After fifteen minutes, Amanda knocked on my door and opened it without waiting for my reply, which she knew would be ”go away!” A tray with two steaming teacups strategically placed in her hands stopped me from throwing a pillow at her.
-This is green tea, lemon flavoured! Have you ever tried green tea before? They say it's really healthy. Antioxidants and stuff. And it tastes very nice, as long as you don't have the leaves in for too long. If you do, it becomes bitter and tastes awful. I bought it today, I thought you might want a cup, and a movie starts at nine, but it's a bit scary, can't you watch it with me? Mom's out with her girlfriends, and dad has the Saracheck. I can make popcorn.
I stretched my fingers. Studied my fingernails.
-What movie?
-Aliens.
I sneered.
-That's not scary! It´s not for real, you know.
Just let me tell you – no movie of any kind can scare me as much as the thought of speaking in public.
-Well, it is to me. Please?

Amanda has never been able to say the words "I'm sorry".
But you don't need words to express regret, and I´m not
the one who holds grudges. Tonight wasn't her fault. All
she wanted was for me to have a fun evening.
-Okay, but I'll get to hold the popcorn bowl!
-No way! I make the popcorn, I get to hold the bowl!
Then I threw that pillow on her, the tea tray at a safe
distance, and we were friends again.

-You've got a letter, Johan!
The surprised tone in my father's voice was justified, since
it was Saturday and we don't get any mail on weekends in
Sweden. We do get the morning paper though, and with
it, there was an envelope addressed to me. Inside, a
beautiful hand drawn card, a black rose with thorns, and
the word "Sorry" in calligraphy.

On Monday, everything seemed to be back to normal.
Some new couples, some breakups, a little giggling and
whispering, but nothing out of the ordinary.
-So, you and Johan? someone tried to tease Lisa.
-Me and Johan forever, Lisa declared without looking at
me.
Agreeing nod from me.
Me and Lisa forever!
Our relationship was happy and without conflicts, because
we barely spoke until highstage. Nothing strange about
that, we didn't have much to do with each other before
either. She was far too overwhelming and intimidating,
not only in my eyes but to most people. She was always
questioning and arguing, never accepted any simplified
explanations or to be treated as a child, even though she
was. She dismissed the arts&crafts supplies with
contempt. Dirty water colours in cracked blocks, how
could we possibly be inspired by that? The piano in the

classroom, when was the last time a piano tuner paid it a visit? And, beg your pardon, the textbooks, were they perhaps written to suit chimpanzees? The fight for better books was in vain, but she managed to find a retired organist who tuned the piano for free, and after about a ton of letters to the art supply shops and all the foundations she could think of, they donated some materials to us. Don't even think about messing with the colours, show the material some respect, will you!

Mostly, the teachers let her be. They had learned their lesson. If they tried to silence her, they got a vivid lecture about freedom of speech and democracy. Trying to argue with her was useless, even at the age of ten her rhetoric could make a politician dizzy.
Every year, we eagerly looked forward to the arguments about Lucia. Pronounced Lu-sii-a, this Swedish feast on the 13th of December has deep pagan roots, so deep that it had to be painted over with Christian colours. There is no reason at all why the Italian saint Lucia should be regarded by us in the North, except for the similarity to the name of the old tradition Lusse. There are Lucia processions everywhere. Lucia herself is dressed in a long white gown, a red ribbon around her waist and a crown of candles in her hair, electric or real depending on age and if you're indoors or outside. Her maids have tinsel in their hair instead of the crown. Both they and the Star Boy are dressed in the same long white gowns as Lucia. The Star Boy is wearing a very tall pointed white hat with stars, holding a golden paper star on a stick, trying to not feel like a big nerd. You can also dress as a Gingerbread Man or an elf. In kindergarten, everyone who wants to can be Lucia. When you're a bit older, there is only one Lucia, most of the time chosen by vote. Every club, every stable, every town, every school have their own Lucia, and there

is a Lucia of Sweden as well, preferably with long blond hair. Sounds Italian, right? Anyway, Lisa resented gender role. She claimed that anyone who wanted to should be given the chance to be Lucia, and you should be allowed to choose any role in the procession. Once, one boy actually did dress as a maid, grinning, trying to be funny. He quickly regretted that. The Star Girl gave him a flaming speech about respect, which made him feel silly rather than funny.

We admired her, we were scared of her, we kept away from her.

Sometimes the classes don't change at all during the nine years of mandatory school, except of course if somebody moves, but sometimes it's considered good for the children to mix them up. You can't have kids getting too attached to each other, they have to get to know other people as well! That was the idea when I started highstage. All the apparent friend constellations were torn apart. Especially the girls took this really hard. Female friendship is a bit different from relations between boys. The parents tried to protest, but in vain. You have to Learn How To Get Along with Everybody! Try that in any adult workplace. Do you work well together? Too bad, then we have to split you up. Have you got issues with someone? Great, then you will Learn!

Obviously, Pontus and I were separated. Lisa also went to a different class, and I soon discovered that I missed her. The lessons were much duller when a teacher just stood there talking, with nobody talking back.

This was a bigger school, more students and more teachers. Some could handle Lisa well, some not at all. Her reputation grew quick and wide, it wasn't long before everybody knew who she was. The troublemakers in black leather, the ones who gave me a hard time, wanted her in their gang. All dressed in black, dyed black hair and heavy black makeup, she would fit in, right? She just sneered. Skip classes to hang around in the corridors, shouting abusive words to passer-bys, just exactly how stupid did they think she was?

-L-l-look! The-the-there's the p-p-poor l-l-little s-s-sissy who c-c-can't t-t-talk p-p-properly!

As usual, I lowered my head, trying to hurry past them. Then I bumped into someone who seemed to have turned on her heel.

-You imbeciles! Has it escaped you that it's the plosives that are causing him trouble? If you're so determined on wasting your microscopic bit of brain capacity to inveigh against your fellow man, then at least do it on correct grounds!

They didn't like that, I can tell you. Not that they understood everything she said, but they were smart enough to get that she, as Lisa would have said, affronted them right back.

-Ey, look how cute she is, defending her boyfriend!

Approving laughter from the entourage.

-You bet I'm defending my boyfriend, and I can easily find out where you miserable creatures dwell.

-Wha?

-Where you live, you morons!

I just stood there, dumbfounded, with a strange out-of-body experience.

-Ooh, so you're going to come and scaaare us? Mommy, help!

The laughter got louder, but Lisa calmly explained:

-I would never condescend to something so disgusting as to approach your foul nest. Besides, you're far too dense to be frightened. However, I will call your mother, and your father, and your older brother -

One by one she pointed at them and told them what their family was about to hear. One apparently had tried to break into the girl's bathroom. The other would be said to have stolen her pocket calendar and drawn genitals in it. The third was told that his parents were going to receive a letter, saying that their son had to go to a gynaecologist as soon as possible.

-Don't think that I won't do it. Idiots like you shouldn't be allowed to roam free. You're lowering the IQ of the entire school by ninety percent just by breathing! Remember that I said that I worried about how I would be able to describe how Lisa talks? It wasn't very difficult after all. I look in a dictionary and use the strangest word I can find.. She doesn't always talk like a dictionary, though. Mostly, difficult words are something she uses as a weapon. Or a shield.

With those final threats, she put her arm under mine and dragged me away from them.

-You okay? She asked

I nodded. Even though I'm shy, I don't blush often, but this was enough to raise the temperature in my cheeks, in my heart, in my whole body.

-I don't remember us breaking up, do you?

My headshake was just as vivid as my earlier nod had been. No, we never did break up after that miserable party where I affectively declared our relationship, simply because I never took it seriously. Didn't think she even remembered it.

-So, we're together then? Lisa and Johan forever?

Carefully I peeked at her. Was she serious, or was this just another rhetorical trick?

She looked earnest though. I still hadn't quite landed from the surreal feeling from the confrontation with my bullies yet, my head was kind of disconnected and I felt my lips form the words:

-I... I... well. Yes. Ok.
-Really?
-Really.
A smile emitted from her eyes, onto her face. Under that
tough surface, she suddenly looked soft and for the first
time I realised how pretty she was. My girlfriend? Really?
Did I have a girlfriend now? A small seed landed in my
stomach, grew rapidly and made my back straight.
-Where are you going now? she asked me.
-English lesson.
-I'll come with you.
A swish went through the classroom when we entered the
room. Johan, who almost never said anything, whom you
didn't notice, the one you forgot, there was supposed to
be 27 in our class but only 26 present, who is missing, why
can't we remember his name, it was a boy, right? And
Lisa! Lisa, whose name was on everybody's lips. What was
going on here? The curiosity felt like carbonic acid in the
air.
The teacher wasn't amused, though.
-Well well, young lady, I think you must have chosen the
wrong door. You don't belong to this class. Please leave.
-We live in a free country. I have a free period. If I choose
to improve my English together with my boyfriend, it
would be lamentable if a teacher was to deny me.
Undeniably a bit difficult to respond to.
-Hrm. Well, as long as you behave!
-Agreed, Lisa smiled and sat down on the empty chair
next to mine.

Soda pop in my veins.
Those are the best words I can use to describe how this
felt.
My dad and Sara loved hugs, so I did get affectionate
contact, but to have somebody who wasn't a family

member this close was something new and totally amazing! Someone who held my hand in the corridor, what a long shot!

We were met by tantalizing cheering in the corridors. I bent my head again, expecting derision, but Lisa answered them with a wide, disarming smile, quite unlike her usual sharp replies.

-Do you want us to hang out after school today, at your place? she asked me when this magical school day reached to its end.

-If you like.

-Yes, I would. If not, I wouldn't ask. That is something you have to learn, Johan, I don't enjoy superficialities. If I ask how you feel, then I really want to know, not the automatic ”I'm fine” even though I can see you're bleeding. I would never ask things just to be polite. Ok?

-Ok.

-In return, I promise to take everything you say seriously. I know that we're considered far too young to know anything about deep relationships, but I don't want any nonsense between us, ok? I'd rather end this here and now.

A hand of ice squeezed my heart. No! I did not want to end this! Five hours of being Lisa's boyfriend, was that all I would get? Not if I had a say in this!

-I'd be happy if you wanted to come home with me, I said firmly and took her hand.

Her smile returned.

I think that's when I started to love her.

My family was just as surprised as my class when Lisa showed up and with ease claimed her space in our kitchen.

-Hi, I'm Lisa, Johan's girlfriend, she introduced herself and stretched out her thin hand to my parents.

My dad was the first to regain his composure.

-Lisa, ah, yes, I know you from the school photo from last year! Haven't you been in Johan's class for quite some time?
-Yes, that's correct, but not anymore. I'm in 7C now.
The sound of a new voice in the kitchen brought Amanda to us, to see what was going on. She had the Saracheck and was playing horse with her. Six years she was now, our little champion, short and almost as wide as she was tall. No, not really, but she did look like a little gnome. She had grown so much in every aspect! After her cleft palate surgery she could eat solid food, and she spoke so well that anyone who made an effort could understand her. Part of the diagnosis is that the oral cavity is shaped a bit differently, so that the tongue seems too big compared to the mouth, which makes it hard to articulate. She still put small things in her mouth, almost compulsively, so we still had to take turns watching her.
-You're Amanda, right? And Sara? Hello. I make the best hot chocolate in the entire world. Do you have any milk? I could make a snack for everyone, if you'd like ? I'm always hungry when I come home from school, it's so exhausting to be forced to spend a whole day inside a flock of sheep. Would that be ok? Or maybe you don't want me to poke around in your cupboards? Some people are a bit sensitive when it comes to that.
My poor mother just stood there, nonplussed.
-Well – yes – that would be fine. Fine. Of course. Just help yourselves!
-I'll make some for you too if you like, for all of you, but I think Johan and I should retire so that we can do our homework. Or perhaps you do it after dinner? I prefer to have it done with as soon as I come home, that makes the evening mine to do whatever I please. What do you think, Johan?

Everybody turned their eyes to me. Could I please answer all their questions, at once and simultaneously if possible? Who was this person? How did this happen? And what to do with the chocolate and homework?

Exalted, Sara sighed:

-Chocklate!

Mom came to life.

-But of course! A cup of hot chocolate would be lovely! I'm afraid my cupboards are a bit untidy, tell me what you need and I'll see if I can find it!

Naturally, not a single little spice jar stood out of line in my mother's cupboards, and by offering to help, she made sure it stayed that way.

Lisa commanded, measured ingredients - Really, cinnamon and black pepper and salt? Trust me! - and talked and stirred and made six cups of hot chocolate. She was so dominating that I actually waited for her to lead the way to my room, which of course she couldn't since she had never set her foot in our house before. She laughed.

-After you, my love!

A hot wave went from my toes to my hairline.

Her love! That was me!

I'll pause in this living dream by telling you about how we address each other in Sweden. We never use the surname, unless it's to distinguish between people with the same name. For example, there are six Maria where I work now, and if more than one of them are working the same shift, we need the surname or a nickname to tell them apart. A surname can also be used as a nickname, especially among teenage boys. That's a bit cool. But never ever would we call an adult "Mr." or "Mrs." or "Ms." whatever. Our friends' parents are called by their first name, and so are our teachers. This has not been the case for very long, though. It wasn't until the late 1960s that people started saying "du" to each other, which is the singular form of "you". The plural form is "ni", which was used to mark a distance, and there were a lot of titles thrown around, lots of status ladders, and grammatical somersaults to avoid the awkwardness if you didn't know if the person you spoke to was above or below you on this ladder. Such as "Perhaps it would be pleasing with a cup of tea?" Fortunately, all this has changed. So, having Lisa talk that way to my parents wasn't strange in itself. The weird thing was having Lisa in our kitchen.

My room wasn't much to brag about. A bed, a desk, an armchair, a wardrobe. No bookshelf, because Sara might climb on it. Nothing smaller than a fist, because she would try to eat it. She ignored sharp things, fortunately, so I could have pencils on my desk, but it was still quite a stripped down place.

Lisa put the tray with our cups on my desk, closed the door and leaned her back against it.

-Phuuu! she exhaled and closed her eyes. Then she looked at me and continued:

-Dear Gods, I was so nervous! Could you tell?

Lisa nervous? I didn't think she ever was.

-No, not at all, I assured her.

-Could we cuddle a little on your bed while the cocoa is cooling? I need to recover.

Cuddle on my bed. Sure. Most natural thing in the world. I woke up this morning as the usual Johan, Johan the Mediocrity, and suddenly someone turned the world upside down and I'm the king of the entire Universe. Of course we can cuddle on my bed! I'd better enjoy this while I can, because tomorrow I will wake up from this dream, just being Johan again.

Isn't it strange, how perfect someone can fit on your
chest? As if there had been a Lisa-shaped void right next
to me, that now was filled. Her hair smelled of lavender.
Even today, I'm awashed by this memory when that scent
fills my nose. This moment was, without comparison, the
happiest in my life. A bit sad for a grown man maybe, that
his happiest day was in his early teens, but this was so
magical that it would take another miracle to trump it.
I did lie to my ex, though. She once asked me to tell her
about the best day in my life. It was quite early in our
relationship, that is, when we still wanted to know these
cute things about each other. I didn't think my true
answer would be very popular, so I had to say: ”The day I
met you, of course.” What else could I say? The day I met
her was not even my top-ten greatest days, in fact, it
wasn't a very good day at all, since I... Oh, well, I'll tell
you all about that later. Let's just say that all of my best
days include Lisa and my ex didn't like her. At all.
-I'm not sure if I'd like to kiss, Lisa whispered against my
neck. Is it ok if we wait?
-Yes, that's ok.
As if this wasn't enough for me, just having her near me!
-I've liked you for so long. Did you know that?
-No. I had no idea.
-Do you like me?
-Yes, I do.
-For real?
There was no trace of the confident girl who just an hour
ago had declared the rules of our relationship. If you said
something, you meant it. However, my gut feeling told
me that this was not the time to remind her.
-Yes. I like you a lot. For real.
With a little relieved sigh, she nestled against me and fell
asleep.

I tried to relax every muscle I had, in fear of waking her up.
My girlfriend was sleeping on my arm.
My girlfriend.
Allrakäraste.

Discreet knock on the door.
-Dinner's ready. We set the table for Lisa too, if she would like to eat with us.
Startled, Lisa sat up.
-I'm sorry!
-About what?
-I fell asleep!
-No harm in that. Do you want to have dinner with us?
-Dinner? Homemade food?
-Yes?
A hint of yearning on her face.
-Yes, please! That would be very nice!
The meals at our house weren't exactly peaceful, so I was a bit worried about what Lisa would think. My mom was too, I could tell, but not to offer her food had been bad manners. We tended to avoid guests during meals. Just because Sara could eat, didn't mean that she wanted to. Every meal turned into a fight and a circus. Meatballs were thrown across the room, spaghetti was stuck in the ceiling and soup was something we hadn't seen on our table for ages. Amanda had tried to suggest that Sara might be disturbed by us and needed to eat before the rest of us, that is, a concealed wish for us to get some peace and quiet, but my mother wouldn't hear of it! We were a family, right? Families ate together! End of discussion. Lisa carefully watched Sara. Turned her eyes to the rest of us to see what our strategies were. Dad used to play aeroplane with the food, sometimes that worked. Amanda pretended that it had rained on the food, wet meatballs

hanging on the fork, dripping into Sara's mouth. Mom tried to coax, speaking baby language. I didn't do anything.
Sara yelled:
-No wanna meatballs!
For the first time ever I was ashamed of my sister. On this day I wanted to at least seem a little cool and impress the person that for some inscrutable reason had nominated herself to be my girlfriend. What if she never wanted to come back after this!
Lisa pinned a meatball on her fork and looked at it sternly, long enough to catch everyone's eye, even Sara's when she realised that she no longer was the centre of attention. Butterflies of worry flew in my stomach. What was she doing? Was it true what they said in school, that she was a psychopath? Had I invited a crazy fork-murderer into our home?
When Lisa felt Sara's eyes on her, she chopped the meatball with her teeth and chewed with exaggerated movements, and exclaimed:
-Gotcha!
You could almost cut the silence around the table with a knife. Lisa repeated the procedure, this time with a potato.
Sara laughed.
-Me too! Me wanna!
Hesitating, I caught a meatball on her fork. Her eyes nearly crossed when she stared at the food and attacked it.
-Gotcha! she imitated, and laughed so hard that she nearly fell of her chair.
Tears were glittering in my mother's eyes.
-What do you all say about apple pie for dessert? I suddenly feel like baking!
It was indeed the best day of my life.

Had this been fiction instead of a true story, I probably
would have added some Dark Secrets to Lisa. She seems
to be the type, right? Precocious, ambitious, litigious.
Surely, she has some kind of problems with self harm,
anorexia, drugs, depression, something?
Some years later she was involved in things I really didn't
care for at all, but in her teens, she didn't have problems
with any of the above. Do you know why?
Thanks to me.
It was one of the most touching moments of my life when
she explained this to me. We sat on the roof on her tall
student residence hall, one of those lovely blue nights in
the spring, cuddling under a blanket. Nights are made for
deep thoughts and conversations. The time is stretched
out and flows in a different rhythm than during day time.
In the night, there is plenty of room for long pauses in a
dialogue. I love nights.
Suddenly Lisa asked:
-Are you aware of that you have saved my life?
I wasn't and asked her to explain.
-I was so tired. Tired right into my very bones, of all the
superficial, childish people in school. Both teachers and
students. Tired of fighting all the time, tired of trying to
squeeze something useful out of the tedious lessons. How
I longed for highstage, thinking that surely there would
be at least some challenges, that the demands would be a
little higher, that I would get some intellectual
stimulation. Hoping the kids would be a little more
mature. Sure, I guess that the workload was a bit heavier,
but the puerility took unbearable expressions, don't you
think? Overnight, the girls transformed into Ladies with
makeup, perfume and pumps, languishing for the urbane
young men in grade eight and nine, and it was impossible
to have a decent conversation with any of them! And the
boys hadn't quite filled their new shoes, chuckling,

scuffling, not knowing which foot to stand on. *Sub Rosa*, Johan...

Sub Rosa, under the rose, this is for your ears only. I didn't know then what it meant, but I looked it up.

-*Sub Rosa*, I went through Kerstin's medicine cabinet to look for something that would either help me endure, or help me end it all.

My heart almost shrunk of retroactive fear, and I put my head against hers. Kerstin was Lisa's mother, who took painkillers for breakfast, lunch and supper, just to be proactive. She didn't have time for headache.

Lisa continued:

-At the same time, I didn't want to give up. I'm far too clever. Too intelligent to start smoking or fall back on any other stupid ways to distract me from the misery. My body is my temple, the only tool I have to fight back against everything I think is wrong. I want to change the world, so I need my body intact. I don't fit in, but it's not my fault, it's the society, this damned, superficial, material community, I wish it could get anorexia and starve itself instead of having the people who try to survive in it collapse under its pressure. I won't play a part in this farce!

I still didn't understand my role in all of this, but then she turned her head against me and looked me straight in the eyes. Not many human beings are allowed to do that, I can tell you. Eye contact is scary. I'd rather look away, or focus on the corner of the eye. Feels much safer.

-When they started teasing you, Johan... I couldn't let that happen. My fight against the entire school culture was like Don Quixote fighting against all the windmills in Holland. You became my Dulcinea, someone to fight for. If you were with me, they might leave you alone. I wanted to save you. I felt so noble!

-Well, you were right, I mumbled and turned my eyes to the crescent. Of course I've always suspected that she only felt sorry for me, but to hear it said out loud still hurt.
-My dear Johan...
Lisa's voice was soft and tender, and she put her head against my shoulder.
-It didn't take more than a few days before I understood that it was the other way around. You saved me. You accepted me for who I was. For who I am. You never wanted to argue with me just for the sake of arguing. You never yelled at me, complaining about the way I looked or talked or was, you just... you were there for me. I could relax with you. Rest in your presence, rest from all my battles. You're the only one that I can sleep peaceful right next to. Everything is simple and easy when I spend time with you. With you, I can stand myself. As long as you like me, I can endure life. Do you think that is selfish?
Her hair still had that intoxicating lavender scent, and I inhaled her. As I told you in the beginning of my story, I have similar thoughts – as long as I have friends, I am valuable. With my nose buried in her soft curls I shook my head.
-No, I don't think it's selfish at all. I'm glad that you're alive. Stay that way, please?
She gave a laugh. Or maybe a sob.
-Yes. I promise. As long as I have you, anyway.

Back to highstage, this cocoon where children enter and pupate in groups to hopefully exit as some kind of individuals.
My highstagetime was good, thanks to Lisa. I was head over heels in love, and I'm sure many of you know how selfish you become when you're in a relationship. Or maybe selfish isn't the right word. Twoish. Absorbed by the twosome.

What about Pontus?
This hurts. Confessions, right? Confessions of an egoist.
Confessions of a quite normal, amorous teenage boy who
more or less forgot his former best friend.
Maybe it wasn't quite that bad, but not far from it. At
least during the first year.

As I told you, our class was shattered. The gym classes
were however segregated, so that the girls didn't have to
share lessons with hormone-fuelled boys who stood
nonplussed with mouths stupidly wide open. So many
bouncing breasts so close was too much for us. Sometimes
we were forced to have joined classes, when the logistics
with the two separate gym halls for some reason clashed,
but that always turned into chaos. Anyway, on these
lessons or what you should call it, Pontus and I kept
together. At almost every lesson, there were these endless
task of working in pairs. A perfect opportunity to add to
the exclusion of the outcast. Kalle, did you end up alone
again? Ok, then you have to be three in a group, who
wants Kalle? Hey, I won't listen to complaints! Someone
has to take him. Or we would play something in teams,
where the two most popular boys could pick their team
and yet again consolidate the ranking. But Kalle, are you
chosen last again? What a coincidence!
I'm sorry if I'm a bit categorical, but how about adding a
little common sense to the mandatory skills taught in the
teachers training program?
-Pontus can be goalkeeper! He fills up the whole cage!
-Why can't we play floor ball anymore? Because Pontus
takes all the sticks and uses them as toothpicks!
-Pontus has to be the last one to leave the pool, if he
leaves, there won't be any water left!

These are just some of the lines that were thrown at him
at gym class. Funny jokes, no harm in that, our so called
teacher thought.
In the corridors, he was called things a lot worse.
Incredible how inventive people are when it comes to
causing pain.

If I showed solidarity? If I wanted to help my large-sized
friend out of gratitude because Lisa had put herself
between me and the thugs who bullied me?
I'm ashamed of the answer I have to give you.
It's not that I didn't want to.
I just... didn't.
Quite Swedish, actually. World War II. You don't mind if
we go through Sweden to attack Norway, do you? Well...
As long as you don't hurt me!
But when it was time for those two-by-two exercises, we
had each other.
Because nobody would have chosen me either.
Two losers, one clearly bullied, one protected by a girl.
Oh yes, I can hear the protest from anyone fighting for
equality. What's wrong with that?
But if you put your idealism away, and see the situation
with the eyes of a teenage boy, I think you know exactly
what's wrong with that.

I really would like to skip this part of my story.

If I could turn back time and at least one time out of ten
not say that no, I'm sorry, I can't come home with you
today, or, no, you can't come with me to meet Sara,
because today I'm hanging out with Lisa.
Silly, isn't it? I don't even know if anyone will read this,
and if you do, I don't know you and you would never
recognise me if we met on the street. Still, I want you to

like me. I promise you that I have one or two stories later
on that will make up for at least some of this cowardly
behaviour. But it's much easier to forgive others than
yourself, isn't it?

Why are there so many films and TV-shows about
high school?
Is it the scriptwriters' way of processing how terrible it
was? Change the story retroactively, focus on everything
that seemed so cool and exciting and make themselves a
part of that? Or is it that they are the ones who were
popular during that period, but didn't have anything at all
to offer once they had graduated, and therefore
desperately cling to the golden era that once was theirs?
Or perhaps masochists who just can't resist poking in a
wound full of pus?
Just wondering.

Around Christmas in eighth grade, Lisa and her parents
were going to Egypt for a whole month. The school had
approved her absence, since she was far ahead in all
subjects. Maybe it would seem like vacation for the
teachers too, if she went away for a while.
Lisa was so excited! One day, she swore, she would travel
around the world! She wanted to set her foot in every
single nation. We went to the stationery shop and bought
the biggest, most beautiful book she could find with blank
pages. This was going to be her World Diary!
I pointed out:
-Don't forget to write about Sweden as well. Many think
that we're quite exotic. Elks and stuff.
She gave me a thoughtful glance.
-You're right, I actually didn't think of that. Ok then.
Sweden, the first of December! Today I have opened the
first door in the Advent Calendar. There was a little

rocking horse in the picture. No snow in Uppsala yet. I'm
having meatballs and lussekatter with my boyfriend Johan
at his house.
Aghast, I protested:
-Not lussekatter! You aren't allowed to eat those before
Lucia!
-Of course you can, you can eat them from the first of
Advent. That's written in the law, you know!

Maybe I should tell you about Christmas in Sweden?
Or should I first tell you about religion in our country.
Sweden is one of the most secular countries in the world.
However, we do like traditions and beautiful rituals, and
churches are indeed often very solemn places to get
married, to bless your child or to say farewell to someone.
But if you ask the parents if they actually mean it with
their whole heart, that they intend to raise the child in the
spirit of God, most of them would probably be a bit
embarrassed and squirm a little. There are Christians in
the country, of course, probably quite many, but no God
is in any way present in the overall society. There is a
political party called something like "the Christian
Democrats", but not even they would dare to use God in
their speeches. "God says it's wrong" just isn't a valid
argument. Anyone who said such a thing would lose all
credibility. But, many of us are spiritual in other ways. We
believe in something. A force, a divinity that is pure love,
maybe not our old Nordic gods, but surely there are
gnomes and fairies in our deep, enchanted forests! We
light candles for our loved ones at All Saints Eve without
believing in any god, we say our prayers to whoever or
whatever might listen out there.
So, Christmas has nothing to do with Christ for most of
us, and everything to do with traditions for most of us. It
starts with advent, the first of four Sundays before

Christmas. We have special candlesticks with four candles, and we light the first candle on the first of advent, the first and second next Sunday and so on. We also put seven-armed electric candlesticks or star-shaped lamps in the windows. It's so beautiful, because so many do this and it's like a warm, welcoming glow from the houses! I really miss that in January. Then, on the 13th of December, there's Lucia which I've already told you about. Then – and not before then if you ask me, but some, like Lisa, think it's alright from the first of advent – you eat lussekatter. That's a sweet saffron bread shaped into an S, with raisins in the centre of the two hooks. Even the ones who don't like raisins put them in the dough, and then take them out again when they're about to eat the buns. We make gingerbreads too, of course, and lots of candy. Butterscotch with almonds can be found in many houses this time of year. Christmas trees and plenty of decorations, of course. Or... plenty compared with the rest of the year. Very few compared with some of the American decorations. To put blinking lights on your balcony or in the garden will make you unpopular with your neighbours. It should be lagom, you know.
We celebrate Christmas on the 24th, with food, gifts and at 3PM, well over a third of the Swedish population (I wanted to say "almost everyone, but I googled it to be correct) is watching "Kalle Anka och hans vänner önskar God Jul", that is, Disney's Christmas Special. Kalle Anka is the Swedish name of Donald Duck.
Christmas is for families, which makes it a stressful time of year for lonely people. Lisa's parents don't celebrate Christmas at all, they think it's just nonsense, so I wanted to invite her to spend the day with us. At first my mother was reluctant, even though she loved Lisa after that first time when she got Sara to eat, she wants it to be just us on Christmas. No other relatives, definitely not friends. On

this day, everything is supposed to be as it always has
been. The same china, the same special glasses with our
names painted on it, the same food of course. It's a
miracle that she agrees to have different gifts. Sorry, that
was a mean joke. But, when we talked about Christmas
one day when Lisa was around, and Lisa shrugged and
said that it wasn't anything special, that she had pizza
from the freezer last Christmas Eve or if it was Christmas
Day, what's the difference, my mother was shocked. This
was too sad! So she invited Lisa, made a glass and stocking
for her, and said that she was welcome to stay for the
whole holiday. That she did. She was amazed and
overwhelmed, and fell asleep on my lap during
Kalle Anka.

When Lisa had left for Egypt in mid-December, I did
what most grass widowers do when they suddenly find
themselves without company – expected that the world
outside my bubble was exactly as I had left it, and looked
for my old friend.
There he was, by the window, at the end of a long table,
crouching, trying to be invisible.
Long tables in a dining hall is another arena for the Game
of Power. The Kings and Queens in the middle with the
court spread around them according to the pecking order.
Long tables for the outcast meant a place in the corner
followed by empty chairs, and maybe some dissatisfied
group who couldn't find a place at the other end.
I started walking towards his table, but stopped when I
saw two rather good-looking girls saying hello to him,
seating themselves in the middle of that table. What was
this? What had happened during my internal twosome-
exile?

Hesitating, I closed in on him, not sure if I would disturb
him or save him by keeping him company. He looked up
and gave me a nod, and then I sat down opposite him.
-Who are they? I whispered.
He mumbled something to his wilted lettuce.
-What did you say?
-Comrade supporters.

The thought was good. In theory. Kamratstödjare,
comrade supporters, handpicked and tutored to help and
encourage the exposed and excluded. The problem was,
that in many cases, it was the bullies themselves that were
comrade supporters, giving them even more power to
abuse. These girls were probably nice people, clueless and
well-meaning, wanted to do a good deed. They had been
taught that they didn't have to be friends with the outcast,
it was enough to do this, to sit at the same table, say
”hello”, because then he would be grateful and feel that
someone at last saw him!
In reality, by choosing Pontus' table, they pointed out to
everyone that he was so lonely that nobody but the
comrade supporters would consider sitting there. Maybe
he wanted to be invisible, rather than being pitied. This
was actually worse than when he bought his friends,
because at least he had chosen that himself.
 I've read that the comrade supporter program works a bit
differently nowadays. I truly hope so.

I'll admit that I'm a bit grumpy, but mostly, I am a man of
peace. Mostly. Bullying, however, has been like a bull's
red cape before my eyes ever since I realised how Pontus
was treated.
I have two utopian solutions.
The first, the primitive, non-constructive is that I
personally, with a cattle prod in my hand, visit each and

every school and workplace in the world. Every offensive word, every scornful giggle, every sly look will be punished with an electric shock. Sorry, but I do dream of this sometimes.

The other solution is the climate barometer and the invisible snare. Whenever the barometer indicates foul behaviour, the snare will catch the perpetrator who will be shown a film of what just had happened, and then have to analyze it, try to understand how it feels like to be on the other side. Is this the kind of person you would like to be? If you change your own behaviour, maybe the atmosphere will change too? You don't have to like everybody, that's impossible, but you can actually stop being mean. It's not that hard. Just stop. Why don't you give it a try?

Amanda has taught me the art of saying "I'm sorry" without saying those words.
-I've got the Saracheck tonight. Would you like to help?
Pontus gave me a radiant smile.
-Sure!
Thus our friendship was re-established.

When Lisa got back, I tried to spend time with both of them. Lisa and I had been together for about a year and a half and I wasn't swallowed up by the relationship anymore. I loved spending time with her, which I did a lot, but I had started to believe that it actually was Lisa and Johan forever. I was no longer afraid that she would go away if I closed my eyes for a second. And I found out that I missed Pontus. As I said, they didn't like each other much, but a lunch hour is short and Pontus was so grateful that the comrade supporters no longer took pity upon him – Lisa had scared them away by her sheer presence – so he endured her lively monologues about everything between heaven and earth. In the spare time

after school, I sometimes was with Lisa, sometimes with
Pontus. He was perfectly happy building his newest Lego
models while I was reading comic books on his bed, and
Lisa loved to just be quiet together with me, so even if I
almost always spent time with someone, it was resting
time. They also helped me with the Saracheck, which was
a great relief since she behaved so much better with non-
family members around.

Mostly, Lisa and I hung out at my place. Maybe it was
because we had food. And some air. Lisa's parents are
almost like caricatures of professors. Their big, beautiful
apartment from the early 1900s was totally cluttered with
books in all imaginable and unimaginable categories. It
might sound rather cosy, but it wasn't. Leif's book mania
is almost pathological. Nothing is to be thrown away!
Once he came home with five huge boxes of discarded
books from the library in a small countryside school that
was shutting down. He couldn't stand the thought of
destroying the books. There are piles of books
everywhere. Literally everywhere. On the shoe shelf, in
the bathroom, in the beds, on the floor in all the rooms,
on the window sills instead of flowers, in the pantry... Ok,
I exaggerate a tiny bit. There weren't any books in the
fridge. Because the fridge was mostly empty. Possibly
there was some milk for Lisa's worldsbest chocolate. The
freezer however was full of different ready meals. They
had a help every second week who filled the freezer and
tried to clean, which was a Sisyphean task. The smell in
the flat was indescribable. The scent in a second-hand
book shop can be quite pleasant, but Lisa's parents
smoked inside and the poor books are forever destroyed,
spreading only the stench of death and stupidity.
Once, we made a valiant attempt to sort the books
according to the library shelving system. During WWII,

there was fuel rationing in Sweden, so the schools were closed for one week in February. During that time, outdoor activities were arranged. After the war, this continued, now for health reasons, and it is still called Sports holiday even though some of us prefer to spend the whole week inside, playing TV games or reading comics. Lisa and I were going to spend an entire week sorting books! We made sketches of the apartment, planning where to put the different sections. So far so good. But the first book was a show stopper, so to say.
-Oh, look at this! An autobiography by an Irish fisherman! I've got to read this!
-But, we were supposed to...
-We will, later! I just want to read this first. It won't take long. You can start with something else while I'm reading.
Feeling a bit awkward, I chose a book.
-Lisa? "Teach yourself how to canalize", what category is that?
-Hm? Put that one away for now.
-But what about this one? It's in Russian! I can't even understand the letters, how am I supposed to know what it is about?
-I'll take care of it later.
In the end, we sorted five books, Lisa read thirty-seven books and I started doing crosswords.

Meeting Kerstin and Leif was a big key to understanding Lisa. When they were at home, there were endless debates about all sorts of things, with those dry, arrogant academic voices that give you the feeling that they don't really listen, they just want to win the discussion.
The first time I met them, I almost died. They engaged us – or, Lisa, I couldn't utter a single word – in an embarrassing debate about different contraceptives. Unwantingly I was told that their only child was the result

of Kerstin refusing to contaminate her body with
chemicals and Leif's laziness regarding condoms and
inability to perform such a natural and simple thing as a
coitus interruptus! What kind of contraceptives do you
use, Lisa? You are being careful, aren't you?
Lisa was used to their way, and answered calmly:
-I'm considering hysterectomy. There are enough human
beings on this planet.
Kerstin gave her a sharp look above the rim of her glasses.
-Hm. Yes. That's a valid thought. I do think you have to
be eighteen first, though.
-Surely you can write a testimonial?
-I'll see what I can do.
Not that we did anything that requested contraceptives,
but Lisa always sought to shock her parents, like a normal
teenager. Just that her methods were a bit unorthodox. I
don't even want to think about how my mother would
react if I told her I wanted a vasectomy. As if.

Another of their discussions gave me nightmares for a
long time, and every time something reminds me of it, I
shudder. It was about stammering. I didn't open my
mouth very much in their presence even before, and never
after that day. For some reason, Leif wanted to share this
with me:
-You know, Johan, there was a German surgeon in the
nineteenth century, Dieffenbach, who did a lot of
research, or rather, experiments regarding different
treatments. His assistant would hold the patient´s jaws in a
firm grip, while he pulled the tongue as far as it would go,
then cut a wedge in it and stitched it together again.
Kerstin commented:
-How intriguing! Did it work?
-Alas, no. Furthermore, there have been attempts with
electric shock therapy, and...

Lisa got up so fast that her chair fell over.

-Are you totally out of your mind, you two! You're supposed to be so bright and clever and educated, but have you ever heard of such a thing as empathy, or social skills? Come, Johan, we're leaving! I've had it with these imbecile... assholes!

No, she didn't use a fancy word for what she thought about them right then. She was too upset. She dragged me after her, I felt numb and my tongue hurt, as if someone had cut through it with a sharp knife for real.

I couldn't speak for days after that.

Lisa cried and cursed her socially inept parents. If only she had some money, she would take her things and move out this very day! She'd be happy to live in someone's old playhouse and use a potty and shower in the rain and search for food in containers if only she could leave that... book mausoleum!

If only...

A thoughtful glimpse awoke in her greengray eyes.

"Young woman with no money seeks roof over her head. Can cook and clean in return."

No. No. Never. Forget it. No, and no. In the trash bin with those replies, Lisa! I know I don't own you just because you're my girlfriend, but if you even think about moving in with Kenneth, 58, who can offer you a comfy place in his queen size bed and is sure that you will come to a very nice and mutual agreement... Just... Don't!

-How about this one, then? An old lady who can't take her cats with her to the nursing home, maybe she could manage a little longer in her forest cottage if a nice girl stayed there with her?

-Does she also have a queen size bed and want a human hot water bottle?

-Doesn't say anything about that part here. Look at the
handwriting, it's so beautiful that she has to be very old
and very sweet!
-What if the sweet old lady is a mad axmurderer?

Yes, I know it should be "axe murderer". The spell
checking program is marking "axmurderer" in red. But
here's where the Swenglish comes in. In Swedish, we
write almost all words together like that. Or should I say,
we're supposed to write them together, because the
meaning of the words change drastically when you
separate them! These kinds of writing errors are common
in Swedish, giving everybody with a sense of correct
writing both agony and entertainment. A classic example
is where the words "brunhårig sjuksköterska", a nurse
with brown hair, turns into a hairy brown sick nurse if you
separate them. The reason for me to keep some English
words written together is that it looks so much better in
my eyes, and this book was supposed to be written in
Swenglish, right? An axmurderer, now that's something
to be scared of!

-Show some faith, Johan!
-I don't want you to get hurt!
-I won't. Why don't you come with me and check it out?
Look at the address, it's not very far at all! Only fifteen
minutes into the forest from the nearest bus stop.
Distressed, I tried to plead to my desperate girlfriend.
Couldn't she try to stand living with her parents just a
little longer? I didn't want her in the forest, or in bed with
Kenneth, 58.
Her venture concerned me deeply. "Social experiment",
she called her ad in the personals in our local newspaper.
She wanted to see what kind of people would reply, what
the answers would look like, but also because she actually

wanted to find out if she could pull this through. Could I please support her in this? She needed me!
Pont-du-John came to my mind. A knight in shining armour, who wanted but wasn't allowed to protect, but who was asked to carry his lady's invisible sword.
I started to give in, but not quite.
-Could we at least bring someone grown-up?
-Like who?
-I don't know...
Of course, any adult we knew would stop us. Lisa got another of her bright ideas:
-Pontus! He's so tall and could easily be taken for over twenty!
-But he's not! He's only a year older than us!
-The old lady probably can't tell.
-Or the axmurderer.
-By all means, be like that if you want to! Would you prefer me to run away and never ever come back, so that you never will see me again?
She sure knew how to persuade me.
-I'll ask, I muttered.
To begin with, Pontus didn't want to hear about it. Adventures were preferably experienced through books or in the cinema, in a safe environment. Look for an old lady, or perhaps an axmurderer, in the deep forest, just because Lisa didn't want to stay with her parents just because they were planning to cut out my tongue or give me electric shocks? Well, no, not quite, but... We're just going out there to... you know... probe the terrain. Like warrior scouts do. But, not for fun, but... for real. Kind of.
-But... what if she really is a murderer?
Pontus' point of view was exactly my own, but I didn't want to lose Lisa and didn't want to go there alone with her. Three was, maybe not a crowd but far better than

two. So I kept persuading him, against my own
judgement.
-Yes, but what if it isn't?
-But...
-I challenge you!
I didn't have the same dramatic authority as my friend,
but I did my very best.
Once more, knight Pont-du-John came to rescue.

Equipped with illegal pepper spray, don't ask me where
Lisa had got that, and kitchen knives in our pockets, we
took the bus and followed the directions. Twenty minutes
by bus, and only ten minutes to walk so the lady – or
axmurderer - probably walked a little slowlier than we.
The evenings in the Swedish spring were getting brighter
each day, but to be on the safer side (there were no safe
sides in this, I felt) we went there on a Saturday morning.
I was nervous and as a precaution I had put a sealed
envelope on Amanda's desk, where I had written "Open if
I'm not back before dinner" and a note inside, telling her
where I had gone. Mom would have opened an envelope
like that immediately, but I trusted Amanda. She would be
curious, and probably furious if she knew what we were
up to, but she would respect my instructions. It would be
too late to save us, but at least they would know where to
search for our chopped up bodies.
The sunlight flowed. If this was to be our last day on
Earth, at least we would die in an almost unbearably
beautiful place! In a glade was a tiny red cottage,
surrounded by a flowering orchard.
Lisa sighed and whispered:
-I would die to live here!
Well, maybe you will, I thought and clenched the knife in
my pocket.
A small, smiling, very old little woman came towards us.

-Welcome, welcome! Would you care for some lemonade? I have set the table in the arbour!
Pontus hissed to me:
-Do axmurderers drink lemonade?
-No, I replied, as if I would know!
That forenoon was like a scene from a fairytale. Homemade raspberry lemonade and freshly baked cinnamon buns. A couple of cats, that seemed only half tame, sneaked around, suspiciously peeking at us, melting Pontus' heart. Of course, in many action movies the villains have cats, but this little sweet lady managed to gain our trust rather quickly. She really wanted to stay in her cottage.
-My sister's grown children want me to move into town, she sighed. They claim that they are worried about me, that they want me to get some company in old age. As if they know anything about me or my wishes! What is the use of that kind of company, to be stuck inside with old raisins that don't even know which day it is? If you're lucky, you can go outside once every second week, if there is enough staff, but there never is, according to the newspapers. You know, children, the only way I will leave my home, is with my feet first! But a little company sure would be nice. And maybe I could get some help with wood chopping by a strong, young man?
She glanced hopefully at Pontus, who proudly straightened his back a bit. Her comment about "children" had made him a little worried, he was supposed to be our adult today, but we soon learned that she called everyone under 80 "children".
-Wood chopping is my speciality, he declared.
As far as I knew, he had never even touched an axe.
Lisa said, with a voice softer than I've ever heard coming from her:
-I would love to stay with you, Frida!

-Oh, please, dear child, would you mind calling me tant
Frida? I think that sounds so sweet
Why aren't there any nice words in the dictionary for "old
woman?" We have several. The perfect Swedish word to
describe Frida is "gumma", but the epithet is "tant". The
adjective "tantig" would be translated into "frumpish", but
there was nothing frumpish whatsoever about tant Frida.
She was genuine, timeless, like Mother Earth herself. I
don't want to use the word "aunt", since that is also the
word for a relative. Frida's nieces and nephews called her
aunt Frida, and since there was no love lost between her
and them, I don't want to use that. So, I will stick to the
Swedish word. I hope it's ok with you.
When you're in school, translation is very easy. Just learn
the word list, and exchange the Swedish word for the
English. Not quite as simple when you do it outside the
textbook. Again, like painting, but I can't find the right
colours.
I blurted out:
-So... so you're not a crazy axmurderer then?
Lisa kicked me under the table, but tant Frida chuckled.
-Ask my chicken!

The next day, Lisa moved in. Even though it made me
feel sick to set my foot in that apartment, I helped her
pack, as a moral support. What are boyfriends for, if not
that? But my nerves were on the outside, if they were
going to talk about ancient treatment methods again, I
would run for my life!
Lisa used that same arrogant, dry voice as her parents
always did when she told them about her plans.
-Since I can't stand being in your presence any longer,
I'm moving out. How would you like me to do with the
practical details, should I report to the authorities that I

have changed address or would you consider forwarding
my mail to my new home?
Taken by surprise, Leif tried to come to terms with what
was happening.
-So? Who is this tant Frida?
-My landlady, thoroughly investigated, with excellent
references.
With excellent references she meant excellent raspberry
lemonade and excellent cinnamon buns.
-Hm. Have you made a budget?
-Of course I have made a budget! With my child benefit I
will do just fine.
In Sweden, the caregivers will get a certain amount of
money for each child until they're 18, to help pay for
some of the necessities. Some need that money to make
ends meet, but Lisa's parents earned enough to let her
have the whole child benefit as pocket money.
-Hm. I'm not sure about this. We need to discuss the
matter with Kerstin.
-I see no reason to. Haven't you tried to prepare me for
adult life ever since I stopped using diapers, and forced
me to make my own decisions and take responsibility?
His face went long.
-Well, yes, but... You're far from coming of age, and I
really don't think...
-Look at it as a gift to Kerstin! What did you say now, I'm
the result of you just thinking about your own pleasure,
right? If it weren't for your selfishness, I wouldn't stand
here arguing with you right now. Give me your blessing
to move out, and take responsibility for your own actions,
that is, me. She never wanted me, so it will be a nice
surprise for her when she comes home from her fancy
professor lunch and finds me gone. Maybe you'll get lucky
again with her, she's far too old to get knocked up now so

it should be safe enough. If you're still capable, that is.
You do look a bit dry and old.
No, I would never get used to anyone talking to their
parents like that.
Leif blushed a little.
-I still think we should visit this tant Frida before any of
us can give any permission.
-Sure, if you suddenly feel the need to act like a caring
parent, go ahead. You could take a taxi and at the same
time give me a ride with my stuff. But I'm still moving
out. Either to tant Frida, or I'll just run away.
-You're being a little overdramatic now, Lisa.
-I'm a teenager, Leif. We're expected to revolt. Haven't
you read about that in one of your developmental
psychology books? I thought now would be a good time
to start my teenage behaviour.
She mixed academic and teenage language. It was one of
her ways to confuse them.

Lisa had actually thought her parents would let her leave
without fussing over it, that they didn't care about her at
all. Kerstin agreed with Leif, though. Of course Lisa was a
free citizen, owned by none, but no, they weren't going to
let her move in with any tant just like that! They insisted
on meeting this Frida person.
Later, Lisa told me about the interrogation. Did the
house have electricity? Telephone? Water? No? How did
she manage in the winter? Did someone make a path in
the snow to the bus stop? Were there mice?
-You should have seen tant Frida! She was so patient, and
explained to those technical idiots that she had lived in
that cottage her entire life, so she was quite sure that she
would be able to keep me alive even without cable TV!
And of course there were mice! Oh, Johan, I'm actually
moving in with her! For real!

She grinned and added:
-I wonder what they would have said about Kenneth, 58!

Tant Frida's small cottage almost became like a clubhouse
for us that summer. If Pontus didn't know how to chop
wood before, he was an expert in the end and made sure
that they had wood for the whole winter. As a bonus, he
got muscles, and with them a better self confidence. If you
are as tall and big as he, it's quite matching to also be
strong as a bear!
My parents couldn't believe their ears when they heard
about Lisa moving out. Of course I had asked them if she
could move in with us, but that was out of the question.
Sara had changed a lot of my mother's thoughts, but in
this case I heard an echo of the past – what would people
say!
People in her salon had quite a lot to say about a teenage
girl moving in with an old lady in the forest just because
she couldn't stand her parents. My mother gave them
plenty of fuel to keep that fire alive, by telling them all
that she knew about the situation. Sara had started
preschool, with a hired resource person to assist her and
keep her from eating unsuitable things, so mom could
work more hours in the salon. My dad knew the location
of the cottage from his newspaper rounds, and took the
opportunity to sharpen his eyes and look around a bit
more, now that he knew I spent so much time there. Tant
Frida's post box was by the main road, near the bus stop,
but my dad started taking his time to deliver the morning
paper to her door. She was an early bird, and of course I
had told her that it was my father who sneaked around, so
one morning she offered him some coffee. Why didn't he
bring the whole family to come and see her? Maybe the
two girls would like to pick some raspberries, she had

plenty! She would be delighted to have them, us, as
guests.
Mom hesitated when dad told her about the invitation.
Was that appropriate?
-Raspries! Sara yelled. Raspries!
It took about three seconds for tant Frida to gain my
mother's trust, and three more before she started teaching
Amanda how to crochet a little star shaped table cloth.

The cottage had a small chamber with room for nothing
more than a narrow bed and a bedside table, a garret with
no insulation that was used for storage, and what we call
an all-in-one room with a wood stove and a kitchen
pullout sofa where Lisa slept. Outhouse instead of toilet
of course. A combined shed for the wood and tools.
Water was drawn from a well in front of the house. The
peaceful arbour. That was it. More than enough. To us, it
was everything. Our paradise!
Pontus and Lisa hadn't exactly become friends, but the
cottage and its surroundings had a calming effect on both
of them. Also, they worked quite well together as long as
they had something practical to deal with. There was
always something to do. Clean the gutters, cook raspberry
jam, repair something, or just sit and listen to tant Frida's
stories. She loved having an audience, and company, and
we loved everything about the atmosphere. I wasn't too
thrilled about digging out the outhouse, though. The
stench stuck in my nostrils for days, but everything else
was fun.

The last months in highstage was surrounded by a vibrant
mix of melancholy and anticipation. So far, we had been
like a bag of mixed candy, everything thrown together
without any thought at all. The next stage in our
education was the gymnasium, equivalent to upper

secondary school or senior high school. This step isn't mandatory, but nobody wants to hire a sixteen-year-old so almost everyone continue studying. This is the first time where we get to choose direction according to our interests, and therefore the candy bags are a little more sorted. Chocolate in one, sweet in one, sour in one. The first step on the ladder to individuality. Division, for better or worse.

-I want to study abroad this summer, Lisa said to me one spring day when we had a cup of nettle tea in the arbour. As you might guess, the Swedish language isn't very useful outside Scandinavia. We begin our English studies quite early, in second or third grade, and it´s popular to go on a languagetrip abroad. Nowadays there are all sorts of courses all over the world for all ages, but when we were teenagers, it was mostly courses in England for about a month.
I blew a little on my hot tea, not so much to cool it down but because I like to watch the steam move.
-Come with me, Johan?
Some tea splashed over the rim of the cup and burned my hand.
-No!
-I think it would be good for you. We could speak English all the time, you and me. Experience something different together. Breathe some new, fresh air, get new influences. Try everyday life somewhere else.
This was in my opinion the worst idea since... ever.
-Don't you think you would be just as annoyed with these teachers and participants as you are with everyone here? You hate school, why do you want to prolong the pain?
She shook her head, restless.
-I'm sure I'll be impatient with them, that's why I want you to come with me! I need someone sensible to spend

my time with. And I actually do believe that it would be good for you. Three weeks, Johan! That's all. Please, give them to me?
-We'll see.

Can you imagine the iron fist that clenched my guts when we spoke about this? My shyness hadn't decreased at all over the years. First, there was the journey itself, being stuck in a bus or a plane together with a lot of people, with nowhere to escape. Stay with strangers. Most likely being forced to talk to them, woe and horror! On top of that, a new study group, new teachers, new people. Everything that appealed to Lisa, repelled me. Soon she would grow tired of me. When the candy bag opened after our graduation, we would be bouncing in different directions. Chocolate and sour.
Pontus tried to give me a pep talk.
-I would love to go on a languagetrip, but mother won't let me go. She's afraid that I would be staying with thugs. Or vegetarians! That would be even worse, however would that end!
I reluctantly smiled a little. Pontus' mother harboured the deepest distrust against vegetarians. When she learned that there were even worse things, vegans, she actually put an extra lock on her front door, convinced that they would break into her house and burn her mink coat.
-You can do it, Johan. I know you can. Do it for me? Send postcards every day and tell me everything, so that I can imagine that I'm there also? Please?
-Maybe my parents can't afford...
-You're making excuses! That's not true, and you know it. You have told me that your grandmother never gives you anything for Christmas and your birthdays, that she puts money in a bank account instead, just so that you will be able to do fun things like these!

-Fun things, yes! Going on a torture camp isn't my idea of fun!
He went quiet.
-Is it that bad?
-Yes, it is!
-Ok. I won't nag you then. But you could have brought knight Pont-du-John. He would probably also want to see a little more of the world than my room and your wardrobe.
The brave knight gazed at me under his helmet, resting on his sword.
-I really do think it's scary, I mumbled to the figurine.
-I know.
-Do you have to do things that scare you?
-Only go to the dentist.
Then he got an idea and lit up.
-But Johan! If you're good at English, I've heard that you can take some sort of exam, and if you do well enough, you will be graded and don't have to go to the lessons! Three weeks of your life, and you might be able to skip three years of sitting in a dull classroom, couldn't that be worth it?
I definitely got something to think about!

Let's get back to my family.
Amanda had chosen a science direction in gymnasium, her mind set to be a doctor. Everything Amanda does, she does thoroughly and methodically. She has her Christmas shopping worked out in detail in September. Who will get what, how much money she can spend, and where she would buy it. Her university plans filled an entire file. Staples, diagrams and boxes to check. What courses she would need in gymnasium to get into the medical program, how high her grades should be, how many points were needed to get the highest grade on a test, how

much she needed to study before a test, when she had to
start studying and when she had to start revising, and
most important, when she could find the time to do this.
Finding time was her biggest challenge.

Yes, we loved Sara and she loved us, and yes, her laughter
warmed the roots of our hearts, but she could scream as
well. One of the nicer prejudices about persons with
Down syndrome is that they are so happy and cosy and
say crazy-funny but at the same time deep and wise
things. Mom is the first one to help spread this myth, and
Sara could be absolutly enchanting around other people. I
don't think she was aware of what she was doing, she was
too pure at heart to be calculating and deceiving. But
sometimes, a bit too often, it was as if she put all effort in
being charming to strangers, and when she came home,
she sort of collapsed. As if she ran out of stamina. She
could sit on the floor for hours, just howling. Or she
would sneak from the person who had the Saracheck, into
our rooms, destroying everything she could lay her hands
on. Amanda had to buy a small safe-deposit box where she
kept her school books and the files with her plans for the
future. I left my books in school, and borrowed Lisa´s
books when we were doing homework.

The Swedish social security system is great when it comes
to helping children with special needs. You can apply for
various support. There are short term homes with staff
where the children can stay a certain amount of days each
month, maybe a weekend, a couple of school days, every
second week, or what suits the family best. The number of
days are decided in cooperation with the caregiver and the
community. The children can also stay with a support
family instead of a short term home. You can also apply
for a reliever, that comes to your own home and looks
after the child, or go with it to different activities. This

doesn't cost anything for the individual. For the taxpayers, a short term home is much cheaper than a parent who has crashed and needs to be on sick leave for a long time. I'm not saying it's always easy to get help. In some cases, the community doesn't want to pay and try to interpret the laws in their own short-sighted favour, and in other cases, often in smaller towns or villages, you might have being approved the right to a reliever, but there is nobody who wants the job.

Subtle hints from my father regarding a reliever were immediately disregarded by mom.

Never in her life! What would people say if she wasn't capable of taking care of her own child? Never, do you hear?

Inch by inch, everyone started to wear out.

Amanda spent a lot of time in the library. She couldn't study in our chaotic home environment. I escaped to tant Frida or to Pontus.

Arguing in the kitchen.

-You and Johan have to spend more time at home, Amanda! I need your help!

-But mom, I have a test next week!

-Is that stupid test more important than your sister?

Foot stomping, tears streaming.

-How can you say things like that! What about us, then? Don't we matter at all? You never ask us anything about what we're doing, how we're doing, what we want to do! I want to become a doctor and help other kids like my sister! I have to live my own life and you can't force me to babysit more than I already do, I just won't do it! I refuse to let you destroy my future just because you're too proud to ask for a reliever!

Front door slamming.

Sara howling.

Mom crying.

Dad rubbing his temples.

In that context, three weeks in England didn't seem like
such a bad idea after all.

With knight Pont-du-John carefully packed, we left for
Hastings a couple of days after our ninth grade
graduation. Lisa had lied to the languagetrip agency, just a
white lie, telling them that we were cousins and wanted to
stay in the same family. She didn't think that any family
would dare to have a romantic teenage couple under their
roof. Not that we were very romantic. After more than
two years together, we still hadn't kissed, but the hosts
didn't know that. My girlfriend, a friend who happened to
be a girl and liked sleeping on my arm. That's all we
needed, I thought.

-It´s much better if we fly, because if we crash, we will
probably die immediately. It's worse with a bus accident
somewhere in Germany. We might end up in a hospital
there for ages and can't communicate properly with the
staff.

I growled at her while my shaking hand fastened the seat
belt.

-Your methods of calming me are totally useless!

This was my first time ever in an aeroplane. The only
thing I knew about flying was that you were supposed to
fake a yawn if your ears felt funny.

Lisa just laughed and patted my cheek.

-It´ll be ok. Planes very seldom crash.

Oh, right. Thanks. I felt much safer hearing that. Not.

We had taken an oath, promising not to utter one word in
Swedish until our feet were on Swedish ground again. For
once, she didn't argue with the teachers, she took a step
back and was content to be nothing more than just a
student in the group, instead of a student standing in front

of the group, waving her arms and explaining things she
thought the teachers didn't do well enough.
One of the first days we stayed after the class and asked
for a word with the teacher.
-Johan and I would like to take the gymnasium English
test as soon as possible in the fall. Could you please
provide us with some extra material, so that we can use
our afternoons for preparing?
Now and then you find a teacher that is like a jewel,
glimmering and vibrant. This was one of them. Not only
did she give us the material we had asked for, she also
found a retired local teacher who would love to help us
for free. If you looked in an illustrated dictionary and
searched for English Gentleman, you would find the
image of Mr Seagrove, dressed in tweed, with white,
bushy eyebrows. In the classroom I was as quiet as I've
been at home. There's something about groups that
makes me uneasy, but the noble air around Mr Seagrove
loosened my tongue and I spoke more during those
summer afternoons than I had done in my entire life.
Disco on the pier? Barbeque on West Hill? Forget it! Just
let me sit here, listening to post war stories, licking on an
intense yellow popsicle, trying to figure out the pun on
the stick, talking to Mr Seagrove! My self confidence grew
by the day as I gave him my opinion about the art in the
museums we visited, about music and lyrics, I poured my
heart out regarding Sara and the colliding feelings of love
and the wish for her to just keep out of my way, I told him
about how badly Pontus had been treated and about my
feelings of guilt, I showed him Pont-du-John and
explained his part in my life.

The more I spoke, the more quiet Lisa became. She walked beside me while I was talking, looking at me as if she was trying to figure out who this new Johan was.

We stayed with a young, newlywed couple on East Hill, who accepted summer students to be able to afford their own house. They were wonderful hosts who took us sightseeing in the neighbourhood, and made us packed lunch that made our classmates green of envy. Vegetarians, what would Pontus' mother have said! Our sandwiches had cheese and lettuce instead of this peculiar pink-grey spread that looks like and probably tastes like cat food. They're called Peter and Lydia, and we've kept in touch all these years. They're the ones checking my grammar, as I told you in the beginning of this story, so it feels a bit embarrassing to admit that we had been lying about being cousins, and I'm not sure about what they will say about what I'm going to reveal about Lisa in the next pages.

Lisa had got a thick bunch of travel checks from her parents before she left.
Scornfully, she asked:
-Are you trying to buy my affection?
-Consider it a part of your inheritance in advance. You might find some books you like.
What Lisa found, was Old Town's Craft Shop, packed with clothes that had ”Lisa” written all over them. Parti-coloured flowing dresses, embroidered maxi skirts, vests with mirror patterns, velvet hats... The look on her face when she entered that shop for the first time was as if she had Seen The Light. Every day she bought something, and on our last day in Hastings, she spent her – and my - last penny in there. She found her style in Hastings, and I found my words.

The last night before we left, Lisa and I had a picnic on East Hill, looking out over the sea. We hadn't caused any trouble during our stay, so Peter and Lydia trusted us when we said that we wanted to stay out late.

The July night was warm, and of course much darker than in Sweden. The last few days, I had felt that Lisa was a bit absentminded. The days were packed with activities and lessons and in the evenings I fell asleep as soon as my head touched the pillow, so we didn't have any chance to just be quiet together the way we used to. It wasn't until now that we had the time an opportunity to both talk and stay quiet.

We lay down on a thick blanket, stargazing. I broke my oath and asked her quietly in Swedish:

-How are you doing, Lisa?

She was quiet for a while, but I could almost hear her thinking.

-*Sub Rosa*, Johan.

-*Sub Rosa*.

-Do you remember that party in school? When I asked if I had a chance on you?

How could I ever forget?

-Mm.

-When I said that I wanted a chance on Åsa?

-Yes?

Another moment of silence before she continued:

-I meant it.

-What do you mean?

-I meant it, Johan. I was in love with Åsa.

Somehow, I was surprised that I wasn't a bit surprised. The thought had never crossed my mind openly, but as I said, we hadn't even kissed for almost three years, so I think I subconsciously smelled some kind of rat.

Our dialogue was diluted yet concentrated with a lot of pauses between our lines. Imagine two youths on a cliff in a foreign country under the stars in the summer night, talking about the most important matter in the world: Love. You need plenty of time to digest and formulate each thought.

-Are you still in love with her?

-No. It didn't last long at all. I thought she was different, but she was just as shallow as everyone else. Or maybe not, but for some reason she wanted to seem average. Perhaps to fit in better.

-Have you fallen in love with someone here? Is that why you look so... sad?

-Yes.

-Would you like to talk to me about it?

She turned to look at me. Our eyes had got used to the darkness, but she was still swept into a veil of dusk that was suitable for this moment.

-Aren't you mad at me?

-Why would I be mad?

-It feels like I have betrayed you. Lied to you.

-Have you?

-It feels that way. I've pretended to be your girlfriend for years, haven't I?

Here's the first of the situations where I feel I redeemed myself a bit for not being a true friend to Pontus when he needed me. A mediocrity without the need to assert himself has the time to listen and watch, and is without prestige.

-You haven't pretended to be my friend, right? That part was sincere?

-Yes, but... I have... claimed you. You could have found a real girlfriend.

I took her hand firmly in mine.

-I'd rather have a real friend than a shallow girlfriend.

Rather a real friend than a shallow girlfriend.
Lisa reminded me of that sentence when my ex had
slammed the door and walked out of my life.
I know she meant well, but at that time, it felt like a
mockery.

Lisa squeezed my hand and whispered:
-So you don't hate me?
I could hear that she was crying.
-I could never hate you. But I want to ask you something.
-Anything!
-Were you in love with someone else? During the years
with me?
-No! No, I wasn't! I would never have done something
like that to you, I... I didn't know! I thought... I had no
idea what it could feel like! I care for you so much, I
wanted to be with you, I really do love you! You mean the
world to me! It's just that...
Laconically, I ended her sentence:
-That you never fell in love with me.
Nothing had been said, but it still felt natural to talk
about us as imperfect.
Lisa sobbed.
-I'm so sorry!
I tried to step into the shoes of the Comforter. Put my
arm around her, placed her head on my chest. My tears
were also flowing, so much for the comfort. It took a
while before I got my breathing under control. I felt
hollow. Like one of T. S. Eliot's Hollow Men.
This is the way the world ends
This is the way the world ends
This is the way the world ends
Not with a bang but a whimper.

-So, what now?

-I don't know, Johan.

-The one you're in love with... Does that person want to be with you?

-Wouldn't think so. It's Lydia.

In the middle of the misery, I laughed, a laugh of despair that Lisa fortunately understood.

-Well, I suppose that complicates things a bit!

She gave me a shove, but started laughing too, mixed with the tears. We both needed to ease the tension, I guess.

-I thought of trying to seduce her when you and Peter went fishing the other day, but I thought that the languagetrip agency might hesitate to send them any more students if they found out, and they really need the money.

-How noble of you!

She replied to my theatrical admiring voice by smashing her velvet bag in my head, followed by a pleading:

-Hold me?

She didn't need to ask me twice.

Lisa, allrakäraste Lisa!

I whispered into her lavenderscenting hair:

-We will always stay friends, you and me. Lisa and Johan forever. Even if I hereby officially break up with you, you will remain my dearest treasure for as long as I live.

Does it sound incredible? Too neat and sweet to be true? The teenage boy who just got dumped and declares his Eternal Love and Friendship? Well, I don't care if you believe me or not. You weren't there, you didn't feel the enchanted electricity in the sea air. Of course I was sad, but Lisa and I were drifting apart anyway. Not just because we were going separate ways after highstage, but also because we didn't need each other in the same way

anymore. What I feared, was losing her altogether. In practice, our relationship didn't have to change much at all. It was platonic from the start to the end. Better to show your hand. Friends. Nothing to sneer at. Girlfriends come and go, friends stay.
Right, Lisa?

Love can be so simple when everything feels right.
Love can hurt like hell when something doesn't feel right.
I'm sorry. I need a break now.

I should probably tell you about Madeleine straight away, to get it done with. Remove the band-aid quickly.
"Keep to the chronology", I hear Camilla say in my head.
"You're far too inconsistent when you write as it is!"
Well, excuse me, then!

So. The gymnasium.
If I hadn't been so withdrawn, people would probably think I was rather arrogant. I was tired of everything from the start. Didn't want to go to "freshman parties", play silly name learning games, and be a part of this hysterical Start Over and Show My New Personality-roundabout. I just wanted to be left alone, thankyouverymuch! Fortunately, everyone was so full of themselves when they got this new start, so nobody cared about me not participating. They asked in the beginning, but always took no for an answer and eventually stopped asking. I wasn't ostracized (yes, I did have to look that word up, we call it "outfrozen" when someone isn't allowed to be a part of a group), I was more... infrozen. I had no idea whatsoever what I wanted to do with my life, so I chose a broad direction with languages and civics. I succeeded in writing the English test, so I took up German and

Spanish. Might be useful if I ever go into the big world again.
Lisa had found a gymnasium with distance learning, which suited her just fine. She still lived with tant Frida and travelled to the school now and then to write exams. Pontus have never been the studying kind, and chose a practical line with vehicle technology, his mind set on becoming a mechanic. While I withered, he bloomed when he finally found friends with the same interests, friends who admired his strength and size instead of mocking him for it.
We still saw each other now and then in our spare time, when I was helping him with his homework, but it wasn't the same. We had nothing in common anymore.

No.
I'm sorry, but I need to fast forward here. I had no idea that writing about my life would be so hard on my emotions. Had I known, I would have taken a toothpick and duelled with Pont-du-John to avoid this challenge. It seemed so easy. Just tell it like it was. Is. Water under the bridge, I've moved on, forgot but not forgiven. The Water Sprite under the bridge rose from the water and grabbed my ankles, trying to pull me down.
Did you actually think that you were over this?
Think again, mister!

So, we're now in the beginning of my random, directionless studies. I was taking independent courses at the university, groping for something to build my future on. Linguistics. History of ideas. Economics, no, I quit that course after the first introduction day, it was nothing more than a desperate attempt to at least try something that might give me a proper job.

My parents are middle class, and I know they have
struggled with the economy from time to time, but they
always put aside at least half of the Child Benefit money
each month for me and Amanda. Maybe for Sara too, I
don't know. Our grandmother had put aside more money
for us than we could ever have dreamed about over the
years. When Amanda found out on her eighteenth
birthday that she had enough money to buy her own flat,
she cried from relief! A condominium was more than just
a place to live, it was an investment. She advised me to do
the same with my money when I came of age, which I did.
And when I talk about more money than we had ever
seen, I'm talking about just enough to get a loan for a
one-bedroom-flat a couple of kilometres from the town
centre.

My flat, in a three-floor-tall building from 1937, has an
alcove where I keep a large bed-cabinet with a king size
bed that I pull out when it's time to sleep. That makes the
flat seem bigger, since you don't see the bed when it's not
used. King size? Lisa spent the night sometimes, and,
well, you never knew. One day someone else might find
their way to my bed.

The dressers in the kitchen aren't in a straight angle, they
sort of lean outwards, all the way up to the ceiling, which
meant that there was a lot of space on the top shelves
since they were deeper. More than once I've come home a
little round under my feet (if that expression is too
Swenglish, it's a way to say that you're just a little drunk),
convinced that the kitchen would fall over me when I was
drinking water from the tap. The kitchen sink is far too
low. Maybe the average woman was shorter seventy years
ago. Pontus jokes about using it as a foot bath. He does
find it useful though, because he never has to do the
washing up.

I wonder what Freud would have to say about the three different kind of people – the ones who prefer to wash the dishes, the ones who rather dry the dishes and the ones who buys paper plates to avoid it altogether.
Procrastination, they call this. Trying to postpone something unpleasant, even though you know it has to be done.
I don't want to write about Madeleine.
I'd rather write about the sloping dressers in my kitchen.

There is something called student nations in our biggest university towns. It's like a small community gathered in the nation house, with a pub, a library, a large banquet hall that can also be used for dancing or theatre or whatever, and rooms where you can study or just hang out. There are lots of activities going on, if you want. From 1667 until quite recently you had to be a member of one of the nations. They are named after different areas in Sweden, and many choose the nation that belongs to your area. You still have the freedom to choose activities in other nations if you wish. I belonged to Upplands nation, but I never went there. I never went anywhere, and Pontus started to get annoyed with me.
-You can't spend your entire life in this flat, Johan! Is there nothing at all that interests you? Look, here's the agenda for all the nations this fortnight, choose one thing! Just one! No? Well, in that case, I'll choose for you! If you refuse, it's the end of our friendship, because your attitude is beginning to pull me down and I won't let you do that to me.
Sara never came to see me or Amanda in our new homes. She couldn't accept that we had moved out. The first and only time she visited me, she tried to destroy everything within her reach. With no Sara trying to eat him, our plastic hero Pont-du-John now lived on my window sill in

the kitchen when it was my turn to host him. Pontus grabbed him and placed him on top of a small square in the agenda on the back of the student newspaper that I never read. His voice had nothing of the humour or the fake drama he mostly used when he challenged me. This time, he sounded angry.
-Here! You're going to... sing in a choir! Look, the knight is challenging you!
I tried to breathe, and Pontus softened a little.
-Seriously, Johan. I know that you don't like groups. Heck, I know you don't even like people very much! But with Lisa in Japan, it seems like you don't see anyone but me, and frankly... you need to find at least an ounce of driving force within yourself. Join the choir, please? Or the photo club, the ornithology club or whatever!
I looked down at my feet, mumbling something.
Pontus took the knight and pushed him down in the soil around my azalea.
-See you around.

It sounds easy, doesn't it? Join a choir! Just do it! Go there and say that hello, do you need a tenor? Sure, why not streak naked at the Nobel banquet as well, just for fun?
I called Amanda and didn't even try to hide how miserable I was.
-Have you got time for fika?
Fika is one of the best Swedish words ever, too complex to translate so you have to learn it now. It's both a verb and a noun. The verb means eating or drinking something nice, the noun is both the concept and the things you put on the fika table. You can fika at work as a short coffee break, fika in a café (also called "fik"), you bring fika to the forest when you're hiking or picking blueberries, you always

have to offer fika when someone is visiting, and you can
have fika all by yourself anywhere, anytime.

My dear big sister who lives her life in boxes has a weekly
square for Family Time in her calendar. Sometimes she
takes Sara to fika, sometimes she goes home to our
parents, and when I called her this day she put my name
in the box.

I didn't waste any time chitchatting.

-Pontus thinks that I should join a choir.

Amanda studied my facial expressions.

-Ok. So, how do we make this happen?

She didn't even ask if it was something that I wanted to
do. She knew I didn't.

-Do you know if there are any... nice student choirs?
That is, please come with me, or, drag me after you, I'm
too scared to climb this mountain alone!

-I'll ask Jörgen.

Jörgen, that was her fiancé, her fellow medical student
who had fallen for her strict charm and in an unattended
moment added "with Jörgen" in the morning box where
she had written "jogging" in her calendar. After a few
months carefully jogging dating, he gave her a beautiful
framed notebook with the text "Amanda's Schedule"
engraved as a Christmas gift. She knew then that he was a
keeper. Someone who understood and respected her need
for structure.

The day after our fika, Jörgen came to visit with his carrot
red hair in a complete mess and frostbitten red nose.
Ok, I'd better admit:
There are times when I wonder if I'm gay, like Lisa. That
might explain why I never wanted to kiss her, why we get
along so well. And I really like Jörgen a lot. But I think it's
more the fact that I would like to be a little more like him.
Happy, curious, positive. Full of initiative, without

jumping into an idea with his head first, like Lisa does. I
don't want to touch him or anything, I just like to be with
him. He always manages to improve my mood. See, just
by writing about him I'm able to tear myself from the
melancholy that wrapped itself around my mind like a
wet blanket when I started to write about Madeleine!
Being gay in Sweden today is, mostly, no big deal unless it
complicates your life on an individual level. The country
is a mix of many cultures, and of course there are scared
people everywhere who are threatened by everything that
is different. HBTQ-rights are discussed everywhere, even
my dentist has a HBTQ-certificate. Not quite sure why it
should matter in that context, maybe you discuss other
things when someone is poking with sharp tools in your
mouth, but sure, it's important to respect human rights
everywhere.
-That's so great, you joining a choir! I've talked to some
friends, and if you want, I'll go with you and check out the
ones they have suggested. It would be fun to go to a
nation again, it's been a while! I don't have much time for
those kinds of pleasures anymore.
It was as if the sun had managed to find its way through a
dirty window, the window to my soul. Somebody was
about to help me break my seclusion!

When you're in the middle of something it's not easy to
be objective, but when I look back on these years, I'm sure
I suffered from a lighter form of depression. Considering
my DNA-code, I might be predestined to fall into slumps
more often than others. Things that doesn't seem very
traumatic can easily push me over the edge. Not that
depression needs a trigger. To ask "What has happened,
why are you depressed?" is just as irrelevant as to ask why
someone gets diabetes or cancer. Yes, I know, there are
people who think that everything that goes on in your

body is a reflection of your mind and your choices, that
diseases is a result of you not meditating daily, not eating
windfall, not being spiritual enough. I think they're right,
sometimes, in some points, but far from always!
Sometimes it's all about bad luck. The body is also a
mechanism, something technical yet alive. The soul can
affect your body, and then the best cure can be to change
your thoughts, but sometimes the body breaks all by itself,
and then you do need medication. In both cases, you
should ask for help. It *is* a disease, a very serious one, that
affects both body and mind. But even today, illness that
affects your mind is considered a shame, maybe not to the
people around you in the way it was earlier in our history,
but to yourself. "I should be able to take care of this on
my own!" Why on Earth should you have to do that?
Nobody expects you to, and you wouldn't think that way
about diabetes, would you? And yes, there are ignorant
people who just don't understand. "Cheer up!" Yeah,
right.

You see, logic has got nothing to do with depression.
When I'm in my down periods, nothing affects me much.
I can see that the sun is shining and that the day is
beautiful, I can eat the most wonderful food, I can watch a
funny movie, and think that yes, this is nice, this is funny,
but it doesn't reach my heart. I do everything I'm
supposed to do during those periods, I eat, sleep, go to my
lectures or to work, I took care of Sara when I was asked
to, but besides that, I could stare out of the window for
hours. Existed, joyless. No wonder Pontus grew tired of
me. At the same time, he wanted to help me and tried to
guess how. Since my mood was so much worse when Lisa
wasn't close to me, he probably guessed right. I needed
more friends.

The first choir we checked out were warming up by lumbering around in the banquet hall, waving their arms, shouting "Hakuna Matata!"
Guess if that seemed appealing to me.
The second felt much better. MinneManneMånne, it almost felt meditative. Friendly nods, welcome to see what it feels like with us, the tenors are in the back.
I was amazed to realise that I didn't find the choir as threatening as other kinds of groups. We stood in a bowed row, not in a circle, not staring at each other. I got to be anonymous, yet an important part of the whole. The song continued even without me, a little weaker though. My voice mattered. It was awesome!
The main reason that I found it so hard to write about my life was that all these old emotions came back and squeezed my chest. But now, when I'm reliving it, and I've had some fika and thought about Jörgen's enthusiasm and kindness, I can look back on that time with sentiment instead of pain. I'll tell you about the grief in due time. Let's have some happiness before that!

Next week, I went to the choir practice on my own.
That's the day I met Madeleine for the first time, and it wasn't a good day because I was so nervous of going alone that I couldn't eat but still had to go to the bathroom ten times.
Madeleine was so pretty! Natural blonde, blue eyes, short enough to fit perfectly by my kitchen sink I thought and got a flash vision of her washing up and me drying after a three-course dinner in candlelight. She didn't have the best voice, but who cared? As long as she could carry a tune and follow the rhythm.
I wouldn't say I fell instantly in love with her, but Wednesday evenings soon became something to look forward to. Something that managed to reach my heart.

Pontus came by a few weeks after our last intermezzo, to say that he was sorry, he had acted like a lout and didn't want to end our friendship – but, hello there, you're glowing, Johan! What has happened here?
Embarrassed grin from me.
-You rascal! Here I am, ready to recant, but you might want to thank me instead?
I punched him on the arm and dug out Pont-du-John from my azalea.
-I challenge you to come to our Christmas concert. Wearing a bowtie!
He laughed and put our hero in his back pocket.
-I'll take the one with snowmen on!

When we were in gymnasium, we joked that we now were Academics and should Dress With Style, and started giving each other ties or bowties for Christmas. We still do. Every last day of term, every birthday or any occasion where we can get away with it, we wear them. Some are alright, but most of them hideous. That's the fun part, to find something really ugly. My antifavourite is a lime green tie with purple flamingos.

The nation choir was small, and our concert was just us singing a few carols to the fika in the banquet hall on the first of advent. Pontus was there in his snowmen bowtie, properly added to our guest list since he wasn't a student and needed permission to enter our noble nation houses.
-That was really good!
-Thanks!
-So, who is the one that brings that radiant smile upon your ugly face just because it's Wednesday?
I blushed and tried to stop my eyes from searching Madeleine. It didn't go very well. ”Don't think of a blue

elephant!" What did you just see in your head? A blue
elephant, perhaps?
Madeleine had a Christmas red velvet dress and tinsel in
her hair. Pontus' smile widened.
-Cute!
-Cut it out!
-Invite her to my Christmas party?
Another tradition that had started in gymnasium was
Pontus inviting all his friends to a big party on the second
of advent. I think that was the best day of the year for
him. Finally, he had friends! Genuine friends who came
just because they wanted to! They didn't even come for
free food, because it was the kind of party where you have
to bring something for the table and a gift to place under
the Christmas tree, and when you were leaving the drop-
in-party you could take a present with you. Sara loved
these parties and declared to everyone that she was going
to marry her Pontus.
His mother was very hesitant the first year. A whole
bunch of strangers? At the same time? What if they were
vegetarians! What would she do then? But she had been
so worried during her son's darker years, and since he
never got that dog or sibling, she couldn't deny him this
just because she was nervous. And when she saw how
happy and proud he was when almost everyone in his class
came that first year, all her doubts evaporated and now
she's as eager as he is. They're planning these advent
parties together at least a month in advance.
I also kind of liked those parties, as long as I had
something to do, like looking after Sara or being in
charge of serving.
-I can't ask her, it's your party!
-Is she dating someone?
I happened to know for sure that she wasn't, that her idiot
ex boyfriend for some inscrutable reason had broken up

with her recently. But I didn't want to admit that I knew
this, and that I cared so much, so I sneered:
-How should I know?
-Trust me. Apparently it was an ingenious move to force
you to join a choir, so I'll keep trusting my instincts.
-Cut it out!
My lines were repeating themselves. I was nervous about
what he had in mind, and hopeful that he might have
something in mind that would lead to something exciting.
He's a bit clumsy and loutish, as I've told you, but he
didn't just go straight to her with an invitation. No, the
old bear was more clever than that! At the fika he sat next
to me, since he didn't know anyone else. After some
presentation and chitchat he said:
-You know what? I use to have a party every second of
advent. What would you say to joining us, giving us some
Christmas carols? I can't pay you, but there is plenty of
food and lussekatter and Christmas candy and spiced
wine. We have open house all day from lunchtime, so
anytime that would suit you would be great!
Quick deliberation. Someone was going home, someone
needed to study for an exam. But yes, at least one or two
in each voice would be able to come, was that enough?
Oh yes, that will be just perfect, because Madeleine could
come, right? It would do fine with just her. Fortunately,
he didn't say that.

Pontus still lived with his mother and aunt. No reason to
move, the house was big enough for all three of them and
they enjoyed each other's company. Better to save his
money. His plans to be a mechanic came to a tragic end
when he developed an allergy to many of the chemicals he
had to come in touch with, but he soon came up with a
plan B. He was going to be a taxi driver. You have to be
21 to do that, so he was working in a grocery store for a

few years, studying the city maps in the whole county and knew every little one-way-path and every roundabout and waltzed through the exam. He got all kinds of tours. Long drives out of the county as well as short drives, he did everything with the same enthusiasm. Most of all he loved driving old ladies, and they loved him for his old-fashioned politeness and attention. Maybe it's the same in other countries, that taxi is also used for transportation service for elderly and disabled. Pontus got to know the people who used this service often, and always remembered what they had talked about on their previous trip, and asked about it. What about your grandson, is he free from the chicken pox at last? Does Skutt like the new rabbit food any better? And you have to tell me the end of that book you were reading, did the nurse end up with the doctor? Really? I would have put my money on the plumber!

Many of the old ladies asked specifically for Pontus when they were booking their trip. If he wasn't available, they would be happy to wait an hour or a day to do the shopping. Just send him, whenever he has time! Maybe it would be appropriate to draw a line between your professional and personal life, but Pontus didn't care.

On the Christmas party that year, there was an odd mix of old school friends, tiny old ladies with hats that smelled of lavender which made me long for Lisa, and the peculiar gang that he had started to play Dungeons&Dragons with, and then the members from the choir dressed in red, me wearing last year's polka striped tie. On top of that, Sara with Amanda and Jörgen who had the Saracheck.

This week's family box. Sara shouted out loud and clapped her hands:
-Johan is gonna sing! Sing! Sing!
Maybe that's when Madeleine noticed me properly. Thanks, my dear sister!

After the concert and Pontus' party, Christmas was getting closer with people going home or away, and there was no need for any more practises. The ones of us that were left decided to have a small end-of-semester-gathering in the nation pub. Madeleine was going, so I had to weigh those two situations against each other – a noisy pub full of people in one hand, and a chance to be near her in the other. The alternative was to sit home alone, regretting not going. So I went, and my heart almost stopped when she chose to sit next to me. My tongue was stuck to my palate, so I could only nod or shake my head when she tried to have a conversation with me. That new Swedish comedy seemed interesting, had I seen it? No? Neither had she, of course, if she had she would know if it was any good, it sure would be nice to see it together with someone!
The opening was wider than a football goal. If I could walk through it? Not. I was paralyzed. She had to do all the work herself. Maybe... if I wanted to see it, maybe we could go together? If I felt like it?
I nodded. She picked the time, and I bought the tickets. Lisa yells at me when I try to pay for her when we're going on fika, she's independent and modern and it's really humiliating! But, I don't know. I understand her point of view, but I can't help feeling that it can be rather nice to play gentleman. I was a bit afraid that Madeleine would be offended too if I didn't let her pay for her own ticket, but somehow she felt as the kind of girl that would appreciate a treat. She was very different from Lisa, which

I saw as a good thing. Of course, watching a movie together didn't make her my girlfriend, but if this led to something, it would be quite nice to have a girlfriend I could kiss. I had never done that. Lisa's more open minded ex Miriam has made me a lot of quite interesting suggestions over the years, but I've never been tempted. Not much, anyway.

Pontus came to check on me before that first date, trying to calm me down when I nervously tried to choose something to wear. Not too dressed up, but I didn't want to look like a slob!
-Don't analyze too much! It's just a movie. And after the movie, you invite her to your place for fika. I've bought three different types of tea. Earl Grey, some flowery shit and herbal tea if she's one of those. And a package of Scottish shortbreads. If she doesn't like them, I'll eat them. And I've bought you some, ehm, well. Just in case. I'll put them in your bedside drawer. You want her to know that you're a responsible young man.
I put my hands over my ears, didn't want to believe what I had just heard. Don't analyze? And he had bought me *condoms?* For real?
I yelled:
-We're going to the cinema, for heaven's sake! And it's scary as hell even without you making a whole chicken farm out of a feather!
-I hear you, but you never know!
He chuckled, complacently. I suppressed a strong urge to hit him over the head with a frying pan.
-Just because you have become some kind of mediaeval Casanova, you know it all? What do you use then? Sheep guts?
-I'm just trying to help! Excuse me, then!

A little hurt in his concern, Pontus put the embarrassing
package in his pocket and moved to the door.
-Leave them, I growled, unable to look at him.
Though I didn't see him, I could hear him smile.

Somehow, I managed to get myself to the cinema. Don't
ask me what the movie was about. I don't remember a
thing. I only remember her scent. Rose. She looked like a
rose as well. She was lovely!
After the movie, we went to a hamburger restaurant. You
didn't think I was brave enough to invite her to my home,
did you?
We sat opposite each other with a milkshake, like in an
American teen movie.
She smiled softly at me.
-You're a bit shy, aren't you?
-Almost pathological, I admitted.
-I think it's rather sweet.
I peeked quickly at her, otherwise my eyes were very
focused on the straw in the milkshake.
-You do?
-Mm. Many guys are so loud and pushy. You're not like
that. I feel that I could really talk to you.
-I hope so.
-My boyf... my ex... He tried to be so macho all the time.
If I tried to talk to him about anything even remotely
related to feelings, his eyes began wandering and he
suddenly had something important to do elsewhere.
That's why he broke up with me. Said I was too deep for
him.
Before I could stop myself I said:
-I can't believe that anyone would ever want to break up
with you.
Madeleine's eyes went misty, and she sighed.

-That's so sweet of you to say, Johan! But I think it's quite difficult to have a relationship with me.
-I refuse to believe that.
Her soft hand over mine.
-I'm getting used to the idea of being alone. He made me feel so worthless!
When I play this scene from my memory and add Lisa's commentary voice, she would have said: "You pathetic, manipulative little bitch! Find someone else to suck self esteem from! Leave Johan alone, or you will bitterly regret it for the rest of your life!" If Lisa hadn't been in Japan during this period, I can promise you that she would have seen that we were heading for disaster even from the start, and thrown herself between us. If I wish she had? Sometimes. Sometimes not. There are days when I would like to erase this experience from my life, but at the same time, it gives me something to compare other relationships with. If I ever find myself in a new relationship. Rather solitude than a bad twosome.
At the time, I couldn't understand at all why she would be interested in me. I was... nothing?
Now I know. Madeleine needed someone to repair her self confidence after being dumped. There's a good English expression for this: She was on the rebound. And I was infatuated by her, anyone could see that. To be adored is a good band-aid for a broken heart.

Madeleine soon learned that my inner driving force is to be compared with the power from a cut-price battery. If she wanted anything from me, she would have to get it herself. Right now, she wanted affirmation. It was right before her eyes, inside me, wrapped in duct tape, a bit difficult to get to, but maybe that was a part of the challenge? Maybe it was her kind of fun, to teach this shy virgin about what she called love.

-I would love to see your place. Would you be
comfortable inviting me to fika some day?
I nodded at my paper mug.
Lisa's imaginary comment would be: "She sure learned
fast how to manipulate you!"
Well, Lisa, you really shouldn't talk. I know you love me,
I know you would do almost anything to protect me from
harm, but when it comes to manipulating me, I think you
are the queen. And you don't even know it.

Most likely, our romance would have come to a natural
end quite soon, if it hadn't been for two factors.
The first: Madeleine immediately fell in love with my flat.
The day after our movie date, she invited herself to my
home and we made tea and scones together. Tant Frida
taught me a lot of her secret tricks and recipes, so I'm
actually quite good at baking. I never buy bread, I
experiment with sourdough and yeast and love the scent
of newlybaked that has stuck in my walls. Madeleine
preferred the "flowery shit", and that alone should have
made me suspicious according to Lisa. Anyone wanting to
drink perfume must be fishy.
The conversation flowed quite easy, since I was in safe
surroundings and Madeleine took the driver's seat. She
asked me about books and music and my studies, and
when I had got used to talking to her, I could return her
questions, that soon became more personal. If I ever had a
girlfriend? Yes, well, I did in highstage, we're still friends
but it was mostly one of those childish "look, we're a
couple"-things. (I'm sorry, Lisa!) No, we don't have any
troubles being friends, by the way, it turned out that she
was gay, so friendship suits us much better.
Somehow I thought it was important to emphasize this. If
Lisa came back, and if this turned out to be something, I
didn't want Madeleine to look upon Lisa as a threat.

Oh, so all your exes turned out to be swine, I'm so sorry,
that's really bad luck, I hope you will find someone good
at last!
-I think I might have found someone, she whispered and
took my hand.
Even I thought that sounded a little too sweet, almost
affected, but who was I to look a given horse in the
mouth! I didn't know what to do though, so I just
mumbled something and poured myself some more tea
with my free hand.

The second factor:
In January, Madeleine would be homeless. She had rented
her student room illegally secondarily, and the person on
the contract had suddenly decided to not continue her
studies abroad, and was coming back.
I don't want to think it was intentional. I have to believe
that she actually was in love with... maybe not me, but
with the thought of a new relationship, a new beginning.
Did I want to come to a New Year party in her student
corridor? Please? It wouldn't be any fun without me!
How on Earth a party would be more fun with me I
couldn't understand, but I promised to come. I was still
more attracted to her than afraid of a crowd.
Luckily, I have to say, alcohol makes me dizzy. If I had
become more relaxed and social, I would have turned into
an alcoholic years ago. When the kitchen drawers are
attacking me, I'm not drunk from a night out, I'm dizzy
from whisky testing with Jörgen. I love whisky! Without
ice. What would you call that, off the rocks?
Some cheap champagne substitute was put in my hand.
-Ten! Nine! Eight! Seven! Six! Five! Four! Three! Two!
One! Happy New -
Madeleine's arms around my neck, her tongue in my
mouth.

Epical, my first kiss ever on the exact turning of the year!
In one area, I'm no mediocrity.
I make love like a God!
The God of Death's cold kingdom, with ice instead of
blood in the veins, as passionate as the cold rocks
surrounding him.

With that said, I still had my virginity intact when the sun
rose on the new year, despite intense efforts from both of
us.
I also had a flatmate, because I had asked Madeleine to
move in with me.
Happy New Year, Happy New Life!

There are a lot of myths and research about how often
men and women think about sex. Some claim that men
think about it every sixth second, others say nineteen
times a day. For the average man, that is. If you combine
me and Pontus, you would get something like that,
because I almost never thought about it, and he did all the
time when we were teenagers. Finally he could take
advantage of looking much older than he was. He could
rent "adult movies" without anyone questioning him.
Well, someone could have, because he happened to meet
one of his teachers in the secret room, but she pretended
not to see him.
The first time he had got his hands on a movie like that,
he wanted me to watch it with him, as immoral support I
guess. I didn't want to, but I was afraid that he might
challenge me and I thought our pure-hearted knight
should be saved from those kind of things. It was also not
long after we had re-established our friendship in
highstage and I felt bad for his situation in school so I
agreed.

Two staring teenage boys, one in fascination, the other in disgust.
-Turn it off! That's just revolting!
At the same time, I was worried about my own reaction. Why didn't I want to try Secret Things alone in the shower? Why didn't I think about sex? Why was I so uncomfortable when Pontus wanted to talk about it?
Lisa hissed between clenched teeth when I told her about the horror movie.
-It's a perfectly healthy reaction, that you don't want to watch that shit! Don't worry. If you don't want to think about it or do it, then don't. You will know when you're ready.

Well, Lisa. I'm still waiting.

In a hectic euphoria, I helped Madeleine move her few belongings into my place. The feeling was related to the last time I suddenly got a girlfriend. Better hurry, before someone pinched my arm and woke me up!
Amanda was a little hesitant. How long had we known each other? Was she really my type? Was I absolutely sure that I wasn't rushing things?
I exploded.
-Well, excuse me if it isn't planned three years in advance in some bloody staple diagram! Can't you try to be happy for me? Everything has been so smooth in your life, you know what you want and where you're going and you have a perfect boyfriend and you will both have interesting jobs and earn loads of money and you will get everything you want, and you can't grant me this?
The silence felt like a crisp, thin ice layer, ready to break and we would both drown.

Eventually, my wonderful, wise big sister, whom I had unrightfully accused, said with a cool but still neutral voice:
-When you're ready to apologize, I will accept it.
She didn't even slam the door.
Why I was so upset?
Because deep inside, I knew she was right.

The first months, we were happy. I was in love with having a relationship, and Madeleine was in love with her new home. She made her own stencils and painted flower edgings near the ceiling. Put up curtains and shelves that she filled with her teddy bear collection that her mother had sent her from Östersund. Geraniums in all the windows. I hate geraniums. Do you know how bad they smell if you happen to touch one? She didn't like my bed cupboard, she wanted the bed down at all time, cluttered with unpractical lace pillows.
I accepted everything, except the small lavender bags that she wanted to place in our wardrobes. I lied, said that they gave me a headache. She was displeased. What kind of home is that, if the wardrobes didn't smell of lavender?
I didn't feel like explaining.
I accepted everything, because I got rewarded with closeness. Cosy closeness, the one I like the best. Someone who snuggled against me on the sofa, watching TV or reading. Someone playing with the hair in my neck, my god, how I miss that! She found my erogenous zone there, and the intimate part of our life finally begun.

I would prefer not to write about my sex life. It's not much to write about, but somehow I think it could be important to remind anyone who might read about this, that it isn't so simple and natural as we're fooled to believe by media. When Pontus got his first girlfriend, he thought he knew it all from those disgusting movies he had watched. Fortunately, she was a strong young lady and quickly put him in place. None of that, do you hear? I think he was quite relieved, because some of the things he had seen were rather bizarre and tacky, and he didn't know where to get the sheep that apparently was needed for some of the exercises.

For me and Madeleine, it was a different matter. I didn't know much at all, and her knowledge came from chic lit novels and Harlequin Passion, and of course from Max, her macho ex. Never had she read about a man who couldn't, well, perform. And contraceptives are far too unromantic to be handled in books like that. I could get an erection (yes, I'm red as a lobster in my face when I write this, please, don't let my mother ever learn English!), but then, there was this matter of putting a slinky, chemical smelling rubber on it. Or, trying to, because I never succeeded. Maybe it could have worked if Madeleine would have helped me, but she didn't want to get that rubber smell on her fingers, it took ages to wash it off! Banana flavoured? Don't be ridiculous!

She started to take the pill again, and it worked alright for a little while. Then I found out that she was a bit careless and some days completely forgot to take them, and that was an even worse romance killer than the condom. ”Have you taken your pills? Of course I have! Are you sure, I thought it said 'Tuesday' on the blister pack and today is Wednesday... Are you checking me?! Don't you trust me? Of course I do, I just happened to see... Well, forget it!”

Once, she wanted us to get counselling. My mother's voice was echoing in my mind: What would people say? And what would *I* say? How could I tell a stranger that I wasn't very keen on having sex with my girlfriend, when I

couldn't even tell her? The thought made me terrified
and I couldn't speak for a whole day. It was like someone
had glued my jaws together. Even eating was difficult
because I was so tense. So she dropped the subject, with a
deep, impatient sigh.
And you know what she thought about my stammering.
She took it as a personal insult that I wasn't relaxed
enough with her. It took a long time before I was
introduced to her family, because she wanted to cure me
first. Kind-hearted of her, wasn't it?

Everything else worked just fine, though. We loved to be
near each other, loved to fika, watch romantic comedies,
even cleaning the flat was fun when we did it together. In
the beginning it was genuine, but eventually it changed
into being a contemporary version of the live role playing
games that Pontus liked so much. We pretended to be
happy, because we wanted to be.

Can you imagine the look on Lisa's face when she came
back from Japan and saw me hen-pecked in a lavishly
decorated doll house?
Very rarely do I see her speechless.
Eventually, she said:
-Teddy bears. You have teddy bears in your book shelves.
-Mm.
-Many teddy bears.
-Yup.
-Ok. Are you happy?
Was I? This tingling feeling that made me slightly dizzy,
that could be happiness, right?
-Yes.
-I guess everything is alright then.

Finally she hugged me.

She had changed her shampoo, and I was struck by a sorrow I couldn't understand.
I wondered where Madeleine had put those lavender bags.

The band-aid has been ripped off, Madeleine has been introduced. You already know that the relationship crashed, and I think you can guess why. We were playing house. Let's wait a bit with the misery, and see what Pontus and Lisa were up to these years! They are a big part of my life so I can't write about myself without including them. And I want to write about them. Their lives are much more interesting than mine, and I don't want to bore you so perhaps I should change the title to "Confessions of a Mediocrity and his cool friends".

Back to the gymnasium.
The most important school Lisa ever went to, was the School of Life in the cottage.
Everything that Kerstin and Leif failed to teach her about empathy and the ability to reflect rather than argue, she learned from tant Frida just by watching her.
Once upon a time, tant Frida had a family. She had bought her siblings' shares in the cottage, since they weren't interested in it, and she had a long and happy life there. Her husband had died from old age just a few months before she answered Lisa's desperate note in the paper, feeling a little desperate herself when the loneliness started to eat her. Their only son had also passed away recently, in a motorcycle accident, so she enjoyed having us around just as much as we enjoyed being there. Her siblings had been much older. The brother was a sailor and had disappeared somewhere. The sister was vital up until her ninetieth birthday party, when she suddenly sat down on a chair and said: "Now it's time for me to leave the party!" and died. The relatives that wanted to put tant

Frida in a home were her sister's step children, so they weren't related by blood, but who else was there to inherit? They weren't exactly nasty, but they desired that cottage. It would be so perfect with a little vacation home so near town! They tried to get tant Frida to modernise it, of course for her own comfort, not at all because it would be so much cheaper for them if she did it now. Couldn't she understand that she needed water in the house? And electricity! However did she manage without that! And no TV! Dear dear, it's about time for aunt to come to a nice service home where she didn't have to be so lonely! But first, get the water and electricity and TV, please!
If they were happy when Lisa moved in?
Guess twice.
They contacted Kerstin and Leif. Their tactic switched between concern about aunt Frida who was too old and tired to have a bunch of teenagers in the house, and in the next breath they pretended to be worried about Lisa who would be so lonely and isolated from all her friends, who in the sentence before invaded the cottage and disturbed aunt Frida.
The professors took the matter with ease mixed with an academic excitement – now they had a chance to play, to twirl the enemy with rhetoric. As I said, they cared more about Lisa than she thought, they just found it impossible to show it in a way she could understand. Now they had the chance! Quotes and theories and reasoning hailed over the poor relatives who had office jobs and were strangers to the terminology and culture of the university. Totally dizzy, they left the smoky book covered apartment, defeated.
Oh well. The old hag wouldn't live forever.
Unfortunately she didn't, but before she left us, something happened that only occurs in newspaper short stories.

Lisa's eighteenth birthday was celebrated with warm
rhubarb crumble pie and whipped cream in the arbour.
-Do you like it here, dear?
Lisa smiled and wrinkled her nose.
-You know I do! I would like to stay here forever,
preferably with you but you might be a little whining
when your hundredandfiftieth birthday is closing in.
Tant Frida chuckled and gave her a brown envelope that
she had glued old flower bookmarks on.
-Then I'd like you to have this as a birthday gift. You have
come of age and I know you are a responsible young
woman.
Inside the envelope was a contract of sale. According to
that, Lisa had bought the property for ten crowns. The
value of ten crowns is somewhere between a pound and a
dollar.
-We have to go into town to get it properly witnessed.
Better make a doctor's appointment as well, so that he can
write an attestation that I'm mentally healthy. If not, my
relatives will probably make a fuss, accusing you of
tricking me into this.
Lisa and I stared at the paper, not fully understanding.
-The cottage will be yours, dearest little Lisa. I would cry
in my heaven if I looked down and saw those couch
potatoes violate my home with electricity and water and
TV and everything else they want to force upon it. You
would never do that.
Quietly, Lisa replied:
-No. I would never do that.
-Do you want it?
Suddenly, tant Frida sounded a bit anxious. Maybe Lisa
had grown tired of the forest and wanted to live in the
city, like other youths?

A conventional person probably would have protested. At least a conventional Swede. We're very focused on balance. A gift or a favour has to be returned with something equal. Something like this would awaken a storm of protests. You really shouldn't. You have to get a fair price for it. Reconsider, you might change your mind! But Lisa looked at tant Frida, long and thoroughly, with her old eyes in a young face, into an old face with young eyes.
-Yes, she finally said. Yes, tant Frida, I would love to manage your legacy. Thank you!
She gave the sweet little tant a warm hug, and repeated:
-Thank you!
Tears of emotion in both their eyes. Lisa gave a little laugh.
-If you behave, I'll let you stay here for free.
Tant Frida patted her cheek.
-You're such a sweet girl!

Before all papers were signed, tant Frida spent her last penny on restoring the cottage. Nothing modern, of course, but the roof needed to be fixed up, and the windows could use new sealing. An expert on old wood stoves showed us how to renovate it to last at least one more century, and some other things were taken care of. The only things that mattered to her these days were her house, her cats and us "children". The money wouldn't do her any good in the grave, as she said.
When the paperwork was done, witnessed by amazed professionals, someone was so touched by the whole thing that he wanted to call the local newspaper. This would be a heart-warming story, illustrated with a picture of the two of them in the arbour!
That suggestion was hammered down with no room for compromise. Neither of them felt like sharing such a

private matter as entertainment. But, it was a very sweet
thought, young man!
The forty-seven year young man blushed a bit and looked
as if he felt like a schoolboy again.

Lisa took a lot of extra gymnasium courses on top of the
mandatory, and while she was at it, some university
courses as well. We had thought that the property was just
the cottage, but it turned out that it was much bigger,
including a rather large piece of the forest. A manager had
been taken care of it for decades, and the income from the
wood covered all the expenses so Lisa wouldn't have to
worry too much about the economy.

One month later, tant Frida died peacefully in the
sunshine.
Somehow, we had thought that she would live forever.
The relatives came very fast. They tried to look sad, but
didn't quite succeed.
Oh, our poor, dear little aunt Frida, we should have
visited her more often, how could this happen, if only she
had taken our advice and moved into a nursing home!
What a sad day this is! Of course you are welcome to stay
in the cottage until the funeral, little Lisa, you have been
such a nice company for aunt these last years, we give
your credit for that.
Their benevolence sunk when they found out who owned
the cottage.
How could aunt have deceived us like this! We did
everything for her! You just wait, you little... the last word
hasn't been said in this matter! We're going to talk to a
lawyer!
Not much a lawyer could do when there was a witnessed
contract and a certificate from a doctor.

-So be it! Then you can bury the old hag behind the
raspberry bushes!
Lisa shouted at their backs:
-Thanks for the suggestion!

We buried tant Frida behind the raspberry bushes.
Everything a funeral agency would do, Lisa and I did.
According to the law, we needed a coffin. It doesn't
matter what it looks like, as long as it's dignified.
Lisa just sneered at the astronomical prices of the
readymade coffins. How hard could it be to make one?
Four walls, bottom and lid. Borrow a car, Johan, we're
going to the lumberyard!

In Sweden, you have to be eighteen to get your driver's
license. Lisa was only eighteen and a month and had no
interest in learning how to drive. My birthday is in
November so I hadn't come of age yet. I was allowed to
take lessons though, which I did from Pontus who was not
allowed to give them but we didn't care. He had his
license just a couple of days after his eighteenth birthday
the previous year, and you must have had your license for
a certain number of years, five I think, before you can give
private lessons. He had bought an old junker that he had
fixed up, and was happy to help. We were all mourning,
and this was our way of handling the immediate grief.
One of the teachers in highstage that had understood and
got along with Lisa was our wood&metal craft teacher.
We went to him. Could he please help us? We wanted to
do it properly, even though it might just be four sides, a
bottom and a lid.
He loved to help out. We spent many hours in his own
carpentry shop. He said that even though the coffin would
be destroyed, we should pay our respect by making it as
beautiful as we could. One entire evening we stood there,

Pontus, Lisa and I, with a soldering iron each, decorating the coffin with patterns and words about how much she had meant to us. That night was when we truly said our goodbyes. Sometimes we were quiet, sometimes we talked. Do you remember when she taught you to make cinnamon buns with raspberry jam, Johan, and you by accident used sifted rye flour and they turned out surprisingly delicious? Remember the old horrible chapbook song she used to sing, about the evil father who drank too much and neglected his motherless children and one day found out that his little girl had frozen to death, and he was devastated and found God? What was it called, Axel and Ester? "Så bister kall sveper nordanvinden..." We sang and cried and laughed and cried.

We covered the bottom with tant Frida's old quilt, so patched that it was impossible to see what the original material was. For the sides, my mom had given us curtains that she had woven herself. For once, she didn't have anything to say about what people might think. Initially she was a bit worried, because she thought it might be too much for us. Lisa sat down with her one day and explained that she had everything worked out and that she needed to do this by herself, she couldn't just hand the whole thing over to someone who didn't even know tant Frida. Mom understood and supported us.

I understand why most people go to a funeral agency that takes care of all the practical details in times of sorrow. We had to get a permit to collect the body from the morgue. Make an identity check. Tant Frida wanted to be cremated, so we had to book a time for that. Cremation is by far the most common way to take care of a body in Sweden, 70% choose that method. We also had to arrange for a dignified car to collect the coffin with the body, and drive it to the crematory. Talk to the county

government and show them on a map where we wanted to
bury the ashes, and get a permission. You can't just bury
or spread the ashes anywhere. Since we wanted to do it on
a private property with miles to the nearest neighbours, it
wasn't a problem.

From the crematory, we got a small bag with the dusty
remains of tant Frida. We put that inside a velvet bag, red
with white hearts, that Sara had made in her textile craft
class. Askew and clumsy and totally perfect.

My family insisted on being present at the interment.
They had been supportive all the way, and wanted to be
there for us to the end. Lisa didn't want to spend money
on an obituary in the local paper. Everyone who needed
to know that tant Frida was no longer with us already
knew. But my father asked if he could do it anyway, as his
own farewell to somebody he had grown very fond of. He
wrote a beautiful litany over the sweet lady, that Lisa, a bit
grudging but yet grateful, approved of.

Even at funerals, there has to be fika.

When the bag and tant Frida had returned to nature, we
had raspberry lemonade and cinnamon buns.

The circle was complete.

When the funeral and everything surrounding it was over,
Lisa sank into the rocking chair, weary to her bones.

-I wonder what it would feel like not to see people for a
year. I think I'll try that!

My heart sank.

She gave me a nudge.

-Not you, of course! You're not people.

I gave her a relieved smile, and she continued with an
affective but mocking tone in her voice:

-By the way, I need someone to do the shopping for me.
How could I manage a whole year without liquorice?

She actually went through with it. Nobody but me came
to see her in the cottage for a year. My mother was beside
herself with worry. Poor Lisa! Tant Frida's death had
really struck her hard. Was she deeply depressed?
Shouldn't you send someone else to talk to her about this?
Are you sure you're strong enough to take this
responsibility, Johan? Does she confide in you? What
does she say?
-*Sub Rosa*, mom.
-Rosa who?
-Never mind.

Lisa wasn't depressed at all. Of course she missed tant
Frida, we all did, but she could feel her presence
everywhere inside and around the cottage. The thin
coffee cups wore the invisible mark of tant Frida's hands,
where she had held them thousands and thousands of
times. The apple trees were carefully pruned by her
hands, and everything was as if Frida would walk inside
the door at any time.
She stopped counting the days and let the nature be her
calendar. In that, she read when it was time for the
autumn cultivation, or when it was time to put extra
spruce around the well. Pontus was people, so the wood
chopping was left to me.
-How equal is this, I protested when I saw the huge pile
waiting for me.
Lisa grinned.
-It's probably good for me to get rid of some of my
principles. Besides, I like watching men chop wood.

-How politically incorrect and nonindependent of you!
Are you sure you're not secretly hetero?

She just laughed.
-Ok, you asparagus, if you'd rather dig out the privy,
you're welcome. That's what I was about to do.
Wood chopping didn't sound so bad after all!

Lisa never understood how much she hurt Pontus by
considering him to be "people", excluding him from his
paradise. He had done more work there than the both of
us combined. Even though he's the least resentful person
I know, he took this hard and it's probably one of the
main reasons that their relationship today is a bit strained.
If it hadn't been for me, they would never have anything
to do with each other. Maybe I should talk to her about
this, and ask her to give him a proper explanation. It's so
sad to see my two best friends being no more than polite
to each other. I still insist on inviting them both for fika
on my birthdays, hoping that they one day will learn to
appreciate each other.

The gymnasium was finally the time and place for Pontus
to fill his own costume. Here, his geeky interest in
mechanics and construction was a great asset, and
suddenly, he was the star of the class! I still helped him
with what is called the core subjects, that is, subjects that
were mandatory in all the programs. He didn't care too
much about those. As long as he passed, it was good
enough for him.
His new friends were playing Dungeons&Dragons, which
opened up a whole new world for him.
On Friday evenings, they set up everything in his
basement – no, mother, we can't sit in the living room,
you have to sit in the basement, it's just the way it's
done – with potato chips, sweets and huge amounts of
Coca Cola. Someone was Game Master, and with

strangely shaped dices clutched like swords in their hands, they threw themselves into fictional adventures.

Pontus tried to explain:

-It's just like when we were playing with my knights! Only so much more fun! You never know what's going to happen, there are riddles to solve and dragons to fight... You have to try it! Come with us on Friday? I can help you create a character!

I agreed to come, but I wanted to watch before I joined. Another of my issues, I'd rather not try new things if I don't know exactly how they're done. It took me ages to learn how to ride a bike. I didn't want to try, because I didn't know how to do it. Logical, right? Baking is the one exception. I love to experiment in that area.

Curled up in an armchair in the corner I watched the eager young men preparing for battle and adventure. You see an old, dilapidated mansion. What do you do? We enter, of course! Rolling the dice. Oh now, a stone falls down and hits you unconscious! You have to stay for... Rolling the dice... Two rounds before you regain your consciousness and can continue. Then I cast a Spell of Healing on him! Rolling the dice. Yay, it's working, he's getting up! What are you doing next? We explore the house!

Quite boring to listen to.

-Want to join, Johan? Let's make you a character!

-I don't know...

-Come on! Sit here next to me. Have some Coke!

I don't like Coca Cola, but I was afraid to let anyone in that company know. I think it would have been just as bad as if I had spit out the communion wine. Coke was like elixir of life to them. If someone had cut themselves, I'm sure Coke would have oozed out from their veins. I took some careful sips, felt nauseous from the sugar and caffeine kick and my stomach protested from both the

drink and the nervousness when they created my character with the dices. Stamina, skill, wisdom, intelligence, strength, courage, attributes... I became a rather stupid dwarf, strong as an ox!
You meet an ogre! What do you do? Johan, try to hit him! You're probably stronger than him. Oh no, a one on a T-20! Maximal bad luck! The ogre hit you so hard over the head that you sink to your ears in the ground! Do you want us to create a new character, we won't mind, this was just too unfortunate!
Thanks, but no thanks. It was probably an omen. I'm going home.
Eventually, hours past midnight, some stumbled home to get some sleep, some stayed on mattresses on the basement floor.
-We have guest rooms...
-No, mother, it has to be in the basement, I've told you!
-But can't I at least cook something decent for you?
-It has to be home delivered pizza! It's all a part of the concept!
She was allowed to cook them brunch though, and she soon cracked the code and brought them snacks and Coke in a steady stream and became the most popular mother in town. She liked that.
The entire weekends were spent in these fantasy worlds. Pontus was happy.
I was envious.

In a fictive story, I would have added something cool to my personality. What if I had spent hours and hours alone in my room, practiced the guitar and turned out to be the next Segovia! Or the master of card tricks, or... just anything. Instead, I just let the hours pass when I was alone. Or baked. I liked that.

Not long after the Dungeons&Dragons debut, Pontus took the step into the forest. LARP, Live Active Role Playing games, became his new hobby. In Sweden, it's called live, but to distinguish it from live music and everything else live, it's spelled as it sounds, lajv. I will keep the Swedish expression. Allrakäraste, lagom, lussekatt, fika, tant and lajv, this is a good start if you want to learn my language!
In lajv, you're supposed to play a character yourself, not by throwing dice, but you had to dress and act like this creature.
-A little hard for you to play dwarf then, I said dryly.
(I told you that I was intolerable in the gymnasium. I'm sorry.)
Pontus didn't let my mood affect him.
-Not a problem. It's all about creating an illusion together! With the right attributes, everyone will understand that I'm a dwarf and then it doesn't matter that I'm over six point five feet tall. I saw the coolest two-edged axe in the hardware store yesterday. I'm going to put it on my Christmas wish list!
Pontus' overprotective mother wasn't very keen on buying an axe for her darling boy. Not keen at all. As long as they stayed in her basement she felt safe. They didn't do anything more dangerous than throw dice and drink a bit too much Coke, but this? Weapons! Do you actually use real weapons?! Pontus tried to calm her.
-Not always. It's more like... jewellery. When we fight for real, we use latex weapons, look, I can hit Johan quite hard and it hardly hurts at all, right, Johan?
I sneered:
-Excuse me, but your dagger looks like a giant butter knife!

You may wonder, as did I, how Pontus could stand me during these years. It wasn't just because he needed my help with the school work, it was to repay his debt to me! Even though he was pariah at highstage, I had still been his friend. Now he wanted to return that loyalty when he saw how lonely I was without Lisa. He told me this much later, when my teenage melancholy and bad attitude had started to wear off and changed into, well, more adult melancholy.

-What do you mean? I let you down! I never defended you when they hurt you!
-It's not always about what you say, Johan, but what you do. You were there. Especially in gym class. Always.
-But... I was with Lisa all the time?
-Not always. And the two of you included me. You made me think that you had lunch with me because you wanted to, not as an act of false goodness.
-But, we did want to have lunch with you.
-There you go.

So, Pontus endured my moods. He remembered the good times we had as kids, and saw something in me that I couldn't see then. He saw *me.* Sometimes I look in the mirror, and try to figure out who I am. I feel that I'm lost both inside and outside myself. All my attempts to build my own person have always been mirrored in someone else's eyes. Madeleine's boyfriend. Lisa's best friend. I even thought about letting Miriam play with me, just to give myself a little substance. I feel like a dough. Rising, collapsing, rising again, wobbly in the bowl, but I can't find any oven. I guess the answer lies within myself. If this had been a book about how I finally found myself and figured everything out, I would have added a Wise Person to Show Me The Way, a way that always was deep inside me, like the musical Starlight Express, when the underdog

Rusty defeated all competition and won the girl when he realised that he himself was the Starlight.

I can't promise you that the book will not end like that. Maybe I will find that wisdom tomorrow. Maybe tant Frida could have shown me The Way if she had lived longer, maybe I will find a secret note from her behind an ancient mirror in the outhouse where she wrote something decades ago, knowing that someone in need would eventually find it and understand the mystery of life. Please, hold your thumbs (which is the Swedish expression for crossing your fingers) that I will find something, anything, to help me enjoy life a little more? I don't mind being a mediocrity, I just want to be... someone.

With Pontus, it has never been like the way I described with the girls. We have friendship, nothing more, nothing less, nothing complicated at all.

It has taken me years to understand this: It doesn't matter if you can't understand why someone likes you. Just try to relax and treasure it!

Lajv needs requisites. Most of all, nice mediaeval inspired clothes.

One of his school friends had a sister who had chosen the clothing technical line in gymnasium. Maybe she could help? Linda talked to her teachers. Maybe she could do this as a part of her school work. They had to do a fashion show, wouldn't it be cool to show mediaeval fashion? And she could write a paper about it, for her textile history course?

Excellent idea!

Pontus thought so too. Not only did he get the best dress in the whole lajv group, real linen and wool instead of crushed polyester velvet and whatever you could find at IKEA, he also found a description in the museum of how to make your own mediaeval shoes in leather. Perhaps not suitable for winter, but on the show they were the icing on the cake! And, on top of that icing, he got his first girlfriend! On the show, he was so proud, wearing every inch of his tallness with pride. The Dungeons&Dragons diet hadn't exactly reduced his overweight but in those clothes it actually looked quite good. Girlfriend and impressing clothes in the same package! He was so happy that his feet barely touched the ground. Could we please stop the time and live in this emotion forever?

The fashion show was held in the evening. Sara wanted to go because she wanted to see her Pontus be a star, and my mother was happy to go with her since she still was interested in clothes and fashion. My own relation to clothes is very simple: It has to be clean and it has to be comfortable. In my wardrobe you will find jeans, sweatpants, T-shirts for the summer and cotton shirts for the winter, boxer shorts and black tube socks, just enough to get me by for a week before I do my laundry. My boxer shorts can be quite artistic though. But hey, why am I telling you about my underwear! That's really crossing the line! (I pretend I have forgotten that you know all about my sex life.)
Sara cheered when Pontus came out on the runway. Not so much when he introduced us to Linda after the show.
-You're *my* boyfriend! she claimed.
He lifted the little gnome and gave her a big kiss on the cheek.
-You will always be my favourite girl in the whole world!
Linda smiled and said that she didn't mind coming second. My little retarded sister probably wasn't any serious threat.

The show made a deep impact on Sara and she kept
talking about it for days.
-Also wanna model!
Mom smiled and nodded.
-Yes, that's probably lots of fun.
-Wanna!
-Mm.
-Wanna! Wanna!
-Maybe you could become a model when you grow up,
sweetie.
Our sweetheart was ten years old, went to a school for
children with special needs and had a confidence much
larger than her small body. Her difficult start was
something we often forgot, because now she never had to
go to the hospital. She was healthy, happy, angry and still
put small things in her mouth whenever she could.
-Wanna now!
-I can't help you with that, love!
I meddled.
-Of course you can.
Mom got confused.
-What do you mean?
-You arranged fashion shows all the time when I was a
kid, and forced us to make fools of ourselves on that
runway. When you finally have a child who wants to do it,
you should be happy!
-Johan! You're being rude! You loved to be on those
shows!
How had she managed to reconstruct the history in her
head? Amanda did it because she was a nice girl, and me,
they had to carry away!
At that time, I didn't feel like quarrelling.
-Ok, mom, I was just teasing. But seriously, they love Sara
at the salon. She would be a big success as a model.
Sara's smile shone like the sun, she danced and sang:

-I'm gonna be a model! I'm gonna be a model! Just like
Pontus!
Mom's eyes went dark and she sent Sara to dad who was
watching sports in the living room.
-Why would you say something like that, Johan! Look at
what you've done! She will be so disappointed when I try
to explain to her that she can't be a model. What would
people say!
I sighed. So here we were once more.
-Maybe people would think it was a rather welcome
change, compared to those skeletons that use to show
clothes that no healthy person could even dream of
wearing. Why can't you do a fashion show for all different
kinds of people? Old and young, disabled, different,
everybody? It would be great if you could get someone in
a wheelchair.
-You can't make fun of people like that! Wheelchair?!
-Yes, mom, wheelchair! Maybe disabled people also want
to look good sometimes?
-I don't want to talk to you! I don't recognise you
anymore, Johan. You have become so... mannerless!
I hid my laugh behind my hand. Poor mom, who
suddenly got such an ill-bred son!
-I'll stay with Lisa tonight, then.
-Please do!

Lisa listened attentively when I told her about my
conversation with mom.
-It's not a bad idea at all! You do get your bright
moments, you know!
-I thought so too. All those fashion magazines are so full
of lies. There are many people with some kind of
disability, why couldn't Sara be regarded just as beautiful
as Cindy Crawford?

-You're absolutely right! If we start by showing the children... She got lost in her own thoughts and got that look in her eyes that I know so well. It meant that she had an idea.

To begin with, the owner of the salon was very reluctant.
-No, dear, it's a nice thought and a commendable initiative, but it's not the kind of operation we do here.
-But would you just think about it? Free publicity, the value of goodwill, new customers... Look at my calculations! It doesn't have to be very expensive. You can get contribution from all sorts of funds!
Hesitating but interested, she glanced at the paper with the figures.
When Lisa wants something, she usually gets it. This was before her year in solitude, and her distance learning gave her lots of free time. She threw herself into the carousel, seeking sponsors, talking to clothes companies, choosing models... In the end, there was a highly acclaimed show, called "A Night for Our Children", where the surpluses went to a fund for children in need. Sara opened the show, just as proud as Pontus had been. Naturally, he and Linda came and applauded her. She waved at them with her whole arm. After her, children in all sizes and colours, with or without disabilities, came parading. Siblings hand in hand, children pushed in their wheelchairs or carried, wearing beautiful, comfortable clothes.
-It was my son's idea.
My mom talked to a journalist and caught me in the arm. I tried to escape but she wouldn't let me. It wasn't as bad as I had thought to be interviewed. The journalist had a clear vision of what she wanted to write. Did I want to emphasize diversity? Nod. Did you want to emphasize everyone's equal value? Nod. And maybe you wanted to make your sister happy? Nod.

That led to a heart-warming quote which made me seem
like a very nice young man. Impressive, that someone so
young can be so mature!

Lisa started a relationship with one of the stylists.
-Nothing serious, she said in a casual tone, removing a
green ringlet from her face. I think her natural hair colour
was a bit like mine, maybe a bit lighter, with soft curls.
-Does she know that?
-I'm sure she does.
-You... won't get hurt or anything? Is she nice to you?
Lisa laughed, a teasing glimpse in her eyes.
-No. She's a very naughty girl!
-Enough! Spare me the details, please!

I'd like to say something about disabilities.
I don't think that the word is used correctly. It's easy to
say that someone is disabled, without stopping to think
about what it means.
You only have a disability when you need but can't get
help to handle a certain situation. If you need glasses,
you're disabled before you put them on. With them, you
are perfectly able. A wheelchair doesn't make you disabled
if your environment is fitted. Sara would never admit that
she had any disabilities! In her case, we were the disabled
ones because we were unable to let her out of sight. And
in my case, my shyness and melancholy is my disability,
not my stammering.

After her hermit year, Lisa wanted to meet people again.
She took a student loan and rented a second hand room in
a dormitory, or in a corridor as we call it. She wanted to
study something that she didn't know anything about in
advance, something where the teachers for once knew

more than she. She begged me to study just one term with her, for old times' sake. We would have so much fun! Celtic languages? What's that?

Apparently, the Celts were not a unit, but different groups of people, with different languages, who had been roaming Europe from about 500 BC until the Romans managed to push them back to the coastlines in Britain and Ireland. Except for the small tribe in Gaul, with Asterix and his friends, you know. Maybe they're still around, hiding in the French forests. Four of these language are still spoken, Irish and Scottish-Gaelic are closely related, but very different from Welsh and Breton. There are two extinct languages, Manx and Cornish, that some enthusiasts try to revive. Oh, Johan, let's move to Cornwall and have a baby and only speak Cornish so that it becomes the first native speaker for centuries! No, let's not.

The only thing I remember is that the longest place name in the world, Llanfairpwllgwyngyllgogerychwyrndrobwllllantysilio-gogogoch, is just a gimmick that the local tailor invented to give the village some PR. It's just words put together, something with St Mary's church near the white hazel shrub and another church and some red cave.

I failed all exams but it felt so good to be with Lisa again! Especially after that night on the roof, when she told me how much she cared for me and that I had saved her life. For a while, everything felt good! Pontus and I had a kind of gentlemen's agreement not to mention how badly I behaved in gymnasium, and Lisa and I saw each other every day.

Until she started experimenting.

It was almost unbearable to watch Lisa burn her candle in both ends the way she did. Maybe she's a little impulsive sometimes, but she's always been sensible. Now, she seemed to be caught in some kind of late teenage rebellion. When I come to think of it, maybe it was me she tried to break free from, despite her words of affection. She almost seemed to enjoy my agony. Sometimes she borrowed my clothes, pretending to be a man. She joined a gay student community and got entangled in a triangle drama with so many components that I couldn't retell them even if my life depended on it. But the worst was BDSM. Horrified, I watched her make a leather whip.

-It's not as bad as you think, she tried to reassure me, or maybe tried to provoke me.

-Do you hurt each other or not?

-It's not like that, Johan!

-What are you going to do with that whip, then?

-Just properties.

-I don't want anyone to hurt you!

Impatient sigh.

-We're not talking about assault here, you know. It's nothing but a way for me to explore myself. Everyone follows the rules, and there are stop words if anyone feels uncomfortable or want to slow things down. And I actually enjoy when someone holds me down and commands me to obey!

My Lisa!

The shock left me speechless and my tongue went tense. I couldn't talk, so I whispered:

-But... What if somebody doesn't obey those rules? If things get out of hand?

She softened a bit and stroke my hair.

-Oh, sweet, innocent Johan. What if a car doesn't stop when I'm crossing the street? What if tant Frida had turned out to be a mad axmurderer? To live is to take risks. If you're too afraid to try something that you're

curious of, what's the point of living? If I die and reach
the Pearly Gates, do you think St Peter would commend
me if I say: "Look, I locked myself into my home my
entire life to make sure nothing bad happened to me, and
here I am, without any experience, but intact!" Or would
he scold me and say: "You only have one life, why have
you wasted it by not trying out all the wonderful things
life has to offer? Shame on you!"
Tears were burning in my eyes and throat.
-But... why have you got to try such horrible things?
She sat down opposite me and made me look at her. That
alone made me even more sure of that she wanted to repel
me. I don't like looking people in the eyes, remember?
-Do you know what I think is horrible?
I shook my head.
-Dough! Every time you stick your hands into a bowl and
touch that sticky goo, I shudder. How can you stand it!
And I know. It's not dangerous to have your hands in
dough. But this isn't dangerous either. Especially not
when there are more than two involved. If somebody
against all odds would flip out, there's at least one more
person there to stop it. And you have to admit, this
leather leash looks really good on me!
That was more than I could take.
I left.
If you're into this BDSM yourself, please forgive me. I
don't want to judge anyone, I just don't understand.
Maybe I would discover new depths inside myself if I let
Miriam chain me to a bed. Maybe I would understand
even more about love and respect if I borrowed that whip.
Who knows, perhaps our sex life had been fantastic if
Madeleine and I had been a little, or a lot, more
imaginative and playful. But to see Lisa in that leash made
me cry.

Remember that Madeleine sighed over her own depth and how difficult a relationship with her must be? Compared to Lisa, Madeleine's profoundness was as difficult to chew as the peel of a tomato, while Lisa's could be compared to a coconut. None of her girlfriends was good enough. In the beginning, everything seemed maybe not perfect but at least as if it had potential. Maybe this was Miss Right, I can really talk to This One, but none of them could bear her intensity and how short tempered she was with everyone who failed to follow her thoughts. Once she tried to have a boyfriend, which hurt me more than I wanted to admit. I felt a bit better when she told me she wanted to break up with him because he was so shallow and only wanted One Thing and she wasn't interested in letting him do that.

Eventually, she grew tired of it all and the destructive carousel she had thrown herself into. Lagom isn't such a bad concept after all.

-I need to get away from all this! Please, look after the cottage for me for a year or so? I could easily rent it out, but I don't want anyone else contaminating the atmosphere we have built up there.

I promised.

Without any plans or any place to stay, Lisa went to Japan with an open return ticket, with a large cheque from her parents in case she found any exciting books.

I borrowed Pontus' car and drove her to Arlanda Airport to say goodbye. It's not like on TV, where you can accompany someone all the way to the gate, so I had to guess which plane was hers and waved at the sky. I felt so empty seeing her go. Even during her hermit year I had seen her every week. This was the first time ever that I didn't have her within bicycle range whenever any of us

wanted to see each other. I wanted to scream to the disappearing plane, even if it wasn't the right one:
Don't leave me!
I'm lost without you!

In Japan, there's something that we could use for the students in Uppsala – capsule hotels! Hundreds of small cubicles stacked beside and on top of each other with nothing more than a bed and a shelf for no more belongings than you could carry. Pontus might have found it tight, but Lisa could sit straight with two decimetres to the roof. There was no kitchen, but a small fast food restaurant. Shared bathrooms, a pool and a lounge with a TV. When you came "home", you had to place your private clothes in a locker and borrow slippers and a cotton robe called yukata. Many of the guests at the capsule hotels are businessmen who have worked so long in the evening that there's no time to go home. Lisa's theory is that the mandatory yukata is a way to force them to relax. It's very difficult to feel stressed in a robe. Lisa brought one back to me, and I love it! Almost all my free time I spend in just my fancy boxer shorts and my flowery yukata, if I'm at home that is. Once, Pontus tried to challenge me to go to my corner shop and buy some potato chips for our Lord of the Rings-marathon. I challenged him back, to accompany me in just his underwear. We spent a few minutes making the challenges more and more indecent until we finally gave up, realising that we would be arrested if we went through with it, and made popcorns instead. In the saucepan of course, with real butter, no microwave Styrofoam, thank you!

Other guests at the capsule hotel were people who can't afford a place of their own and rent their cubicle by the month, men who had a little too much to drink and are unable to find their way home, and the occasional backpacker.

Lisa was fascinated by Tokyo. She spent her days just walking around, studying the people, the surroundings and the atmosphere. The street fashion intrigued her with the mix of absurd playfulness and bright colours, and she wanted to try it. She went into a fashion boutique and asked for help. Destiny would have it that on this particular day, they held an audition for a fashion show. The staff just assumed that she was applying, gave her a number and showed her the waiting lounge. While waiting, she wrote a postcard to Sara:
"My dear sweet cool Sara!
You can never guess what I'm about to do! I'm trying out to be a model, just like you, because you're my Leading Star and I want to be like you! Keep your fingers crossed, will you? I'll tell you all about it later!"
Naturally, Lisa got to be on the show, and was offered a model contract. She had something that is quite unusual in the fashion world – she didn't care about it. That gave her a relaxed air and the photos of her looked natural, like she posed for fun, not because she wanted to impress someone. The whole fashion universe was far too superficial for someone like Lisa. However, she thought it would be an interesting experience, it was an income she could live on during her stay, she could use the endless hours in the makeup lounge to learn Japanese, but most of all, she did it for Sara. Every week she sent her a postcard, writing about something fun. Sara was overjoyed! She brought all the cards to school and read them to everyone, so proud, so proud that she knew a celebrity! I also got to

see the newspaper cuttings she sent, and read the postcards, that often had a "kiss Johan on the nose from me" written on them. Now and then Lisa called me with a lively background noise. Her life was too hectic for any longer conversations, so I never really got round to tell her about Madeleine. It was all about her. As usual. Mostly there were photo shoots in those bizarre street outfits and the occasional fashion show, and soon she moved on to the screen where she did commercials. They loved her Swedish accent when she talked about how wonderful this noodle soup or shampoo or whatever was. The idea of a TV show started to grow. Lisa in Japan! They wanted her to travel around the country, learn Japanese and about Japanese culture in a screwed slapstick way that always ended with someone getting wet, falling down in a bathtub filled with yoghurt or some other strange twist. Lisa agreed, as long as she wasn't the one getting wet. She was prepared to do many things to try the experience, but she certainly could live without being covered with lemon curd! I tried to joke about it when she called me and growled because they wanted her next photo shoot to be of her inside a giant cupcake with a huge jelly cherry on her head. "Look at it as a gastronomic form of BDSM". She didn't share my sense of humour right then though. She told me to shut up and chop wood because she was coming home! Enough was enough.

Have I gathered all loose ends now? I think so! We have Pontus as a happy taxi driver, lajving in the forest, changing girlfriends as other change their clothes, which was why I called him a mediaeval Casanova earlier in my story. Amanda and Jörgen had both come a long way in their MD program. I had yelled at her, and we had not made up yet. Sara was in highstage and was a Teenager

with a capital T. I had managed to overcome my
depression by singing, and was surrounded by hundreds of
teddy bears. And then Lisa came home from Japan. Yes, I
think I've got it all covered now.

The winners write the history, but the losers are the ones
who get to describe their exes.
I try to be fair regarding Madeleine. She probably has
many good qualities. My mom adored her! She was
interested in fashion and knitting, and look how sweet she
was to Sara!
Too sweet, if you ask me. Like aspartame. Unnatural.
Madeleine talked to her as if she was, well, ok, retarded.
Maybe you couldn't discuss politics with Sara, but she
sure knew everything there was to know about boy bands
and all about love and feelings. She was in love with a boy
in her class, so there! You didn't need to sweeten your
tone when you spoke to her. Madeleine was aghast once
when I yelled at Sara for destroying something. "You
can't shout at her like that! She's just like a baby, she
doesn't understand!" Of course she understood! Maybe
she couldn't help destroying things and keep trying to eat
everything smaller than a tennis ball, but she wasn't
stupid!
What else can I say in Madeleine's favour? What kept us
together those years, except for her love for my flat and
my wish to get an identity through her?
We had the same taste when it came to film and TV.
Romantic comedies, costume dramas, British crime. She
also loved to watch all the sitcoms about groups of friends,
as I've told you. Her secret dream was to be a part of such
a group, and she never gave up on trying to pull me into
her artificial circle of friends.

There is a fable about a Nightingale visiting a King. The King wanted to give the bird the very best! Wine, the finest meat, delicious candy. Nothing suited the Nightingale, who became weaker and weaker. Eventually, the King called for his advisor and asked what to do, and got the answer: "The secret is that you should find out the needs and desires of your guest, not offering only whatever you think is the best." The King dug up a worm from his garden and treated his guest. Out of gratitude, the Nightingale sung the most beautiful song the King had ever heard.

What can we learn about this?

Madeleine should have learned not to try to force me into activities that she herself enjoyed, when she saw how much I hated them.

It's rather tricky. If nobody pushed me at all, I wouldn't do anything. But while my friends have the ability to push me into things that turn out to be good for me, like languagetrip and the choir, and the sensibility to back off when they notice that they have pushed me into something that's not for me, like lajv, Madeleine never even tried to learn that. She always wanted me to go with her to parties, couple dinners, pub crawls and all kinds of social horrifying activities. The difference between her and my friends is that she never pushed me because she thought it would be fun for me if I just got used to it, but because she never gave up the hope of changing me. Wanting to change your partner from the start is not a very good foundation for a healthy relationship.

Take my word for it.

Was I the perfect boyfriend, then?

Of course not.

To begin with, I never told her about the cottage. I was afraid that she would want to borrow it while Lisa was gone, pretend it was ours, maybe even bring some of her dreaded teddy bears, "contaminate the atmosphere" as Lisa had said. When she had her girl nights, with hundreds of giggling friends in every corner of my flat, I said that I would spend the night at my parents house to give them some space. They thought it was so sweet and conciderate of me! It was a lie, though. I fled to the cabin and savoured the blessed silence there.

The week before Lisa was coming home, I asked Pontus to go with me to chop some wood. He hadn't been there since tant Frida's funeral.
-I use to dream about this place, he said quietly and took some deep breaths to inhale the peaceful air.
-You do?
-Mm. Sometimes I dream that I'm sitting here with a glass of raspberry lemonad. Suddenly something happens and I'm banned, and I never understand why. Or I dream that some rich snob has bought it, torn it down and built something modern and ugly with electricity and water and a huge TV. It feels strange to be here again. As if the dreams were more real than the memories.
There was some raspberry lemonade left in the pantry and I gave him a glass.
-So, have you got any interesting lajv coming up?
That question always does the trick. Pontus lightened up and started telling me about an epic drama where the King, who had been a fair and good King, had crossed some magical line to another world, and had come back totally changed and evil! He had already started to change his kingdom, enslaving his subjects. Now they must find a way to stop him!

Once, I had gone with him to a lajv. Maybe I would enjoy this more than Dungeons&Dragons? This was more like theatre, without spectators of course, you would be one of the actors yourself. I could be The Mysterious Stranger In The Corner, with a dark hat to hide my face. If anyone tried to talk to me I would just hold up my thumb and index finger like this. Then everyone would know that I belonged to a special monastic order and had given a vow of silence. How they will know? Because the order is well known in this area, you can read about it in the mailing. Everyone participating have to read all background texts thoroughly and learn about the important roles, so that you don't break the illusion. You don't have to do that if you're staying silent of course, but I'm playing an envoy from Tuvallia and since my character knows everyone of importance, I have to know it too. We're having a pre-meeting before the big lajv in July, where we get to know each other in real life and will recognise each other once we start playing.

The lajv itself hadn't been so bad. The trick with the fingers worked, they left me alone, and it was much more fun to watch real people in fantasy-mediaeval clothes improvise a drama together, than to watch pale teenage boys rolling dice. Sometimes the lajv went on for a weekend or even a whole week, where they put up homemade tents. On other occasions, they just had a one-day lajv. Some lajvs were a part of a big story that went on for years, even decades. Then you could play the same character every time, or you could create a new character to try out something new.
-Isn't it confusing? I mean, if you play this envoy now and the next time you're something else...?

-No no, it's all about the clothes and equipment!
Everyone knows that I'm the envoy when I'm wearing my
green hat and tunic.
I was invited to a one-evening lajv in a scout hut, that
Pontus thought would be suitable for me. He was right,
five hours of mystery and intrigues and magical rituals and
just sitting around waiting for something to happen was
about all I could take.
What he hadn't warned me about, was what happened
after they had stopped acting in the evening.
Everybody hugged everybody!
Hello, I haven't seen you before, are you new? Oh, you
were so cool, sitting there in the corner looking
mysterious, wasn't it difficult to be quiet the whole
evening? I could never do that!
I thought I was going to die! I've never felt such panic.
Pontus came to my rescue, dug me out of that corner and
practically had to lead me to the car. When I could
breathe again, I admitted that I had enjoyed myself up
until then, and that I was glad I could see and smell and
feel what he was talking about. However, once was quite
enough!

Even though I never went to a lajv again, it was still
entertaining to listen to him talking about his adventures.
He's a very good story teller. After one of his first lajvs he
got a rather nasty abrasion on his shoulder, not from
weapons but from a sharp twig, and his poor mother was
beside herself and wanted him to stop this dangerous new
hobby! Couldn't he go back to his dice, please? He still
did some of that, but lajv was so much more fun! He *was*
Pont-du-John! But to be on the safe side, he always
landed at my place. Here he could borrow my shower and
check for wounds, and then collapse on the sofa, telling
me everything in detail. Then he called his lajv friends,

put on the telephone speaker and once more went through the events, giving me a wider aspect of what had happened. Meanwhile, I made pizza. It should be home delivery pizza, I know, but mine is so much better so he accepted this new routine. I loved these Sunday afternoons! After my initial teenage sulk, I really enjoyed listening to him. I think that's one of the reasons that our friendship survived and grew stronger during these years. Lajvers never grow tired of talking about old and new adventures.

Madeleine wasn't amused at all. A muddy Pontus clashed with her teddy bears. And the smell! Three days of sweat! And all those blankets and whatever is in those sacks, just thrown in the hallway... What if there are bugs in it, crawling out on her newly vacuumed floor!
The postlajv visits came to a halt. But when Madeleine left, my home was yet again a middle zone, a place to land between two worlds.

The introduction of Lisa to my girlfriend was no success. Lisa had brought a whole box of photos and newspaper cuttings from her career. We sat close on the couch and laughed when Madeleine came home from her lecture. Automatically I moved an inch, as if I had been doing something I shouldn't.
-Hello, Lisa said with a broad smile and stretched out her hand with long, decorated nails. Her wavy hair was in spikes, except for her bangs that were pointing down like an arrow. She wore the Japanese exaggerated makeup just to joke a little with me.
Madeleine smiled politely but deprecatory.
-Hej.
Never before had she got any reason to be jealous. How could she, I never talked to anyone but her. She

commended herself by not having a single little gene for jealousy. Not even when all the girls were after her ex, she had been jealous.

Since I'd never told her about the cottage, she never knew how close I was to Lisa. The postcards came to Sara, so all she knew was what I had told her in the beginning, that I once had a girlfriend who still was my friend. When we first started dating it didn't seem like a smart move to tell her that I loved another woman even if it was strictly platonic, and later on I never found a reason to bring it up. I felt a bit uneasy not telling her about the cottage, but I knew how she was going to react. Oooh how cute! I closed my eyes to the warning lamp. Wasn't it enough to have a relationship? Did it have to be good, too?

Lisa immediately picked up Madeleine's aversion but tried to be nice anyway. I think. Or maybe she was being provocative when she asked if Madeleine wanted to join us, we were just looking at some weird pictures of her. I tried to buy some time and got up from the sofa.

-I'll make some tea.

-Earl Grey, please.

-I know.

Evil glance from Madeleine

Reserved, she sat on the couch with a clear distance to Lisa, and started looking in the albums. She became more and more rigid. When I came back with the tea tray, I hardly recognised my partner.

-How interesting that your friend is a model, she said in a crisp voice.

I didn't know how to respond. Lisa shrugged.

-Nothing very special. It's just a job, a little weirder than the average maybe. Did he tell you about the latest, with the cupcake?

-No, he didn't.

-No? Let me tell you, it was so funny...

With vivid gestures, Lisa described how they wanted her
to pose inside the giant cupcake. I couldn't help laughing.
I'm naive. It's not until now, when I write about this, that
I realise that I was in the middle of a very subtle catfight.
Not over me as a person, but over me as a territory.
Madeleine didn't even smile. She looked at me, almost
accusingly.
Lisa stayed late, and I offered her to sleep on the couch.
She glanced at the Lady of the Mansion and said thanks
but no thanks, she had missed the forest so much, she
wanted to go home, why don't you visit someday soon?
Of course!
Madeleine spent the rest of the evening in silence. Her
back turned against me in bed. No goodnight kiss.
-I've never heard you laugh before, she said laconically to
the wall.

The next day, we had our first quarrel. A very civilised
one, at breakfast.
-I would appreciate if you asked me before you invite
strangers to stay over. I live here too, you know.
Her hand was so elegant when she poured us the flowery
shit from the teapot. I didn't drink it, but I liked holding
the cup, smelling it. Nowadays, that scent only reminds
me of bad things.
I was honestly surprised. She had never ever asked me
when she had her friends stay over. Not to mention the
afterparties, loud strangers in various stages of
intoxication, invading my home, playing the stereo so
loud that I had to apologise to our neighbours, throwing
up in my bathroom, falling asleep wherever they could
find a spot. I always fled, unable to bear it, not knowing
where to flee to. I still had the key to my parents house,
but mom was terrified of burglars and of course I was
more than welcome to spend the night, but please, call in

advance? Not an easy thing to do, since the afterparties usually started at one thirty AM. A telephone signal at that hour would give her a heart attack. Pontus might have the early shift so I didn't want to wake him up, so I sighed and took my bike and went to the cottage. It was even worse when I came home from the night shift at work, so tired that I almost wanted to throw up, and found a bunch of people in my bed. Then the lies came easy. I called my parents, sorry to wake you up so early, but I wonder if I can come and sleep in my old room today? Madeleine has some guests and I don't want them to feel that they need to be quiet for my sake. Oh, Johan, how considerate of you, of course you can!
I was surprised, and hurt. Somehow it felt like a personal insult to me, that she didn't like Lisa.
 Muttering, I replied:
-Stop dragging people home for afterparties and I won't invite Lisa.
She froze.
-What's this? All of a sudden, you want to set up conditions?
-Yup.
-That's very childish of you!
-Then I guess I'm childish.
The rest of the breakfast was accompanied by frosty silence.

In time, I found out that Madeleine's way of arguing followed a pattern. Yes, I call this an argument, even though some of you with hotter temperament might smile at me. For me, it was.
She punished me by being silent the rest of the day after a skirmish, then she woke me up sometime in the middle of the night for make up sex which worked surprisingly well, because I didn't have time to think about it. If I was in the

middle of an interesting dream, it even worked very well. The next day, everything was sunshine and everything was unresolved.

This first time, however, I didn't know that we would make up so fast. Her silence was like torture! She didn't even look at me and I was sure it was over between us. That thought gave me conflicting feelings – I both feared and wished that it was true.
By lunchtime, my nerves were so frayed that I had to do something. Anything.
I took a long walk which led me to Amanda. On her doorstep I whimpered:
-I'm sorry! I'm so sorry!
Amanda might live by her schedule, but she can easily rearrange it when something happens, like if her distraught brother disturbs her in the middle of her study hour.
With a steaming cup of real tea, I mean Earl Grey, in my hands, crying, snot running and the plosives uncooperating, I told Amanda everything.
Gently, she stroke my back and asked:
-What's the worst thing that can happen now?
-I don't know! That it will be like this forever! That she never wants to talk to me again!
-What's your own opinion, do you think you've done anything wrong?
I dried my tears with the sleeve and looked for something to blow my nose in. The napkin would have to do, even if it was a cheap kind that I knew would dissolve.
-Maybe I should have told her more about Lisa.
-Do you think it would have made any difference?
-Not really.
Amanda took my hands.

-Listen to me. Madeleine is a nice girl, but she's still young and immature, and a strong personality will scare her. It doesn't matter if you explain that Lisa isn't a threat.

Which I couldn't do, since I wasn't sure it was true. Jörgen and I took Amanda's clean-the-kitchen-box in her schedule, which she could fill with her studies to catch up. Strengthened with a whisky I went home to some more silence. It felt terrible to go to bed without saying goodnight, and terribly strange to have sex in the middle of the night. I didn't complain though. Anything was better than silence.

My independent introduction courses piled up together with the residue exams and I wasn't allowed any more student loans. Pontus helped me study for taxi driver's test, no Johan, you don't have to chitchat with your passengers, most of them prefer to sit quiet in the back seat. But before I got that far, Amanda showed me an ad in the weekly job newspaper that she thought would suit me. They were searching for a personal assistant to a five year old boy with autism, who had a reduced need for sleep and needed someone to keep an eye on him during the night. A happy boy, they added. That's almost mandatory to write in an ad like that, whether it's true or not. If they told the truth, that the children might bite you, not many would want the job. The rest of the ad was the usual. "Flexible, positive, responsive" etcetera.
-Why don't you apply? You have plenty of experience of children with special needs.
I took her advice and I got it! My first real job!
Samuel and I got along just fine. He fell asleep at six o'clock in the evening. He looked at the watch and didn't have any daylight-saving time issues. If it said six, it was time to sleep. Four hours later, he woke up. My shift

started at ten, which gave me some time to talk to the parents about the day. We talked about if something had happened that I needed to know, what the plans were for the next day so that I could prepare the schedule in the hallway, and it also gave them the opportunity to get to know me a little better. This was the first time they got help. Until now, they had managed on their own, sleeping in shift. Now Samuel's mother was expecting again and they were desperate enough to welcome almost anyone in their home to help out. I was a bit worried the first time, but I think they were even more nervous than me and somehow that had a calming effect.

Many would probably think this job was incredibly dull. Samuel minded his own business. His only toys were plastic animals, hundreds of them! Every night, all night, he arranged them in spiral patterns and moved them around according to a secret system, quietly talking to himself in a strange language. Now and then he went to the kitchen to get some ice cubes to eat. He always left the freezer wide open but didn't protest when I closed it. There is a wonderful tool called time stick. It's a digital tool with twenty small red lamps, each marking one minute. When I wanted to prepare Samuel for a new activity, I set the time stick on ten minutes and placed a pictogram on it. When one minute had passed, a lamp was put out. When the ten minutes came to an end, the time stick would beep, blink or vibrate. One of the common issues with autistic people is that they find it difficult to go from one activity to the next. The time stick gives them time to prepare. When I put the time stick on the floor, not too close to the animals but close enough for Samuel to see, he knew that it was time to round the game up. Not unlike Amanda, he had his daily schedule, with pictograms showing the activities. Twenty minutes past five I set the time stick on ten minutes which was the perfect time for him. Then I prepared two slices of bread with nothing on and a glass of milk in his favourite glass with Curious George. After that, the image of brushing the teeth and getting dressed. Meanwhile, his parents woke up and took over, grateful for a full night's sleep. My shift ended at six thirty. After my first weeks, they almost started to feel like human beings again.

I was working three nights in a row, and had two nights off, when a colleague I never met took care of him. To be awake all night and sleep during the day wasn't a problem, but I found it difficult to sleep the nights I was free. My body couldn't handle the constant turning of the rhythm. Now, when I'm single, I have completely turned my days and nights around. I stay awake even the nights I'm free, and sleep until three every day. In the winter, I don't pull the curtains. I have forced myself to get used to sleeping in a light room because I know the body needs some sunlight. I feel much better now when I'm consequent. The job was perfect for me, and I was perfect for the job. Samuel wanted to be left alone, and I left him alone but kept my eyes on him. During the long nights, I read a lot, did crosswords and just sat there and thought about everything and nothing.

Nights are strange. A night with deep conversations can last forever, while a night in silence flies by. This was when Lisa was dating Miriam, who was deep into the New Age-movement and had some interesting thoughts about time. She said that time is a learning device, a spiritual tool that was portioned out to everyone according to the individual needs. There is no such thing as ”I don't have time to do this”, time is something you're born with, something that is yours and can't be taken away. The only question is what you choose to do with that time.

Maybe Miriam is right. Maybe time isn't linear, but flowing back and forth, capable of stopping for the one who needs it, rushing for others. Silently laughing at us for trying to capture it and measure it. These are the kind of things I think about during the nights.

I'm a bit reluctant to tell you more about Miriam, because sometimes she scares me.

Lisa invited me to Miriam's place, because she was curious of me. She only lives two blocks away so I had seen her now and then before I knew who she was. You couldn't miss her. She was the image of New Age, with long, henna red hair, layers and layers of colourful clothes and vests and shawls and jewellery and an air of incense surrounding her. Of course I didn't want to come, but for some reason, Lisa said it was important to her that I met Miriam. That made me both scared and curious.

Miriam's place was just like her. Full of symbols and candlesticks and textiles and strange books and tarot decks and wooden boxes and everything you can imagine in that area. Lisa almost had to push me over the doorstep. In my plaid shirt and jeans, I felt misplaced. She kissed Lisa, and looked closely at me with her nut-brown eyes for much longer than is socially accepted.

-Yes, she said with relief. Yes, he's the one!

I was the what?

Fika is so deeply rooted in the Swedish national spirit that even in New Age circles fika is mandatory. Miriam had prepared a tray with something that smelled like smoked dandelions. Which it was. You understand why I had to introduce the Swedish word, because you can't call a cup of brewed weed "coffee break".

There was no chitchat. She went straight to the point.

-I've known you in a previous life. Every time I see you in the corner shop, I want to talk to you but believe it or not, I'm not quite that pushy. When Lisa showed me some photos of her friends and I realised she knew you, I could feel my heart beating faster and I felt that the spirits had led Lisa to me. Through her, I found you. We were once closer than any sisters could be.

She started telling a story about ancient Egypt, where she claimed we had been slaves, working in a kitchen. The house caught fire one day and we were trapped inside the large pantry. We then made a promise that we would search for each other in our next life. Or the next. Or the next. And now she had found me.

I didn't want to, or rather, I didn't dare to disappoint her so I just nodded, even though I felt uneasy. It was difficult enough to be Johan, I didn't want to have to deal with other lives as well. Furthermore, I don't believe in reincarnation. I think.

My new day rhythm didn't have a great impact on my relationship to begin with. I came home from work not long before Madeleine had to go up, so I made us breakfast and we ate together before I went to bed and she went to her lectures. When I woke up at three I wanted some fresh air, so I went shopping and had dinner ready when she got back. I still had the choir but she had joined a photo club instead and had many other activities in the evenings, so we didn't see much of each other except during the meals.

The best part of my job wasn't that I for the first time had a proper income, but that I had an acceptable excuse for not going with her to all those social things. No, I'm sorry, I can't go to the pub even for a little while, I need

to rest before I go to work. Do I look happy about it?
Sorry, I didn't mean to.

A couple of years went by. Both Pontus and Lisa changed
girlfriends now and then. Sometimes I saw Miriam in the
corner store and if we both had time we went for a walk.
She talked about spiritual things mixed with direct and
intimate questions and suggestions. Would I like a
Polynesian massage, I looked so tense? Or maybe fellatio?
She could feel my lack of sexual energy, she would love to
help me with that, as a friend.
Not today, thanks.
I don't know why I didn't say "no, never in this life or any
of the other lives I might have".
Maybe because I was just a little bit tempted.
I didn't want to cheat on Madeleine. I thought that
infidelity was so... tacky.
But the thought of some of the things Miriam offered
during our walks gave me a tickling feeling.

In a healthy, equal relationship, it should be ok to tell
your partner about your dreams and fantasies. There were
two, no, three things that stopped me. Once I was more
or less forced to play a board game with Madeleine and
two guests during one of these nightmare couple dinners
she loved so much, a game where we were supposed to
reveal our secrets about this or that. Just another version
of my antifavourite spin-the-bottle-game. Maybe I had
died and gone to Hell. The only thing missing was the old
classmates. Anyway. The other man in the company got a
question about what kind of sex he liked the most. His
answer made Madeleine shout: "Ew, you *pee* with that
thing!", killing all my dreams of ever mentioning
something like that to her. And when she, giggling and
drunk, revealed what she secretly dreamed of... Well, let's

just say that I was afraid to ever ask her when she was
more sober, in case it was true. When it was my turn, I
went to the bathroom and threw up.
That's the two first reasons. The third you have already
guessed. We didn't have a healthy relationship.

The story gets nearer to the crash.

The main reason why it hurts so much to write about this
lies elsewhere.
I don't know if you've noticed. When I write about Sara, I
always use the past tense.
Sara is no longer with us.

I need another break now.

Miriam spoke a lot about life and death. She claimed that
death was just an illusion. The concrete body might be
limited, but the soul is immortal. If you speak to someone
who no longer exists in the physical world, they will still
be able to hear you. Always. Speak, use your heart to
listen and you will get an answer!

Sara, are you there?
Can you smile at me, in your special way that always made
me warm inside? Please, comfort me? Life is so empty
without you.
So inexpressibly, unbearably empty!

Sara's big, boundless heart gave up.
Heart failure is a common problem for people with Down
syndrome. We had buried our heads in the sand, had
chosen to believe that everything was alright after all
those surgeries in her childhood. They had fixed her,
right?
The average lifespan within the diagnosis was almost fifty-
six years. I read this in an article and was never able to
erase it from my memory. The thought that we could lose
her earlier never crossed my mind. Average didn't mean
maximum. She could grow old enough to play with my
grandchildren!
But she didn't.
I wish her end could have been as peaceful as tant Frida's.
Fast, easy, painless.
It wasn't.
Everyone worked their hardest to save Sara's life. Acute
surgery followed by intensive care. We took turns sitting
by her side. My parents, Amanda, Jörgen, Pontus, Lisa
and I. Madeleine claimed she suffered from hospital
phobia. Maybe it was true. Maybe she just couldn't handle
the situation.

The intensive care could just as easy have been a room
inside the experiment house of a mad professor. Tubes
and probes to and from the patient. Devices beeping too
loud and too often, with frightening curves that we soon
learned to keep our eyes on. Eighty-five in oxygen, we
knew from experience that wasn't enough. High pulse,
does that mean she's in pain? We can't tell from her
motionless, expressionless face.
Does she understand what's going on?
Does she know we're here?
Can she feel our presence?
We read her favourite books and sung silly little songs,
close and quiet, trying not to disturb the other patients in
the room. People being kept alive by machines, locked
inside their own invisible bubbles. I have never been able
to watch The Matrix again after this.
I took Sara's hand. It was warm. She was still with us.
At the same time, she was already gone.

Without telling Madeleine about it, I took some days off
from work while we were watching over Sara. Madeleine
was so uncomfortable when I spoke about the hospital so I
didn't want to talk to her at all about it anymore.
The thoughts I had during those nights were too difficult
to handle with Simon around. The common
misconception is that autistic people can't read other
people's feelings. Sometimes it might be true, but often
it's the other way around. They notice everything. When
they walk into a room, they are awashed by everyone's
emotions and need to shut it out, leaving them looking
blank. Simon knew that I was sad, and I wanted to spare
us both. Just as the night strengthens the depth in a
conversation, it also deepens the self-reproach.

Why hadn't I appreciated Sara more?
Why hadn't I spent more time with her?
Why couldn't I have been more patient?
Why?

Mom wanted to be by Sara's side at all time, but we forced her to get some sleep at least a few hours every day. If Sara wakes up – ok, ok, *when* Sara wakes up, she will need you, mom. You need to rest. Please. We'll call you as soon as... We'll call you.
I came home around ten, the same time as I should have started my shift. Madeleine wasn't there. Probably out with friends, I thought.
Around four, I texted her.
"Are you ok?"
No reply.
Half past six in the morning she came home, tousled and rosy-cheeked.
-Are you home already?
Something seemed to move in my stomach. Some kind of instinct maybe. I lied:
-I just got home. Samuel's grandmother was visiting and she's an early bird, so... so she said that I could leave the morning routines to her, as long as I showed her how the time stick works.
She sounded a bit relieved.
-That's nice! I must have fumbled when I set the alarm clock yesterday, it rang an hour earlier! I was so tempted to stay in bed, but I thought that if I did, I would oversleep so I went out for a walk. Ambitious of me, wasn't it?
Did her giggle seem nervous? Perhaps.
-Very ambitious.
-How is Sara?

-Not so good. I'll try to get some sleep now, and then I
want to spend some time with her before I start my shift. I
won't be coming home in between, ok?
She gave me a hug, no kiss, and if she had tried, I think I
would have backed off. My subconsciousness knew more
than I wanted to admit. Maybe that's why I lied to her
about going to work. It would have been the perfect time
to tell her that I had taken a few nights off.
-It must be so awful! You have to take care of yourself too,
don't forget that!
-I won't.

I hate that expression.
Take care of yourself.
What's that supposed to mean?
Take care of yourself, because nobody else will.
I don't want to take care of myself.
I wanted *you* to take care of me!

Sara died with me and mom by her side.
The curve of Death is straight and still.

After saying goodbye, I needed to be alone so I went
home.
As if I knew that I was going to be alone there.
Madeleine didn't come home that night either.
All evening and all night I sat still on the couch, staring
into the nothingness. Tried to grasp the triple sorrow.
Sara's death. Madeleine's betrayal. The end of my
relationship.
The doorbell rang. Lisa's voice in the mail slit.
-Johan? Are you there? Please let me in?
A little later, Pontus voice.
-I'll sit here outside for a little while. You don't have to
open, I just want you to know that you're not alone.

Later, I let them know that I appreciated their gesture. It did make a difference, knowing that my best friends didn't want to intrude, yet didn't want to leave my side.
If it had been just about Sara, I would have let them both in.
As it was, I needed my space.

This time, she came home at five thirty. The old grandmother couldn't wake up that early, right?
Quietly, I asked:
-Where have you been?
-My god, you scared me! What are you doing here?
-Where have you been?
My voice was toneless, neutral.
For a moment, she seemed to debate with herself. Was there any plausible explanation she could serve me? How long could I have been home, would I believe that she had taken a morning stroll again? Not likely, she was very morningtired.
Attack is the best defence, she decided.
How could I have the nerve to accuse her! I, who had hidden my past with a Japanese model! Didn't I think she knew that I still saw her? Her friends had told her, they had seen us in the park, so there! Who was I to blame her for seeing someone behind my back too? Besides, we hadn't had sex for months, apparently I wasn't interested, and the few times we ever did, we never did anything fun, she could just as well have been an inflatable doll, did I think that her self confidence was boosted by that? Was it so strange that she had found someone who had the good sense to appreciate her a little more, and was able to give her an orgasm, yes, orgasm, had I ever heard that word, unless Lisa had explained it to me? Max had made her cry out of pleasure, while I only made her cry out of anger because she had wasted so much time on me, and yes, she

had been naive, gullible, fooled to believe that I was
different, which I was, but not in the way I had made her
believe. I was dull beyond belief, without any driving
force whatsoever (direct quote from me, from the first
days of infatuation when we listed our faults, her biggest
flaw was being far too kind, please dear Madeleine, look
yourself in the mirror during this monologue and repeat
that phrase?), a mediocrity with lack of ambitions (there
you have the phrase from page five!), pathologically
unsociable, she had sacrificed *so* much for me, *so* much
time and energy and the best years of her life trying to
help me have a richer life and not be so incredibly boring,
but now she couldn't take it anymore, she gave up, she
didn't need to stand here listening to my accusations and
harsh words, she deserved *so* much better, enough is
enough, she was leaving now and expected me to be gone
when she came back tomorrow, she was generous enough
to give me time to pack, not that I needed much time to
rake together my useless belongings, she could even give
me one of her dotted IKEA bags to throw my ugly clothes
into, because I probably didn't own a bag since I never
wanted to go anywhere, had I even been outside the city
borders, except for that rotting old hovel in the forest,
yes, she knew that I sneaked out to go there, I had lied to
her, lied all this time while she always had been honest
and sincere because she, unlike me, had given everything
to this relationship, had done everything to make it work,
but apparently I expected her to carry the whole burden
herself, and sure, she had dreamt about children but never
dreamt that she would have to mother a grown child like
me, who didn't even dare to wipe my own bottom if it
wasn't the exact same toilet paper as my mom had used
when I was a baby, which I still was by the way, and damn
it, Johan, she thought I was better than this, but I was just
a big bastard and a bloody parasite who had been using

her, she wanted me out of her life, no more of this sucking the life spark out of her, I could sit in my oaf friend's basement and play my old LPs and wake up when I was ninety-three and wonder what had happened to my life and why nobody came to water me, like a giant fucking plant I was, the kind that leaves a white, thick mucus when you break it, and you just want to wash your hands with alcogel when you'd had anything to do with me, goddamnit, how could I be so mean to her, she had never done me any harm, never had she complained about how fucking rude I had been to her friends whenever she had invited them to her own home, she had been so ashamed of me, it wasn't easy to try to cover how weird I was, for god's sake, I couldn't even speak properly, whether I was too stupid or too lazy to learn she would never know, and she had to lie to her friends, telling them that I had a lot of good, well hidden qualities that still made her stay with me, don't think that they haven't asked why, whatever did she see in Johan who is the biggest bore they have ever met, and she had told them that at least I was better than Max, but to be honest, I wasn't, he was better than me in every single aspect, he treated her like a queen, and said that she was beautiful and funny and loved to touch her, caress her, make love to her, did I hear, he liked doing all those things with her, enjoyed it, not like me, doing it out of some kind of duty, and he had grown and matured, unlike me who had rather regressed, sometimes she thought that I too was retarded like my annoying little sister -
She stopped for a second, partly to catch her breath, but I could see by the insecurity in her eyes that she suddenly remembered that the annoying sister was in the intensive care. Which she didn't anymore. She was in an anonymous box in the morgue. In my imagination, they

had wrapped her in a fuzzy blanket. I didn't want to know the truth.
Somewhat less agitated, she repeated:
-I expect you to be gone tomorrow.
Then she slammed the door.

So, how did I feel after that downpour?
Numb.
It was like all the drops, all these words, hovered above me, just waiting to fall down on me, one by one.
Stiff after motionless hours in the sofa I carefully stretched my body. Thought about possible strategies to avoid the pain that inevitably would come after a night like this. Alcohol? No, that would only make me dizzy and even more sad. Some other kind of drugs, maybe, but then I would lose my job, and it would be all that hassle with finding it, confronting family and friends when they found out, and then having to quit. Cut yourself? One of Lisa's girlfriends had done that, because the physical pain covered the emotional. With the scars to remind you for the rest of your life how bad you once felt. Didn't seem very attractive.
While those absurd thoughts spinned in my head, I went to the kitchen, took out a bowl, looked for a recipe in my mental card index, set the oven on 220 Celsius Degrees and put all the ingredients I needed on the bench.
Without thinking, I made madeleines. I always made them on her birthday. She said that it was so sweet of me.
Egg and white sugar whipped to a white fluff.
Vanilla sugar, wheat flour and baking powder sifted and carefully mixed with the white fluff.
Add milk and browned butter.
Fill the baking tins.
Eight minutes in the oven.
Cool.

Lemon zest, vanilla powder
mixed with
three tablespoons of salt
instead of sugar
because you're not sweet, you treacherous bitch
three tablespoons of salt,
turn the cakes in the salt and throw them with all your
strength from the balcony into the backyard.

Even though I've known deep down inside that this facade
would crack sooner or later, I still think her timing could
have been a bit better. I can understand that the
circumstances were difficult for her too, when she was
expected to be supportive in a time of sorrow that fit
badly with the kind of life she wanted. Had she said: "I'm
sorry, this is too much for me, I think we should take a
break", I think I would have understood and agreed. The
last thing I needed when I came home from the hospital
was having to keep up this stupid game we played,
pretending to be happy. A break would probably have
done us both good, leading to the final break with much
less bitterness. But this? Infidelity? As I said, tacky. A one
night stand I might have forgiven, but as it was, she had
deliberately deceived me. For how long I don't know and
I don't care.

All her poisonous words soon began to fall from that
invisible bowl, one by one, and burned holes in my mental
skin. The unfair stung, but the truth hurt even more.
Worst of all was how I felt my self contempt grow. Not
because of what she had said, but because I had betrayed
myself during these years. Why had I stayed with her?
Definitely not for the sex, that I could have done without
even if I miss the kisses. Not for her intellect and
interesting conversation. I only pretended to listen when

she complained about some cute guy being sent home from one of these endless song contests on TV. I nodded and lied and said that yes, indeed, she was right. Not for fear of being alone. I like being by myself, I preferred it when she was away.

So why?

Because I lack driving force.

Just when the last cake had landed, the phone rang. I didn't want to talk to anyone, but it kept ringing so I answered just to shut it up.

It was Amanda.

-Finally! Thanks for picking up the phone, I was starting to worry about you. Lisa is here and demands to get your spare key or she would smash your door. How are you feeling?

-Tired.

My voice sounded almost metallic in my ears. Funny. I wonder if that's how other people hear me? Like the tin man.

-Me and Jörgen spent the night here with mom and dad. Please, come? We miss you. Jörgen can come and get you?

-Not now.

-Ok. But I don't think you should be alone. Is Madeleine there?

-No.

-Is it ok if Lisa comes by? I don't want to leave mom, I gave her something to sleep on but I want to be here when she wakes up.

-Yes, you can tell her it's ok. More than ok. But... tell her...

Amanda waited for me to continue. I took a few deep breaths.

-Tell her to take a shower and use the shampoo she had
before.
A second of surprised silence.
-Ok, I'll tell her. I'll call you tomorrow.
-Thanks. And, Amanda?
-Yes?
-I love you. Even if I never say it.
-I love you too, Johan. Difficult words to say, but you
know I do.
-Thanks for looking after me.
-My pleasure.

A couple of hours later, Lisa came with damp hair. It
hadn't been easy finding a shampoo that were made more
than a decade ago. Impossible, in fact. She had to go to
her parents flat and dig through two wall-high layers of
books to reach the wardrobe in her old room where she
thought she might have left a bottle. While she was at it,
she reconciled with her parents.
-I still think they're a couple of archkretins, but on a day
like this, atonement seems justified.
-Or betrayal seems justified.
-What's that supposed to mean?
With my nose in her hair, like the scent was a mental
pacifier, I told her laconically what had happened and had
been said.
Lisa was quiet for thirty seconds. I counted, because I
needed something to focus on.
-She commanded you to move out?
-Mm.
-Has she forgotten that it's your flat?
-Apparently. Or she reckons that she has made it hers. I
can't fight a whole army of teddy bears.
-Do you want to move out?
-No.

-Just wanted to be sure. Wait here! I'll be right back.
In the corner shop near my apartment – *my* apartment! - you can find rock hard pick&mix candy, bread made of wheat flour and preservatives and some other things that cost twice as much as anywhere else. Except for the imported beer. It's suspectly cheap.
Five minutes later, Lisa was back with three rolls of garbage bags.
-You start with the clothes. Please, let me take care of those teddy bears? My fingers have itched for two years now, just wanting to place them inside a black bag!
-What...?
-We're helping your ex girlfriend to move out.
A vague protest, not stronger than the wing beat of a butterfly, moved inside me. Could you really behave this way? I went out on the balcony and watched the crows feast on the salty cake crumbles on the ground.
Yes, I thought it could be therapeutic for me to behave a bit unconventional.

With The Damned's Music for Pleasure thundering, we got started. Carefully I folded all Madeleine's clothes and placed them into the garbage bags. Lisa wasn't quite as gentle with the teddy bears. One swiping movement with the arm, and one shelf was cleared.
While Lisa enjoyed removing everything lacy and cute, my pleasure lay in packing her books into the moving boxes that had been gathering dust in the attic. "Why do we keep them, Johan, I never want to move, but of course, when we start a family we might need to buy a house, ok, let them be.
Near the end, we had an argument when I wanted to go through our bookshelf and give away books we never read.
-Jackie Collins! Do you actually read this crap?

-Sometimes! They're a part of my youth, and if they bother you, maybe you could take a look at yourself in the mirror and put away that silly plastic knight?

Lisa smiled at the look on my face when I touched those books.
-Do you want me to buy some rubber gloves for you? she offered with an innocent tone that made me laugh for the first time since I couldn't even remember.
The laughter was the key to the tears. I let the book fall in the box and myself fall on the floor. Lisa hurried to my side, held me, whispered:
-She knew how much you loved her.
I knew she didn't mean Madeleine. Between the sobs, I asked for more assurance.
-Do you really think so?
-I know she did.
-I should have...
-You did everything you should have done. Always. You went with her to the cinema and watched that awful movie with the digitalized Smurfs, twice! You went to every vernissage at her art school and bought at least one painting every time. You sent her postcards with puppies that would kill a diabetic. And at the end, you were with her every single day. She couldn't have asked for a better big brother than you, Johan! You were always proud of her, never ashamed, you let us be a part of her life and that is something both Pontus and I value. I'll never forget the first time I had dinner at your place. I was so proud that I could inspire her to eat those meatballs. She made me think about what's important in life. You could never fool her by pretending. She saw through the facade, straight into your heart, and liked people for who they were, not for what they had or did or what they could give her. To have known someone so wonderful as Sara is a

privilege. As long as we remember her, and think about her, she will stay alive. And we'll never forget her. Never! It felt so good, just lying there on the floor with Lisa's arms around me, crying together. In the middle of the pain, I felt a warm happiness.
-Do you believe in what Miriam said?
Lisa thought about it for a few minutes.
-Somehow, I think I do. Whenever I'm sad and lonely in the cottage, I think about tant Frida. Then it's like someone is giving me a hug, or, giving my soul a hug if you know what I mean. I feel that she cares for me even if she's no longer here. Miriam thinks that you can talk to the dead through a medium and get answers in words, as if the one you're talking to exists just as he or she was in life, but in another dimension. I'm not so sure about that. I think it's more as if the emotions people had when they were alive can linger and sometimes manifest themselves. Like haunted houses, where bad feelings stay and affect us, some of us more than others. Miriam says she can see human shaped shadows in some houses, and who am I to question other people's truths? At the same time, there are places that feel so peaceful and full of positive energy, like tant Frida's cottage. I think that if an animal or person has truly loved you, the love stays with you. If you call for Sara and ask her for guidance or consolation, and feel something like I do when I think of tant Frida, it won't be Sara herself that speaks to you from the other side, but her love for you that's still inside you that gives an echo of your own calling. I'm rambling a bit, but can you follow my thoughts?
-I think so.
-Let's try! Sara? Sara, please let us know that you still love us! The world is so empty without you. We miss you so much!
I lay still, echoed Lisa's words in my head.

A calm but vibrant warmth spread inside me, like Sara's smile, from my toes up to my head.
Then I knew for sure:
Yes.
It's true.
Love can never die.
Never.

Towards the evening, I had my door lock replaced.
Lisa thought that throwing out the cakes was a great idea and wanted to do the same with the garbage bags, but I wouldn't let her. The salty cakes had been my way to let off steam, no need to overdramatize. Almost all the furniture was mine, only the white rattan shelf that had hosted her favourite teddy bears was hers. It was easy to carry that down to the hallway outside the laundrette in the cellar, with the rest of her stuff. I put up a note to the neighbours: "Sorry about the mess, this will all be gone tomorrow." Even though I had calmed down, I wasn't reasonable enough to keep her things in my flat until she realised she would have to move.
-Do you want to stay in the cottage for a few days?
-Yes, later. I just need to... take care of everything first. Make sure she understands she doesn't live here anymore. She might call a locksmith.
-Do you want me to stay?
-Thanks, but I think that would make things worse.
-Are you sure?
I nodded. Of course it would have been nice to hold Lisa's hand through this, but believe it or not, a small spark of pride still burned deep down inside.

Restless periods of slumber during the night turned into a deep sleep sometime after sunrise. Angry signals from the doorbell followed by even angrier hammering on the door woke me up. I took my time to go to the bathroom and wash the sand from my eyes before I opened up and faced a furious Madeleine.

-Have you *changed the lock?*

-Yup.

-Give me the keys!

-No.

-I live here!

-Not anymore.

Trembling lower lip.

-What do you mean?

-It's my apartment.

-It's more mine than yours! I made it what it is!

A tasteless cavalcade of cuteness, I thought but kept my mouth shot. I didn't want to argue.

-Your things are in the cellar.

-You... you have poked into my things?

-I have no interest in poking. I've helped you pack. Everything is neatly folded. Except the teddies, they might be a bit upside down.

She gasped.

-You have moved my teddies?!

-Mm.

-You'll regret this!

-I think not.

-I have rights! The partner law...

I interrupted her. Yes, there's a law that gives partners who live together a lot of rights. But I had an ace in my sleeve.

-You don't officially live here, remember? All that paperwork is so boring, and it's so cute to see your mother's handwriting on all the dull envelopes from the authorities when she has to forward your mail.

Tears in the beautiful blue eyes.

-But... I have nowhere to go!

-Too bad.
-Can't we... try again? I was... I said some nasty things yesterday, but I didn't mean them! I was just so upset!
-What about Max?
She tried to row without oars.
-It didn't mean anything! It was a huge mistake, I...
-You and I were a huge mistake.
-How can you say that! You have to forgive me!
There are very few things in life that you absolutely have to do. There's almost always a choice, even if the consequences are so dramatic that it feels like you're forced to do it. For example, I don't have to stop at a redlight. I can choose to run the little tant over. I can also choose not to go to the bathroom, and die from constipation. To forgive Madeleine was one of the many, many things that I didn't have to do, and the consequences of not forgiving her would not affect me in any negative way at all.
-Not now.
-But... there is a chance? For us? To start over?
When she uttered those words, it was as if a primal scream wanted to break free from inside my chest.
No!
I took a few deep breaths to gain control of myself and not let that scream out.
-No, Madeleine.
-Please! Let me in, let us talk this through, you can't just throw away the years we've had together!
-We can talk outside.
-But...
-I'll make some tea. Wait in the backyard.
Defeated, she left.

I called Pontus. Could I please borrow his car?
Sure, he could drop the key off in about an hour, was
there something else he could do to help me?
Yes, if he could spend the evening with me?
You bet!
The flowery shit was in the bottom of one of the garbage
bags, so I made two cups of Earl Grey. Even in a situation
like this, fika was important. Something to keep your
hands and eyes busy while you were talking. Or listening.
Or trying to kill time.
Madeleine hated Earl Grey but didn't say anything. She
was still crying when I came out to her. Suddenly, she felt
like a stranger.
-Is there anything I can say or do to make you change
your mind? she sobbed.
I shook my head and gave her one of the steaming cups,
the one with milk in. After all, I wasn't heartless.
-Can't I stay for a few days, while I'm looking for a place
to live?
-I'll help you drive your things to Max.
-But I can't stay with him! I don't want to!
He didn't want to either, I'm sure of it.
-I'm sorry, but that's where you made your bed.
Quietly, we sat there with our tea. I drank, she didn't.
-How's Sara? she asked when nothing had been said for
almost ten minutes.
-She's dead. That's why I came home earlier that night.
Madeleine almost dropped her teacup and spilled hot tea
on her flowery tights. She stared at me in shock.
-What are you saying!
I focused on my tea. Didn't want to talk about it. Most
certainly didn't want to cry again, not in front of
Madeleine, didn't want to share my pain with her. She
resumed her crying, though.

That might have been the longest hour of my life. I was so relieved when I saw Pontus in his taxi waving at me. I got the car key, told Madeleine to wait while I rode my bike to get the car at the old stone house where Pontus still lived.

Someone might think that I was too nice, helping her move, even if she didn't want to. I could just have left her things in the basement. But right then, I wanted to forget the reason for our break up, wanted it to be as smooth as possible. Partly because I didn't want to fight, not at all and not so close to Sara's death. But also, I knew that I was in no way an innocent victim. I carried half the responsibility for this. I had pretended to be satisfied, let her believe that I was ok with all her lace and teddy bears, let her pour me a cup of flowery shit every morning, never tried to explain why I didn't want to go with her to all those parties and events, sneaking off to Lisa to breathe without telling her where I'd been. Nothing to be proud of. When I come to think of it, that's an even worse form of infidelity.
We both needed something important that we couldn't get from each other.
We should have ended this long ago.

Everything fitted in the trunk and back seat, so we only had to take one turn.
I could feel her agony.
-He's probably not at home at this hour.
-You'll have to wait for him, then.
-His flatmate won't accept it.
-I'm sure you can charm him.
-Johan...
Max lived on the second floor in a tall student building with two-room-flats. Madeleine didn't lift a finger. I had

to carry everything myself but I didn't mind. Soon there was a large pile outside his door.
-Please!
She threw her arms around me and tried to kiss me. Instinctively I backed off, disgusted when I thought about her and Max together, but... another memory came through. When she had kissed me on that New Year's eve. My first kiss. Would this be my last?
All other thoughts pushed away, I kissed her back, desperately, pushed her against the door to her lover's home, and didn't stop until she broke free when she heard someone coming. I couldn't hear anything, there was a silent noise inside my head.
 It was just a neighbour, who looked a bit amused but minded his own business and went inside without any comments.
We stared at each other, her eyes full of hope, mine probably bewildered, before I tore myself from the situation and ran to the car. She called my name, over and over again, ran after me but lost a shoe in the stair just like Cinderella at midnight, but this prince would never look for her again.

Sadly, I was right.
I haven't kissed anyone since.

Even if you hire a funeral agency, there's a lot to do. Mom wanted the farewell to be perfect. Not because of what people might think. This time, she did it for herself. As long as the planning of the funeral service occupied her mind, she could keep herself up.

Afterwards, she fell apart.

Where I work now, I see a lot of caregivers devoting their lives to children with special needs. When the child dies, the foundation for their whole existence disappears. No longer do they have to fight or discuss with authorities, staff at the habilitation, school, daily activity centre and sheltered housing, with personal assistants, speech therapists, physiotherapists, with the hospital and uncomprehending doctors, all the people in the social security net that had been spun around your child. All of a sudden, they're alone.

Who are you without your child that needs you, mom?
Can you remember your dreams and plans?
If you do, will you be able to fulfil them now that you're free to do so, or do you have a bad conscience because you longed for a lazy vacation in the sun?
Do you feel the need to punish yourself for not being able to appreciate every single second with your child? Do you feel that you don't deserve to do all those things that you're finally able to do?
Dearest mom, nobody could have been a better mother to Sara than you! It's not your fault that her heart gave up. Your words about not wanting another baby so many years ago didn't cause this. Her heart would have been defect even if she hadn't been a surprise.
Try to understand that?
Please mom, try to forgive yourself!

Pontus had been feeling unwell for some time, with stomach ache and lack of appetite. To begin with I wasn't surprised at all. A diet of fast food, chips and soda will eventually take its toll. But it didn't get any better when he cut back on the sugar, so finally I told him that he had to go and see a doctor. I had just lost Sara, so I was uncharacteristically harsh when I spoke to him, because I was so worried that I might lose him too.

Pontus didn't want to.

-What if they find anything wrong with me!

-You moron, that's what we want! There *is* something wrong with you, and the sooner we find out what it is, the sooner we can fix it!

-But what if they say that it's cancer!

That's what I was afraid of too, but we couldn't both be scared. Someone had to be the pushy one and while my own fuel tank is almost empty, I have a spare tank for my friends.

-If you do have cancer, does it go away if you don't get it confirmed?

-No, but...

He looked so miserable, and had lost so much weight, which didn't suit him at all. Some people are meant to be big.

Knight Pont-du-John stood on my window sill. He had been unemployed for a long time. During my years with Madeleine, we had taken a break from our game. Now was the perfect time to throw him back into the battle. I put him in front of Pontus.

-I challenge you.

-That's not fair! he whined.

-Never said it was.

He beheld the figurine, and I could almost see the memories playing like a movie in his head. Then he looked me in the eyes. Our friendship had survived a lot. After everything with Sara and Madeleine, it was stronger than ever.

-Will you come with me? I'm scared.

-Of course I will.

The verdict was a huge relief for me, and a disaster for Pontus.

Celiac disease!

His life was ruined. No more bread! How would he survive without freshly baked bread? And pizza! And pasta! And what would his mother say? People who didn't eat normal things, that is, everything she ate, made her nervous. He didn't want to listen to my attempts to give him a little perspective. At that point he would much rather have heard that he had a tumour that could be removed, or something else that could be cured with a medicine. Stupid scientists, how hard could it be to find a cure for celiac disease? Well, see if he cared! He had endured stomach ache for years, he had got used to it. He wasn't going to change his life style because of this!

I was so angry with him! The kind of anger that's born out of fear. I knew enough about gluten intolerance to realise that he would get sick for real if he continued eating the way he wanted to, and that if he changed his diet, he would get well. All he needed to do was to avoid eating things with gluten. It's not like other allergies where you get symptoms by just being in the same room as the allergen.

I decided to play even more foul.

-If you don't take care of yourself, I'll talk to your mother.

Pontus' eyes went very dark and if he had been able to use one of those lajv spells on me, I think he would have.

-Don't even think about it. I'm warning you.

He knew what his life would be if I said to his mother that I was worried about him. She was still overprotective. Her sister had grown tired of the Swedish winters and had recently moved to Spain, so there was nobody else she could spend her energy on.

The Swedish winters, by the way, can be so depressing.
We live in a very long and narrow country. In the
southern parts, it doesn't snow very often. When they do
get snow, there's panic and cars in the ditches every few
hundred meters. In the north, the first snow can fall in
August and stay long into the spring. In Uppsala, you
never know. Some years we have wonderful, white
winters, where the snow stays from late November to
March, but often we get snow a few days, then it melts
into a greybrownish sad slush, or it melts just enough to
form a smooth surface of ice. A little rain on top of that
makes it really interesting. I have winter tyres on my bike,
but it's still an adventure to conquer the winter roads.
And, just because there's snow doesn't mean you can build
a snowman. It has to be the exact right temperature. If it's
too cold, the snow is just like a dry powder, impossible to
mold.

Pont-du-John had been in Pontus' pocket since the last
challenge, as a talisman. Maybe he could protect us from a
bad test result. Now he was thrown back at me.
-I challenge you, you bloody optimist! If you manage to
bake a bread that I can eat, that actually tastes good, I'll
shut up and endure this shit. But if you give me anything
resembling to that pale miserable things they call bread,
that you can find in the shop freezer, you can shove your
annoying positive attitude where the sun never shines and
shut the fuck up, alright?
Optimist? Positive attitude? Being called that felt truly
refreshing and I started experimenting. I went to the
library, checked the internet, tried different flours and
mix of flours, different temperatures, different liquids and
spices and discovered a whole new world! You had the
classic alternative flours with almond, corn, millet and
buckwheat, but also exciting ancient but for me new flours

of sorghum and teff, and flour of coconut and peanut that I had never used in bread before.

It wasn't cheap compared to wheat flour, but Pontus was happy to pay. Happy to being able to eat bread without his stomach protesting.

His attitude had changed, because it had to be changed in order to calm his mother. Her son had a lifelong disease! -No, mother, not exactly a disease, it's just an intolerance. It's not a big deal. Look here, Johan has found a recipe of gluten free scones, they're delicious, and I can still eat your plum jam with it, everything can still be as it always has been, just without the gluten!

I spent a whole day in the kitchen with Pontus' mother, teaching her everything I had learned during my experiments. This was the first time that I spent time with her as a person. Before that, she was just a friend's mother, someone I said hello and goodbye to and yes, school is fine and my parents are healthy. I realised I knew nothing about her. When I commended her for learning so fast, she blushed and looked as if she never had got a compliment in her life. I kept sending her recipes whenever I found something new, and she showed me her own baking secrets. Even though they had different personalities, it somehow felt as when I was baking with tant Frida. Sometimes we experimented together, giggling, having fun.

Finally, I had found something to start defining who I was. I'm that guy who likes to bake.

Madeleine also liked to watch docusoaps, like Big Brother where you threw a bunch of people together and forced them to interact. If you weren't cool enough or entertaining enough, you would be kicked out and there would be a Winner. The coolest and most popular would get money and fame that would last for a short while in

the nightclubs in Stockholm. When interviewed about
their strategy before the show started, they all said more
or less the same thing:
”I'll just be myself.”
I've never understood that expression.
You're always yourself, no matter what you do. It's just
that different people and different situations winkle out
different sides of you. With Madeleine, I put up an act,
but it was still me trying to pretend to be something I
thought I should be. At parties, I'm also myself, a self I
hate because I feel so bad.
Miriam says that you need to push yourself outside your
comfort zone to grow as a person and to learn more about
yourself. Why do I need to grow if it makes me
uncomfortable? Why can't I just stick to the people that
make me a myself I like?

How I enjoyed my single life!
No afterparties. No teddy bears. I could see my friends
whenever I wanted to. Solitude wasn't a burden, it was a
relief! I didn't want to listen to Pontus' suggestions about
finding someone new. Did he want to start eating gluten
again? No? Stop asking, then, because I get stomach ache
just by thinking about it.
But if the Right One is out there?
Well, ignorance is bliss.

One evening, Samuel's father wanted to talk to me. He
looked serious and immediately I was worried. Had I done
something wrong?
-I've been offered a job I can't say no to, in Copenhagen.
We will have to move next autumn. It's almost a year
from now, but we thought it was fair to let you know. We
sincerely hope that you will stay with us until we leave,
because you do a fantastic job with Samuel. He's always

much calmer the days when he knows that you're coming. And if you ever think about moving to the Öresund region...?

I shook my head, feeling a lump in my chest. Lose my job and my safe routines? Lose Samuel? Even though he never spoke to me, never even looked at me, we had some kind of connection and he was an important part of my life.

Samuel's father sighed.

-I guessed you wouldn't. Of course we will give you the best references even if you want to look for another job right away, but it would mean so much to us if you would agree to stay until then. You seem to enjoy this job?

Nod. Today was harder than usual to form the words.

-Have you ever thought about becoming a nurse assistant?

Now, this is a tricky word to translate. Undersköterska, the Swedish word, is a job you can have in all kinds of places where you take care of other people one way or another. If you work in a sheltered housing for people with special needs, or in a home for elderly, or help people in their own homes, there are no nurses so it feels strange to call it "nurse assistant".

My academic non-career had given me nothing but debts, and I was scared to pick up the books again. There are two ways of becoming a nurse assistant. The first is to choose that program in gymnasium, which obviously was too late for me. You can also go to adult school and take the same courses as in gymnasium, in a classroom or by distance learning where you study on your own. You send the assignments via email and only go to the school to write the exams and on the few mandatory lessons like CPR and First Aid.

I knew what my friends would say. "Of course you can do this! We believe in you! Look at it as a challenge!"

Amanda would probably be able to give me a more objective view, but I didn't want to risk getting stuck in her net of planning and leave with an hour-by-hour plan for the next two years before I had decided for myself if I wanted to do this. Mom was still grief-stricken and my relation to her is still a bit strained after all the years I've felt set aside. She hadn't even noticed that Madeleine was out of my life and I didn't feel like telling her, making her even more sad. Maybe she would find out eventually. Everyone else knew though. Hard not to notice. Unless you were locked into your own world of mourning.

It was Sunday morning, and I had thought about this all night during my shift. Dad always takes a morning walk, so I went to my old home when I had finished my shift, knowing that I wouldn't be able to sleep unless I talked to someone about my possible plans. He was glad to see me, but a bit worried. This wasn't something I had done before, asking if he wanted company on his walk. Please, no more troubles?

He was relieved and excited when I asked him if he thought I would become a good nurse assistant.

-That's an excellent idea, Johan! One thing I have learned during all these years with Sara in and out of hospital is that everyone around us had their own important part in the big machinery. The workmanship of doctors and nurses might be the difference between life and death for the patient, but they almost never had time to sit down with the patient or the family. The nurse assistants did. You have the most important skill a nurse assistant needs – patience, and the ability to listen in times of pain!

Forgive me. I'm not being fair to my mother. She fell into a depression after Sara's death. She couldn't help it. But she refused to accept help, and that wasn't fair to us.

Pontus and Lisa gave me the encouragement I knew they would and cheered me on, and Amanda was thrilled to help me with the studying strategies. I chose the distance learning, so that I could study at work. Some courses were very easy if you had a little life experience. It wasn't news to me that women in some cultures wore a hijab or niqab, or that it might be more profitable to look for special offers when you were helping a tant with the shopping. These courses were indeed for the gymnasium age. But when it was time for the medical course, I needed Lisa's help. She still loves to learn new things, and thought the bloodstream and autonomic nervous system and liver diseases were exciting. She read the text, retold it to me in her own words, drew pictures and gave me examples to make me understand. It's always been easier for me to learn that way, instead of just reading. I passed the exam, all thanks to her.

During these three semesters, we had to get work experience from three different practice placements, four weeks each. I had to take some leave of absence from my job during the first two placements. Just before my third semester started, Samuel moved to Skåne. Funny how much you can miss someone who doesn't interact at all! The first placement was in the home care, when we went to elderly people's own homes to help with shopping, cleaning, personal hygiene and other things. That nearly made me give up the whole idea. The constant chatting, the smell, the rotting wounds, the filth, the aggressiveness, the crying, the prompting, the wish for us to stay a little longer, or the wish for us to stay away forever. I hated every minute. Samuel was the only reason that I endured. With this education, it would be easier for me to find work with other disabled children when he had moved.

Second placement was much better, a sheltered housing
for adults with neuropsychiatric disabilities. These people
truly were disabled, unable to relax in a world they
couldn't handle. This month made me understand Samuel
and his parents much better. In the nights, he wasn't
disabled at all, because he was left alone. He could do
what he wanted to do as long as he didn't want to do
something dangerous. In the daytime, he was awashed
with thousands of demands and impressions each minute,
and was unable to sort them. The nervous system is
constructed to sort out unimportant impressions. If
someone ask us what we saw through the bus window
when we went into the town centre, we might remember
the art museum, some trees, a traffic light, and hm, wasn't
there a big red house somewhere? Someone with autism
might be able to tell you the shape and colour of every
brick in every house, the name of every tree and the birds
on the branches, and describe the pattern of every curtain
in every window we passed. When everything you see and
hear and smell and feel seem to be of the same
importance, no wonder life seems overwhelming!

One day, there was a problem with the food delivery. The
manager muttered:
-No bread! No cereals! Johan, could you please go down
to the corner store and buy something?
I almost shivered when I saw the range of so called bread
they offered. What if I could... would it be too bold?
Ten minutes later I was back with the least disgusting
bread they had, along with some flour, syrup and yeast
that I had bought with my own money.
-I thought... maybe someone might enjoy some
homemade bread. It doesn't take long to make, and... I
thought... If the scent isn't too disturbing...

-Of course it's not disturbing, it's a wonderful idea! If you feel you have the time?
As a trainee, I had lots of time so I used it where I thought it was best.
The scent of warm bread had a magical impact. One of the most reserved, who never left her room if she wasn't forced to do so, stuck her head out to see what was going on. And the malnourished man, who never wanted to eat anything except green apples, ate three large pieces of bread with butter.
-Please stay with us! the staff asked me and smiled. Whether they were serious or not I don't know, but it felt good to hear!

My last placement was in one of the wards in the Children's Hospital. I'm glad it was my third because the previous had tought me to get more used to being around so many people. My shyness hadn't disappeared, but I had learned how to handle it better. I couldn't manage the small talk, but I didn't feel the need to hide.
On my last day, the head of department asked:
-Would you like to stay with us?
She was definitely serious, and here I am now!

Lisa's life was far from mediocre.
Her Japanese agency didn't want to let her go. There were thousands of Swedish girls with dreams about being a model, but from the beginning, Lisa's lack of interest was what made her special in their eyes. She went back now and then to do the occasional job, if they guaranteed there was no nonsense! She could do photo shoots and commercials, if they didn't put her in any giant pastries, and no more game shows. Without Sara, Lisa didn't have any incentive to do silly things.

New idea. The TV show where Lisa had travelled in Japan had been quite popular. What if they made a show with Lisa in Sweden? They could bring famous Japaneses to Sweden where they could discover exotic environments with her. And of course they wanted to film Lisa in her home -
No way.
But...
No TV team in a mile's range of tant Frida's cottage!
But...
Under No Circumstances!

Even if Lisa and Pontus weren't on the same wavelength, my birthday fikas with both of them were nice. During the Madeleine years we had the fika in the cottage, because I kept my promise not to invite Lisa to our home. Not that Madeleine stopped having afterparties.
With big gestures Lisa told me and Pontus about the constant nagging of the agency and the producers. It was such a great idea, there was already a line of advertisers who wanted to pay an insane amount of money for a spot in the show. Everybody wanted to learn about Lisa's life in that strange country. She almost had an obligation to show them!
Why wouldn't they take no for an answer? She had already signed the contract for the show where Japanese celebrities came to Sweden, but she needed tant Frida's cottage as her sanctuary.

Pontus said:
-They should buy their own cottage, the Japanese. An old ramshackle, that they could restore, like the Swedish TV show, you know, and have the camera follow every move. When you buy it, fix it up, go to flea markets to look for furniture and stuff, and...

Lisa fell in:
-And they could make another show after that, a docusoap where ordinary Japanese people came to live in the cottage, trying to survive without modernity! We could have some cows and chicken and Johan could teach them how to make bread and I could teach them some Swedish...

The production team loved the idea!
Lisa got involved in the project on all levels. She wanted to learn more about what happened behind the TV camera. How did they catch the best picture? The most interesting angle? What did the whole production line look like? What kind of personalities would be suitable for a docusoap? What would be the best house and environment for the project?
I don't know how many miles we travelled to find the perfect, lagom scruffy cottage. Pontus helped, both by looking and acting as an alibi when I told Madeleine that I was going away for a whole day. When driving his little ladies, he asked them for help. Perhaps they knew something about old houses nearby?
They were thrilled, and told him everything they remembered, generously spiced with intricate stories about who lived where and who was married to whom and who were cousins, once and twice removed. He took them on reconnaissance trips in his own car. Some of the places they remembered were in ruins, some weren't there at all, some had been restored or torn down to leave place for something new, but eventually we found the perfect place, only an hour's drive north of Uppsala. It had a spacious kitchen, two smaller rooms, an attic, and a row of outhouses. It had been for sale for a long time, so expensive that nobody wanted to buy it since it would cost

a lot to fix it up, but the production team had the money
and saw the potential.

Lisa loved to have a hand in everything. She found
trustable craftsmen who taught the Japanese builders how
to save old Swedish houses. The interpreter was also the
host of the show. They wanted Lisa but she said she
would rather stick to the role as Swedish teacher and help
out with everything else. The interpreter, Akemi, didn't
quite manage to stick to her part. When they let her loose
at the flea markets, she was beside herself with excitement
and bought loads of things for herself. That gave rise to a
spin-off show called "Akemi's Treasure Hunt". To see
someone be so happy about a worn Dala horse was almost
touching. She was so sweet and I think I fell in love a little
bit with her. She was twenty years older than me, which
wouldn't have been a problem for me (and I didn't give a
damn what people would say!) but by then I enjoyed my
life as single far too much to try to flirt with her. First of
all I would have to learn how to flirt, and I had my studies
to focus on and I might say or do something wrong that
would destroy the whole project and I was scared and,
damn, it's not until now that I realise how much I liked
her. These confessions come as a surprise to me too,
they've been hidden so deep somewhere inside.

Thousands of people wanted to be on the show, so the
production team immediately decided upon doing more
than one season, with people from one region at the time.
Lisa found a shrewd little farmer who was trudging
around and taught city slickers from Tokyo how to
harvest flax and make sausages. Between the real life
sequences, there were animated parts with very basic and
not particularly useful Swedish phrases. Suddenly, a
purple pig could emerge from nowhere, saying: "Gris! Jag
är en gris!" (Pig! I am a pig!) with the Japanese translation
flowing around, the beautiful characters dancing. So, Lisa

wasn't needed as the teacher, but at the end of each day, she sat in the cosy kitchen with the participants, asking them what they had learned and what they thought of it all. None of this stupid "one has to leave"-nonsense. It wasn't a competition, it was an experience to be shared. She lived an intense life, my allrakäraste Lisa, but she still managed to find time for me. She said that she needed me to keep her sane in this whirlwind.

Pontus drove his taxi and went on lajv adventures and was happy.
Until he met Bella.
They had met at the gym, not long after Sara's death. She had asked him to stand behind her while she was doing bench lift and he admired her strength and ability to focus. They continued training together and soon fell in love.
-She wants me to move in with her, he told me one day, just a couple of weeks after they had started dating.
My experiences of moving in together too fast wasn't the best, but I remembered how angry I had been with Amanda for pointing that out to me so I tried to lay low.
-What do you think, then?
-I'm crazy about her! I think she might be the one. She says that I'm the only one that truly understands her. All of her previous boyfriends have been total bastards.
-Really?
-Mhm. She says I'm perfect! Nobody has said that to me before!
He sighed and looked so happy that I couldn't reveal my thoughts. But I decided to keep a close eye on him.

Bella was nice to me. Very nice. But I didn't like the way she talked to Pontus. Or, talked for him.

”He's given up that stupid lajv thing, you've grown out of
it, haven't you?”
”He's thinking about buying a truck, and quit the taxi
driving, because it's not very profitable, right?”
”He needs to lose some weight, so we're going on a diet.
We won't be needing your bread anymore.”
We never spent time alone anymore. He always made
some excuse, or brought Bella to our movie marathons. I
didn't know what to do. His eyes looked just like when he
was begging me to go to that class party ages ago, but they
rested on her instead, waiting for approval or permission.
Sometimes she would raise him to the skies, sometimes
she talked to him as if he was an imbecile.
One day, he wore a scarf on a hot spring day. He never
wore scarves. Not even in the middle of the winter.
Another day, he had sunglasses on a rainy day.
I needed to talk to someone, preferably to someone with
professional secrecy. Both Amanda and Lisa were so
terribly efficient, they would probably push things too fast
if they knew about my worries. But here is where my
shyness became my disability. I couldn't bring myself to
look for someone.
-Sara, I whispered into the sky. Please, help me! What can
I do? What can I say to him? I won't stand still and watch
someone hurt my friend again!

To find an opportunity to talk wasn't easy. Eventually, I
found an opening. Sometimes he got long drives, outside
the county. Even though it was strictly forbidden to take
friends with you, Pontus and his little old ladies didn't
care, so now and then I went with them. This time he was
a bit reluctant though, as if he knew Bella wouldn't like it.
But since it wasn't allowed, and therefore a secret, maybe
she didn't need to know.

When we had left the little tant at her daughter's place, it was just us in the car. My heart pounded and my mouth was dry when I tried to find a way to bring it up. The time when I could get him in a relaxed mood by asking about lajv was over. After some forced stories about the cottage and TV project, I started telling him about Miriam. Or, I started lying about her, because what I was about to say was something that I had read myself, but I didn't want him to know that. Telling him that Miriam had said this was just a bridge, from one subject to another.

-Miriam told me about a discussion she had in an internet forum. There was a woman who lectured about women who abuse men, and she got threatened by feminists! How short-sighted and idiotic isn't that? I mean, if it's equality they strive for, it's not very constructive to close your eyes for the fact that there are also women who mistreat men. Not only the other way around. But the community isn't ready to accept that. A man who gets beaten up by his woman, that's almost a little ridiculous, right? He's so much bigger and stronger, he should be able to take a slap! Except that three out of four women use some kind of weapon to compensate if they're not as strong as the man. Isn't that terrible, Pontus? That men are afraid of admitting to being mistreated, because they don't think they will be taken seriously?

My eyes had been focused on the motorway. Now I glanced at him. His eyes were wide open, kept on the road but I could see his pain, sadness, fear and something that made me think of a wounded animal, looking into the rifle barrel, knowing it was about to die but didn't understand why.

Then I knew that I was right.

-There's a phone support line...

-I don't want to talk about this!

-You're not alone, you know.

-They will laugh at me! You can't force me!
This was way too serious for Pont-du-John. He could
challenge me to write this book, and to get Pontus to the
doctor, but now was not the time or the place for him.
-What would you have said to me if Madeleine had hurt
me?
-But she didn't! And Bella doesn't! It... it will be alright,
she's just... not herself now, she didn't mean to, and by
the way, it's not true!
-You had a black eye the other week.
-It was from the training! I don't want to talk about this,
ever again, do you hear me?
I closed my eyes and sighed.
-*Sub Rosa.*
-What?
-I won't say a word to a living soul. But please, be more
careful when you're training.

Not to a living soul. But dead sisters tell no tales.
I talked to Sara, and she gave me inspiration.
Pontus kept away from me, didn't return my calls and
didn't pick up the phone when he saw my number on the
display, so I had to think of another way to get in contact
with him. I called his mother and asked if she would be so
kind to show me how to use a wafer iron. I said that I had
just found tant Frida's in a cupboard and couldn't work
out how thin the batter should be. She was pleased that I
remembered the homemade wafers that she used to serve
ice cream in, and invited me for a lesson.
After a pleasant afternoon, I lied about having left my
mobile phone at home, and asked if I could borrow her
phone to call Pontus.
-Please, don't hang up!
I could imagine him looking over his shoulder to see if
Bella knew it was me.

-Hello mother, he said.
Of course. They had a display on the answering machine
in the hallway.
-It's Sara's birthday tomorrow.
-I know.
-Come with me to the grave?
-I don't think I've got the time.
-Please. I need you.
-Couldn't someone else drive your friend to the
graveyard?
I waited in silence. Finally he gave up.
-Sure. I'll pick her up at noon.

No makeup in the world could cover the bruises on his
face, but he had tried so I didn't comment on it.
Sara loved glögg, the spiced wine that we drink around
advent and Christmas. Of course Sara got the non-alcohol
version. She would have drunk it all year if mom had
allowed her, but glögg was for the winter!
 I had saved a bottle and filled a small red paper mug with
glögg and put it in front of her beautiful small white
tomb. Dad would have preferred to spread the ashes
somewhere, but mom needed a grave to look after.
We stood in silence for a few minutes before I said as soft
as I could to the grave:
-Happy birthday, my sweet sister with the pure heart.
Will you please give Pontus the strength to take care of
himself? He won't let me. I know you would have if you'd
still been with us. You wouldn't have let anyone hurt him.
Not even himself.
Pontus fell on his knees, tears in his eyes.
-You tricked me. This isn't fair!
-No, it's not. I didn't know what else to do.
I sat down beside him, put my hand on his shoulder. He
flinched.

-Pontus... I don't understand what's going on here. Please tell me!

Eventually, I got the whole, sad, classic story.

In the beginning, she had told him he was perfect.

Then, not perfect enough.

Not perfect at all.

A big freak, hopeless, stupid, smelly, fat, clumsy, ugly, he should be grateful that she let him live with her, he would never find anyone else who could stand being with him, just look at his earlier relationships, nobody stayed! Go figure!

-I don't understand, he cried and wiped his nose on his sleeve. Why does she stay with me, if I'm such a loser? It's my fault that she gets so angry, it must be, she doesn't want to hit me, but she can't help herself when I act a certain way or have a certain tone, and then she promises she will never do it again. She cries and says she's sorry. If I just stop provoking her this would never happen. Why can't I ever learn?

-Listen to yourself, Pontus! I asked you once before and I'm asking you again – what would you do if Madeleine or anyone at all had treated me like Bella treats you?

-You're not as stupid as I am. Nobody has to beat you.

-It's just as bad without the physical damage! Can't you see? Even if she hadn't laid a finger on you, she's still abusing you emotionally!

-She's only telling the truth. I am stupid.

Yes, you are, I thought, but said instead:

-So if Sara had a boyfriend who called her stupid, would that be ok?

His eyes went black.

-Of course not!

-Why not? She probably deserved it.

-I won't let you talk about her like that!

-And I won't let anyone talk about *you* like that! Not
again, not ever again, do you hear me? If you want me to
fight dirty, I can promise you I will!
-Stop threatening me!
-Tell me what to do then!
-Just leave me alone!
-Never!
I don't know how this would have ended if Amanda and
Jörgen hadn't showed up with a small bouquet.
-What on Earth are you two doing! she demanded. And
Pontus, what's happened to your face!
Warningly I kept my eyes on him. He wouldn't dare lying
in front of Sara!
He looked back at me for a few, very long seconds.
Looked at the grave. At Amanda. At me again. At his
hands. Finally he said in a low but calm voice:
-My girlfriend is abusing me and Johan is taking me to a
shelter.

It took time to rebuild Pontus' self confidence. At the
shelter he got the chance to talk to other men in his
situation. Nobody laughed at him, their stories were more
or less the same. Bella begged him to come back to her,
she had changed, she loved him, she needed him, you
selfish idiot, can't you see that I'm the best thing that ever
happened to you, no, no, I didn't mean it like that, if you
just come home you'll see how sweet and gentle I can be!
Don't you believe me? Are you accusing me of lying?
How dare you!
In front of the staff at the shelter, Bella completely lost
both her temper and her mind, grabbed the nearest chair
and smashed it in his head. He didn't want to press
charges, but the staff did.
She got probation and fines.

Pontus got good help from a psychologist, but the best healing power came from the Labrador Queenie who moved into the old stone house. With the aunt in Spain, the reason for not getting a dog was gone. His mother was a bit worried, she never had animals, but Queenie soon won her heart with her calm charm. Finally Pontus had his dog! She was a bit like Sara. Forgive me for comparing my sister to a dog, but it's a compliment. Queenie didn't complicate things. She was full of love and trust. She made him laugh. When his mother complained about dog hair in the sofa, he smiled and said:
-She might shed, but at least she's not a vegetarian!

Camilla and Pontus first met at a lajv, then again at a dog training course. Pontus was still wounded from his experience with Bella, so he was very careful when they started dating. Someone, I can't remember who, said that you can be infatuated by a complete bastard, but you can't be friends with someone you don't like. That's what he was looking for. Friendship. If the friend turned out to be someone you could fall in love with, he could feel safe again.
-Friendship should be the foundation to any relationship, he said when he told me about their first kiss.
Thanks for the input.
Even if Camilla is a bit pushy sometimes, she treats Pontus like gold. She doesn't try to stop him seeing his friends, and never tries to change him.

-How can you work with sick children!
Camilla gasped when she found out what I do for a living. I shrugged.
-Someone has to. And I like it.
-How can you like it! Isn't it awful? What if they have cancer! How can you cope?

A common opinion, that childhood cancer must be one of the worst diseases in the world. Of course it's terrible, but believe me, there are far worse things that can struck a child. The neurological diseases are so cruel that I don't want to talk about them. And there are other illnesses and deformities that inevitably will make life difficult for both the child and everyone around it. I wish my job didn't exist, that there was no need for a Children's Hospital. But you can't work in a place like this if you think it's heartbreaking. You have to learn to see the children with different eyes, see the healthy spirit of the child inside the sick body. Most of the time, they handle their illness much better than adults. The children happily drag IV poles after them in the corridor, jump around on crutches, find a way to play unless they are in a very bad condition. It's tougher with the teenagers who just got a frightening diagnoses. They have a wider perspective, have just started to taste independency and now have to look Death straight into the eyes.

How I can cope?

By doing the best job I can!

I can't cure them. But I can treat them with respect. Listen if they want to talk. Be quiet if they don't. Bring a glass of water or an ice cream. Change the sheets to make them more comfortable. Help them change position in bed.

Earlier in the nursing history, the parents were just visitors. If the child was upset when the caregiver left, it probably was best that they didn't come at all. Now, at least one caregiver has to be present at all time, taking the main responsibility regarding the care of the child. Some teenagers might insist on sleeping alone and that's ok, but mainly, the nurse assistants are only there to help, not to take over.

Night shift suits me best, so I've continued working
nights. I've got used to the rhythm and enjoy it, and when
you're shy, it's just too many people around during the
days. Doctors, physiotherapists, cleaners, dietists, staff
from the hospital school and play therapy, scientists,
secretaries, and above all this, all the visitors and all the
new patients and their families who needs to be shown
around. It's too much for me.
Night time is down shifting time. Just a few nurses and
nurse assistants. The doctors only come if there's an
emergency.
Sometimes, one of the nurse assistants is needed to stay
close to a child all night for various reasons. It can be that
it has a tracheostomy, maybe a respirator, or has other
issues that make it necessary with someone who's awake
all night in the same room. Since the parents keep watch
during the days, someone has to help them during the
nights because they need to rest.
I love to be on night watch! Some of my colleagues hate
it. They need to keep moving in the night to stay awake
and prefer all the night duties like cleaning, change water
in the dishwasher, prepare breakfast and of course check
on the patients. For me, it's a bit like when I worked with
Samuel. It's just me and the child, and sometimes a lot of
technical equipment that I need to keep an eye on. No
need to talk.

There's a small kitchen that the parents can use if they
want to cook. Mostly they eat microwave food, but there
is an oven. I use to make bread rolls with sourdough at
home, let them rise during the night in the fridge at work,
and put them in the oven right before my shift ends. Is
there a better way to start the day, than to feel the scent of
newlybaked bread? Nobody in their right mind wants to
be in a hospital, and this is my way of making it as

pleasant as possible for at least a few minutes of the day. While the bread is in the oven, I clock out, take a shower in the changing room and have breakfast with my colleagues. I make enough rolls for them too. It's not a deliberate strategy to make myself popular, but it has that effect and I don't mind. It's like balm for my self confidence, hearing colleagues joke about wanting to change their shifts so they can adjust it to mine. I might be mediocre, but my bread is not!

Maybe this would be a good place to end the book? I think it is! Pontus is happy. He and Camilla is planning their wedding and I have said that he doesn't have to give me anything for my birthday or Christmas for as long as I live if he doesn't ask me to be his best man. Since he told me they were getting married, I've had nightmares about standing in front of the guests, naked, trying to hold a speech with a knife through my tongue.

Lisa is in the middle of her project with the Japanese at the farm. She spends the night at my place now and then and let out the steam to me when the culture shocks frustrate her. She has the occasional relationship, but says she doesn't have time for nor interest in something serious. She can manage alright with her battery powered little friend - thanks but I didn't need to know that.
Mom is still depressed. Dad tries to cheer her up, takes her to weekend trips, theatre, concerts, and she smiles and acts grateful but the smile never reaches her eyes. Madeleine called the other day, crying, begging me to take her back. Max had cheated on her. Karma, my dear.

My life is rich. I enjoy my work. I have friends. Tonight, I'm going to Jörgen and Amanda. Jörgen and I are having another whisky testing night. We have a fancy leather address book we use for the ”whisky alphabet”, trying to find brands from A to Z and write comments about them. The Swedish alphabet also have ÅÄÖ in the end, but the only Swedish whisky is called Mackmyra which is no help to us so we stick to the English alphabet. Jörgen has found something that is said to be whisky that begins with Q, but he strongly suspects it might be some kind of chemical dissolvent. When I get home, I'll try to come up with some sort of catchy ending with an encouraging moral about being a mediocrity but still have a good life.

Catchy ending:

Fucking Hell!
Jesus Fucking Christ Goddamnit!

What's happening?

We have whisky. Both the disgusting Q nonwhisky and
others. I get dizzy as usual, but drink it anyway. Jörgen
isn't affected in the same way, he just gets giggly. Experts
never swallow the whisky when they're testing, they spit it
out, but we're no experts, we drink everything and I lose
my foothold and when he playfully puts his hand around
my neck to say something I can't hear because I can't
concentrate on his words, I drown in his eyes, something
sweet and heavy spread from my heart to the rest of my
body into arteries I thought were dead and forgotten,
something I've never felt before, I care for him so much
that I want to cry, he's so close to my face and to my heart
and this is going straight to Hell, or no, he backs off at the
very last second so the road to Hell is crooked but
inevitable, he gently removes a strand of hair from my
forehead and says, I don't know what he says because once
more I can't hear, there's noise in my ears, I nearly kissed
my sister's partner, I wanted to, I ached to, I don't give a
damn if I'm bisexual or whatever this is, it's not the point,
I've had my suspicions for a long time, but Amanda's
boyfriend, for God's sake, this was going to be a mediocre
autobiography, not some cheesy Greek drama or an
episode of one of those stupid soap operas that Madeleine
liked to watch, I can't get up from that ugly brown
corduroy sofa from the Salvation Army, you have to cut
me loose from it, I can't move, then Amanda comes and
asks why I look so strange, she says I'm pale but how
could I be when I'm burning inside, not stuck after all
because I fall on the floor and she thinks I've had too
much to drink and I almost throw up but manage to
suppress it by breathing deep and get even dizzier from
hyperventilation and Jörgen tries to help me stand but I

can't stand his hands on me, want nothing more than his hands on me, and I scream, howl worse than Sara, Amanda tries in vain to calm me, calls Pontus who comes for me, drives me out of town, lets me out somewhere I can scream and scream until my throat is sore and then I cry and try to hurt myself but he holds me tight, too strong for me, holds me until I calm down, my head pounding, doesn't try to talk to me, knows I'm incapable of listening, drives me to Lisa who also holds me, allrakäraste Lisa, I try to push her away but she won't let me, just holds me together with Pontus, two pairs of arms around me on tant Frida's kitchen couch, no words, just closeness and love and I love them both but I don't want to be a part of this world anymore! Just let me sleep and never wake up!

Eventually, I fell asleep, exhausted and empty.

The cottage lies in a blessed radio shadow, far from the reach of any mobile telephone reception. Lisa leaves her mobile phone in a plastic bag in her mailbox by the main road. No need to bring it to the forest. The TV production team was furious with her, they wanted to be able to reach her any time of the day but she just shrugged. She would be there when they had agreed to, she refused to be some kind of slave. They had my phone number as well, for emergencies, but it wasn't helping much since I pulled the cord out when I was sleeping during the days and often forgot to put it back.

Pontus has never been able to lie convincingly, so Lisa went to the mailbox, called my job and said that sorry, but Johan has caught a terrible flu, he won't be back for at least a week, he's lost his voice, so I have to make the call, yes, I'll tell him to get well soon, and I'll let you know how he feels in a few days!

Get well soon.
What kind of expression is that?
Do we really need an imperative when we're down?
Like it's something we can decide for ourselves. Get a cup of coffee. Get a life. Get well.
Sure. As soon as I feel better, I'll get onto it.

The first days, it felt as if I did have the flu, so I stayed in the pullout kitchen sofa with a clear conscience. Someone was always with me. Lisa or Pontus. Dad. Mom came for a few hours and seemed truly concerned. Is this what it takes to make you care, mom? That your child is sick? Amanda had a big exam coming up, but sat by the kitchen table and studied. She said it was the best place for studying that she'd ever tried. Nothing there to disturb her.

On the second evening, Jörgen came.

Nobody knew what had happened, why I suddenly had fallen apart like this. Nobody but Jörgen, who might have a faint idea.

Carefully, he sat down on a three legged stool beside the kitchen couch where I lay, wrapped in one of tant Frida's many beautiful quilts.

-How are you feeling?

My throat felt like sandpaper.

-Not great.

-Are you too tired to talk?

I nodded.

-Is it ok if I talk, and you listen?

I wasn't so sure about that, but I nodded anyway.

Jörgen looked out of the window for a few minutes. The snow had begun to fall, and we would soon be in the middle of an idyllic Christmas card.

-Things got... out of hand, didn't they.

It wasn't a question.

-I'm sorry, Johan! Can you forgive me?

I was surprised.

-Forgive what?

-I'm not sure. Anything? Everything? I have to say or do something to make it right between us again, and I have no idea what. Can't we just... forget it? I don't want to lose you as a friend.

Forget it... Maybe it would be possible to pretend that whatever it was never happened. On the outside, nothing *had* happened. My inside was a different matter, but my own matter.

If Amanda ever gets her hands on these confessions? God forbid.

But I think she would understand.

I think she might have understood already.

And, you can't choose your feelings, but you can choose
your actions. Jörgen and I looked at each other and chose
to pretend to forget.
Smelling from sweat and overall unfreshness, I sat up in
my temporary bed. Someone must have put little socks on
all my teeth. Hygiene matters in the winter is a bit
challenging in the cottage. Lisa likes it, it's a bit like the
Japanese way, slow and thoughtful. You have to think
about every step on the way and be careful to not waste
the hot water. Sometimes I enjoy the ancient procedure of
melting snow and heat it up on the iron stove, but
suddenly I felt the desperate need of a long, hot shower in
my own home. Amanda and Jörgen didn't own a car, they
had borrowed my dad's when they came to look after me
here. I asked:
-Can you give me a ride home?
-Of course. Is everything ok between us?
He sounded anxious. I nodded again.
As a thank you to Lisa, I took all her laundry with me and
left a note saying how grateful I was, that I felt better and
would return her clean clothes in a day or two. Pontus got
a similar message on his voicemail, thanks for everything,
I'm going home, feel free to bring beer and I'll make pizza
if you're free someday soon.
Meaning: I need to be alone for a little while, but I know
you want to check on me and I want to thank you for it!

Life got back to normal.

No more whisky for me and Jörgen. What else could we
do together? The testing of different brands had been fun,
something in that area maybe? Non-alcoholic glögg at
this time of year. No more alcohol thankyouverymuch.
Julmust, of course. Julmust is the classic Christmas soda.
All breweries have their own recipe, quite similar but with

small differences that we loved to discover. Coca Cola has tried for years to claim space on the Swedish Christmas table, but it won't happen in my generation. The TV commercials about Santa Claus drinking Coke, we find ridiculous. Everyone knows that he drinks julmust. Later, we found other things to try and compare. Quality chocolate. Liquorice. Chilli! When we had something to focus on, we regained the lightness between us. Everything I might have felt for him in forbidden ways was buried in a chest of steel with seven locks. I refused to think about it, but was aware enough to avoid long walks in the sunset and anything that might make me lose control. Glögg with no alcohol is boring, but better safe than very very sorry.

My so called flu was over within a week and it felt good to be back at work.
One day, we got a tiny baby, premature, only half the size of other babies his age should be. He would have to stay with us for a long time. The parent, a single mom, took care of everything in the daytime, but needed help in the night since this baby needed to be watched all the time. It's best for the children to have as few people as possible around, so I was asked if I would be prepared to take care of this child on all my shifts. Of course I agreed.
The little one didn't want to lie in his own bed. Not! Even if he had a heat mattress, it was lonely and scary. I put a pillowcase on my chest to see if that was better, and immediately he fell asleep with a little satisfied sigh.
In this job, you need to keep a distance between you and the children. Your skin has to be soft enough to care, but hard enough to cope if they get worse, or die. And if they get better they will leave, so it's no good getting too attached. Not very professional either. But this one... It was impossible to not let my guard down. Night after

night he slept under my chin, wouldn't accept anything
else. I started to love him and dreaded the day he was
going to be well enough to leave.
I had never thought much about children of my own.
Until then.

One good thing came from my mental flu. Pontus and
Lisa finally realised that they both had grown and
changed. The love from Queenie and Camilla combined
with long talks with a good psychologist had stripped
Pontus of the insecurity that bothered Lisa, and she,
well... She was still intense and dramatic but less of a
besserwisser and didn't use strange words just to be
superior. The night Pontus brought me to tant Frida's
cottage, I heard them talk when they thought I was asleep.
The invisible wound from when she shut him out of her
life and the cottage was cleaned and healed.
-We all have our shields, she said. We try to protect
ourselves by building walls, not understanding that the
only way we can protect our souls is to surround ourselves
with people who love us, in environments that give energy
instead of stealing it. I'm so sorry that I denied you the
peacefulness of this place. I didn't understand how
important it was to you, or, I was too selfish to even think
about your feelings. Tant Frida's legacy isn't mine alone,
it belongs to you and Johan too. Do you think you can
forgive me?
The question was honest, not the usual "forgive me" you
would say as an excuse.
I could almost hear Pontus thinking before he said:
-Yes, Lisa, I think I can. We have been stuck in old
patterns. Maybe it's about time we got to know each other
all over again.
They spent the whole night talking in soft voices. Night
talk. The best therapy ever.

What a beautiful wedding!
The ceremony was held in an old church in the countryside outside Uppsala, and the party was in a house close to it. The guests were allowed to wear what they wanted, but the theme of the party was mediaeval. Instead of gifts, they had asked everyone to help out with decorating, cleaning, entertaining, bring something delicious for the buffet. I made the bread, everything gluten free, and got the great and frightening honour of creating the wedding cake. To my colleagues delight I spent months experimenting to make sure everything would be perfect. Not during my shifts of course, but someone had to try what I'd made. Camilla brought one of these cakes to the school where she's working as a secretary, but most of her colleagues were on diets and forbade her to bring anymore, ok, maybe just one or two more. Pontus fellow taxi drivers got several cakes but were of no help at all. ”Tell him that he has to make another one, this one won't do!” they criticized with greedy smiles and licked every crumble from the plates. In the end, I made a lemon and orange cake with rum cream, decorated with wild strawberries and edible flowers. No horrible sugar paste!
Lajvers can be very picky, and someone commented in an uppish tone that oranges didn't feel very mediaeval! Lisa pretended to agree, said that no, this was very troublesome, because oranges had been around since BC, which wasn't mediaeval. And South Asia wasn't mediaeval either, was it? Oh no, the whole party was ruined! Well, what did she know about mediaeval things, dressed in kimono as she was! This would have been a golden opportunity for Lisa to give a lecture, but she had matured enough to just smile and walk away. Later, she told me the reply she wanted to have given, and I'm glad for Pontus' and his guest's sake that she didn't.

Since I had the bread to focus on, and helped out a lot
with the rest of the food, I could relax and didn't have
time to be shy. Parties where you have to mingle and then
sit still at a table the whole evening, having polite and stiff
conversations with strangers, is another of those levels in
Dante's new inferno. Camilla however rose to her feet
and spoke to the whole room without hesitating. Her
mother is from Denmark, where they have a tradition to
let the bride give a speech to her new husband.
-My beloved Pontus. The first time I saw you, you had a
two-edged axe on your back, introducing yourself as
Ongulf the Dwarf, looking for the princess Bloomhilde. I
was her maid and had to bend my neck backwards to be
able to look you in the eyes, and I thought: "Don't bother
with the princess, I can be your queen!"
The guests laughed a little, and she went on:
-Today, I'm not only marrying the most magnificent
dwarf I've ever seen. Not only the man of my dreams, the
love of my life. I'm marrying my best friend! For better or
for worse, I know you will always be by my side, just as I
will be by yours. Infatuation might come and go in waves,
but our friendship is solid and will carry us through
everything.
You know how you can feel when someone is looking at
you?
My eyes searched the room. Lisa's thoughtful eyes met
mine. I know what that look means. She's got an idea.
I just didn't know what kind of idea.

One morning a couple of months after the wedding, Lisa
came to see me at work just when my shift had ended and
I was enjoying some newlybaked cardamom breakfast
rolls. I had invited her several times, just to show her
where I spend a great deal of my life, but she had been

busy so this was the first time. I was surprised but happy
to see her and invited her to join us in the staff room.
My colleagues know three things about me: I prefer to sit
in a room with a child all night if there's need for it, I
make great bread and I never say anything if I don't have
to. Lisa's surprise visit was like a gift to the ones that were
curious. Johan's friend? Girlfriend maybe? Please come
in, sit down and tell us everything about him! No, they
didn't say that. At least not in words.
She wasn't wearing any makeup today, no fancy hairdo or
clothes. Just her curly Mohican hanging softly over her
left cheek, and a maroon hooded sweater. She smiled at us
and said that no thanks, she just wanted to see if I would
like some company on my way home. She had been to the
early drop-in at the blood centre, donating blood.
I finished my roll and said goodbye to my colleagues.
Before we went out into the sunlight, I gave her a quick
tour around the ward
-How was your night?
I would never reveal any details to Lisa or anyone, but
she's bright enough to combine my short answers with the
news if something big has happened. Not a very good
night, combined with a story about a car accident with
children involved... Ah. No need to explain.
This morning I smiled at the morning sun, the warmth of
the little boy still lingering on my chest.
-It was good!
-Would you like to have children of your own?
-Hm?
-Would you?
We had never talked about these things before so I was a
bit startled.
-Sure, that would be wonderful, but... Well, I would need
someone to have them together with. Why do you ask?

She walked beside me, so quiet that I had to stop and look
at her.
-Lisa, what's the matter?
Flashback. My new, first girlfriend who looked at me,
serious like now, and told me that if she said something,
she meant it. Between the two of us, there should only be
honesty.
For a moment I thought that she had got pregnant, and
wanted to discuss her feelings about it with me, but I
didn't have time to react to that possibility before she
asked:
-Would you like to have a child with me?
She looked so vulnerable that I had to put my arms
around her. At the same time, it was a perfect way to buy
time. Thank the gods, she hadn't washed her hair with the
old lavender shampoo. If she had, I would have said yes
without thinking about it, just for the fear of losing her. I
mumbled into her hair, my voice unclear.
-How long have you had these thoughts?
-Long enough. My biological clock is ticking, it's getting
louder every day, and I can't shut it off even though I've
tried to. And this... all this entertaining nonsense with TV
and stuff... I don't know anymore. There must be
something more to life. I try to reason with myself, that it
would be selfish, but my whole body is yearning. We're
nothing more than biological creatures after all, right?
The meaning of life for all other species is to reproduce,
why should it be any different for us?
My mouth went dry and I let go of her.
-You want to use me for reproduction?
-No! No, Johan, that's not what I'm saying, I just...
Forget it!
Her voice was trembling and she started to walk fast.
-Then, what are you saying?!

-I'm saying that I... I could go to Denmark and pay for insemination, or I guess I could go to the pub and get drunk enough to drag some man with me into a wardrobe, or I could ask someone else, but, damn it, you're my best friend and... And I think you would be a terrific father. The best.
That might have been the greatest compliment I've ever got. However, I still felt rather uneasy.
She stopped.
-I'm so sorry. I have thought about this for months. In my head, I could explain everything to you. We wouldn't have sex or anything, there are other ways to do it. And... I'm so sorry. It all came out wrong. I wanted you to be the father of my child. Of *our* child. Not just a sperm donor.
I stroke her cheek, dried a tear that had escaped from the corner of her eye.
-Let me think about it?
-You're not mad at me?
-How could I ever get mad at you. Come here!
Once more she was in my arms.
No, Lisa, I can never get mad at you, not even when I've had reason to.
Sometimes I think that bottle in middlestage was magic, and that you cast a spell when it pointed at me.
Did you?

One of the reasons that I manage night shifts so well is that I'm able to sleep when I get home, almost no matter what. This thought was so huge and potentially life changing that I forced myself not to think about it. Don't think about it. Don't think about it. That mantra went through my head until I fell asleep and dreamed that I was pregnant, but I can't be, I'm a man, right?

I woke up far too early with a strange tingling feeling in my body. It felt like Christmas Eve morning, when you knew something exciting was going to happen. Had it been a dream? It must have been!
But I knew it wasn't.
Who could I talk to about this? Pontus? No, I didn't want to break into his newlywed bubble of happiness. My parents were out of the question. Amanda too, she was far too efficient and even though I probably would ask her for emotional support if this ever became true, these initial thoughts were far too intimate to share with my older sister. My younger sister, however...
Still in bed, I talked to her in my mind:
-Sara, help me sort my thoughts? Would it be selfish of us to do this? You know, the community has changed since I was a kid. More children have divorced or single parents now. Rainbow family is a concept. It's perfectly acceptable for a woman to go to abroad to get an insemination, and two women can get help with insemination at the hospital. Is this so terrible, then? We would both love the child, and I think our friendship is solid enough. What if I never meet someone else to start a family with? This might be my only chance.
Lisa had given me this chance.
What if she changed her mind and went to Denmark!
Something invisible punched my solar plexus.
Then I knew for sure that if Lisa was going to have a child, I wanted it to be mine!

Not fully awake, I brushed my teeth in a hurry and took my bike to tant Frida's cottage, praying that she would be there instead of at the farm with all the TV people.
She was.
The smile must have reached my ears, when I said to her:

-So, how do we do this?
-Do you want to?
-I do!
-Really? Are you sure?
-Totally. I just needed to sleep on it.
Lisa threw herself around my neck, and I lifted her up a few inches from the ground.
-We're going to have the most brilliant baby in the whole world! she laughed.
-Of course we are, I replied with confidence.
With a cup of Earl Grey in our hands, we sat close on the kitchen sofa and discussed the arrangement. The traditional way was out of the question for both of us. Lisa could have sex with some of her friends just for fun, but not with men. For me, the thought of that kind of intimacy with her made me shudder. I wouldn't say she was like a sister to me, but it still was unthinkable.
-There are several ways to do it. Some use a teaspoon, some use a plastic syringe. The syringe sounds more effective, and I'm not overjoyed with the thought of having to put a spoon in a place where you don't usually place spoons.
-Understandable! I can steal some syringes from work. And then, I...?
-You give me the seeds. I'll plant them.
The image made me laugh.
-Flowers and bees, right?
Lisa grinned.
-When we're done, we will have revolutionized how they teach biology in schools!

We created a strategy. Lisa would check her ovulation and let me know when the time was right. Then I would, hrm. Well. Try to get some seeds in a galipot, give them to her, and take a walk while she was planting them. None of us wanted me present during that procedure.

I'd read about ovulating when I was studying, but never thought that it would have something to do with me. Some mysterious female thing. Now I learned everything about it. Amazing how many get pregnant by accident when the "right time" is so short!

 Lisa didn't need any tools or kits from the pharmacy to know when she was ovulating. She just knew. "Don't ask me how." She says it's the same thing as being hungry, you know when you want to eat, right?

For me, it was much more difficult. To begin with, my libido isn't very strong. Furthermore, I'm shy even in front of myself. Believe it or not, when I take a shower I take a shower, nothing else, and I sleep with my hands on the cover, so to say. If I wake up from interesting dreams, I wait for it to calm down or take a cold shower. The thought of someone, anyone, knowing what I would have to do to produce these seeds wasn't exactly a turn-on either. The first time Lisa called me and said it was time, I was paralyzed. Couldn't bring myself to do it. She was concerned when she saw the look on my face when she came over. My tongue was completely glued to my palate, so I had to write to her to explain that she would have to ask somebody else. We had never talked about these things before, at least not from my point of view, so she had no idea that I didn't use to, hrm. You know.

-I'm so sorry, Johan. I didn't know. Are you sure you want to give up?

I just looked at her, miserably, unable to answer even in writing.

-Let us try a bit more? I'll think of something. Ok?

I nodded and she gave me a hug.

What she thought of was Miriam. Lisa had arranged for the two of us to take a walk, nothing more, and talk about what could be done. Miriam had also changed since we first met. She had spent time on different retreats and energy centres and learned so much about herself and ancient healing methods. Her voice and charisma was much softer.

-Lisa told me that your sexual energy is blocked, she said as if she was talking about a blocked nose.

-Mhm.

-Before I start any treatment, I want to know if this is her idea, or if it's something you want for yourself.

There was mist over the Fyris river and mist in my head. I tried to pretend that this was all happening in my mind. At the same time, I gave her question some serious thought. Sex seemed to be such a big deal to people. Maybe I'd been missing out on something all these years.

-For myself.

-Good. Then I would like to start with giving you a massage, to ease the tension in your whole body. You're very tense, you know.

No, I didn't know.

-Just a massage?

-Yes. You can keep your underwear, and bring some music you like.

Finally someone got to see my fancy boxer shorts!

With Porcupine Tree's Nine Cats on repeat, Miriam released me from years of tension. I had no idea that I was so stiff! After the first session it felt as if my whole body was disconnected. After the second, she asked if she could give me something called Rosen therapy. That's a kind of psycho-somatic bodywork that might help me to relax in my mind as well. The idea is that the body remembers everything the mind tries to forget, and that a sore back can be so much more than just physical. Sure, why not. I didn't believe in it, so what harm could it do?

A lot of harm, as it turned out.
No, I'm being unfair. It did me good in the end. But after the first session I could hardly stand, and as soon as I got back home – thank goodness Miriam still lived close – I had to drink three large glasses of water and ate a whole package of salty crackers at once. Then I fell on the floor and cried and tried not to throw up.
Many feelings hidden in my poor body.
All my instincts shouted at me to never do that again, to keep my guard up and my doors locked! But lying there on my old, beautiful wooden kitchen floor, I decided that it might be time for a change. Time to come out of my shell a little more. Time to get inside my shell a little more. So I went back, again and again, each time feeling a little better. It's hard to describe what it's like, and probably it's different for everyone. Miriam was so gentle, asked questions that I didn't have to answer to her, just to myself if I could.
 “Anger usually stays in the calves, yours feel almost as hard as a tree branch, do you keep any anger there?”
Oh yes, I thought. I was still angry with my mom. With everyone who hurt Pontus. With myself. With Bella. Not with Madeleine, I've finally come to peace with all that. Now I can even miss some of the things we had together. After one of these sessions, Miriam thought it was time to move on.
-Next time, I would like to come to your place, if that's ok with you. I'll look at your energies, and if I manage to unblock something, I will leave you alone.

The unblocking was done through zone therapy. A wonderful foot bath followed by massage, and then she started to follow some invisible lines that awoke something in me that I hadn't felt since...
Since I almost kissed Jörgen.

-Stop! I'm not ready for this!
Immediately she wrapped my feet in a soft towel.
-I'll come back three days from now. If you say no, I will respect that, so you don't have to worry.
She must have said that because she knew I wouldn't call her. So I waited for her.
Waited, and practiced.
I started with my hands. Looked at them, touched the skin, felt the muscles when I moved it, was grateful for them, without them I couldn't bake or work. Went on to my arms. My face. It felt good to rub my earlobes, they were so soft! I tried to think like Miriam, that I was beautiful and special, yet a small part of the great Universe, that pleasure was a part of life. I didn't even feel silly when I spent half an hour caressing my own chest. I felt as if I was fulfilling those words that are said to someone who's not feeling well. Take care. My friends had taken care of my soul, and Miriam taught me how to take care of my body.
The next time, she managed to set the energy free, and left just as she had promised.
Even though I had some good moments with Madeleine, it felt as if this was when I truly lost my virginity. This time, both my body and soul enjoyed it.

Lisa was discreet enough not to mention anything about my new relaxed appearance when I gave her the galipot the next time we decided to try. That first time I felt quite awkward giving it to her, knowing that she knew what I

had done, knowing what she was about to do with it. With
Springsteen's "Born in the USA" pounding in my MP3 I
took a brisk walk and could barely look at her when I got
back. We soon got used to it though, and created a
routine. After my walk, we cooked dinner together,
watched a movie or read something loud to each other,
and she spent the night in my bed, right next to me.
Harmonic and a bit weird at the same time.

Miriam hadn't been told why my energy needed to be
unblocked. Sara was still the only one who knew what we
were trying to do, so she was the one I talked to when we
still hadn't succeeded after more than a year. I whispered
to her white tombstone:
-I'm scared, Sara. I didn't know that you could yearn so
much for someone who doesn't even exist. What if there's
something wrong with me? Or worse, with Lisa? What
should I do?
As always, I felt I heard an answer within me. "Talk to
Lisa. She will understand."
The next time Lisa came home to me and stated that we
would have to try once more, could she *please* have some
dark chocolate *now,* I gave her the chocolate and carefully
suggested:
-Maybe it's time we had a check-up.
She sighed and took another bite.
-I guess so. You're aware of that they will check you first?
If there's nothing wrong with your seeds, then the
problem must lie with me.
I insisted on calling it seeds.
-But Johan, aren't you being a bit silly now, we've always
been able to say things straight?
-No! Not this time! I refuse! I won't do it if you use the
correct word!
-Ok, ok, I'll keep saying seeds. I promise.

I had already read everything about the procedure, and was incredibly grateful for living so close to the clinic that I could produce what they needed at home. I could never have been able to do it there, in a "secret" room with disgusting magazines and DVDs to inspire, while everyone knew what you were doing. It's not helping one bit that it's their job and are used to men producing test material. *I'm* not used to it!

Too many people in white clothes forget the patient perspective. Don't worry, little tant, I've seen naked breasts before. Maybe so, but nobody has seen this little tant's breasts since her husband died thirty years ago! She might not worry about the doctor, but about her own dignity.

Another way to gather seeds would be to use a vibrator, or a thin needle. Show me any man who doesn't wince when sharp things are mentioned in the same sentence as their private parts! So I did it at home, tried to pretend that this was just the usual routine, that these seeds were for Lisa and nobody else. She helped me by taking it to the clinic. I would have died on the spot if I'd met a colleague in the corridor!

The second Sunday in November is Father's day in Sweden. I spent the weekend in the cottage, preparing it for winter and playing Scrabble in candlelight. Lisa always wins. Her vocabulary is twice the size as mine. I went up before dawn to light the fire in the stove and crawled back into the kitchen sofa where I enjoyed the crackling sound of the fire, and how the warmth slowly spread into the room. It's luxury to wake up in a warm room in the town, but this definitely has its charm!

Lisa came into the kitchen in her slippers and padded yukata, and I moved my feet to make room for her. From the sleeve, she pulled out a small package and gave to me.

-It's nothing yet, you know that, but... Happy Father's Day anyway.
-The wrapping is marvellous! Did you learn this in Japan?
-Just open it.
-It would be a shame to destroy this.
-Open it! she growled and pinched my toes. I'm very ticklish so I laughed and nearly kicked her.
Inside the wrapping was a dark green velvet jewellery box. Inside the box, a plain golden ring.
My head was very still.
-Will you marry me, Johan?
Her soft voice startled me so I nearly dropped the beautiful box. I looked inquiringly at her.
-But if we don't succeed...
-Then I still want to spend the rest of my life with you. If you will have me. As I am.
She removed the ring from the velvet slit and took my left hand.
-Could I just... try it on?
I nodded, almost in trance.
She put the ring on my finger, pulled the yukata tighter around herself and asked anxiously:
-How does it feel? Is it too big?
Through the trance, a strange heat spread from the ring, through the finger and hand, into the arm and made my heart burn. I gasped and felt the tears behind my eyelids. The only thing I could think of to say was:
-I haven't got a ring for you.
-I... bought one for myself... just in case...
-Put it on.
-Are you sure?
-No. Let me put it on.
She took out a similar box from the other sleeve, with the exact same ring, only smaller.
Before I dared to land in this, I had to know:

-Are you absolutely certain of this, Lisa?
In that moment, she looked so small and fragile, not at all the tough street-smart Japanese model and TV star. She looked like the girl who had fallen asleep on my arm that very first day.
My god! She was my girlfriend again!
Suddenly I had so much more to lose if this was taken away from me.
-If I put this on, it'll be forever. No turning back. I won't allow you to change your mind. What if you fall in love with someone?
-If I fall in love, I will get up and brush it off! It's just infatuation, it's not for real and it will go away. I *am* in love! I love *you*! Love is an act of will, and I want to choose you, for all time and eternity! Please, don't reject me?
-I won't. Give me the ring.
Solemnly she placed the ring in my palm, and with equal serenity I put it on her thin ring finger and declared:
-I now pronounce us husband and wife to be!

Something had changed inside me. Miriam had showed me a new path. Not that I had become newagey, but I felt more content, more self confident, and I finally found a way to include myself in my small circle of friends. My personality hadn't changed though. I still liked to be on my own, but now it was an active choice, not a passive because I lacked driving force. I became more interested in other people when I wasn't stuck inside my own gloomy bubble. Yes, that's the best way to describe it! I had been living inside a bubble. A few people had managed to get inside it, but the rest of the world was beyond my reach except for a few moments of interaction. Mr Seagrove in Hastings had reached me. The little boy at work hold my heart in his tiny hand. Let's not mention

Jörgen, ok? Even my sister was a stranger. Miriam hadn't touched the bubble, but she showed me how to start destroying it.
Lisa's golden ring on my finger gave me the last key to liberate myself. As I said, love can be so easy when everything is right. We talked everything through. Gave each other the freedom to have other relationships to meet our physical needs. I wasn't sure I would use that freedom, but it was good to know that I wouldn't hurt her if I did. Also, I was relieved to promise her that she could do whatever she wanted with her friends, as long as it made her happy. As she said, if people can have sex without love, why couldn't we have love without sex? A marriage was a promise to take care of each other, respect each other, help each other, simply share your life with one another. In reality, it wouldn't be much different from what we already had, yet it was a huge change for me and the way I looked at myself.

Finally, mom had agreed to try some medication to break her depression. As you hopefully know, the medicines doesn't make you "happy", but they can help balancing the chemical substances in your brains, enabling you to cope with everyday matters. She was sad when she learned that Madeleine was gone. When she tried to convince me to patch it up, I chose to be honest. "Madeleine cheated on me, that's why we broke up." Oh. Ok then.
 My parents were happy to hear about the engagement. They like Lisa and I'm not sure they knew that she was gay. Dad clapped my shoulder and said something about how old love never dies. Amanda raised an eyebrow but congratulated us. Jörgen looked away and Pontus laughed out loud.
-Well, that's about time! You two have been like an old married couple since you were teenagers!

Leif and Kerstin got caught in an endless, boring discussion about divorce statistics and various wedding rituals. No thanks, you don't have to slaughter a goat, we're just going to the city hall one day with two witnesses. No big deal. We just want to be together. For the rest of our lives!

There was nothing wrong with my seeds, so they examined Lisa and found an intergrowth on her oviducts. A simple keyhole surgery would fix that and increase our chances of a natural pregnancy.
Lisa was terrified!
I've never seen her truly scared before. She was always the brave one, the one who had taken care of me, comforted me, thrown my girlfriend out, fixed everything. Now it was my turn to be strong. Not that fear makes you weak, but you know what I mean.
Sometimes it's my task at work to prepare the children who have surgery early in the morning. When I do, I never lie to them. Yes, it will hurt. Yes, it's scary. But we will try our best to make it hurt as little as possible. To respect their worries is to respect themselves. No need to be dramatic, just calmly tell them the way it is. I kept that attitude with Lisa. It didn't matter to her that the hole in her body would just be a few millimetres. There was still something wrong with her that someone else had to fix by opening her up and put strange tools into her, and they would have to sedate her and she would lose control! She always had control, even during her BDSM-experiments. At work, we use a method called guided imagination. It's almost like a very mild form of hypnosis. Someone talks to the children or ask questions in a very soft voice, trying to distract them from the unpleasant thing that has to be done with them, like taking blood tests or giving them a

shot. I tried that with Lisa when I was sitting by her side, waiting for them to sedate her. I talk very slow and soft when I do this, and, I don't stammer when I do it, come to think of it. Interesting. Maybe loosening my vocal cords ease the tension on some nerves?
-Describe a scent that makes you feel relaxed!
-Mm... Your bread, Johan! When I smell your bread, it's like there's no evil in the world.
-Ah, thank you, that was kind of you to say! Now, imagine that you've been on a wonderful walk in the forest. When you come inside, you feel the scent of freshly baked bread with rye and honey. Can you see how beautiful the kitchen table is? Tant Frida's embroidered table cloth with autumn leaves, and the candlestick is lit.
-Be careful with the tablecloth!
-Of course, the candlestick stands on a tray, the old silver tray that you found in the attic, remember?
Lisa had almost fallen asleep, but suddenly looked at me with her greengray eyes wide open.
-I want to sign you up for a TV baking contest!
A ball of fear bounced inside me but I wanted to get her back to the calm state so I played along.
-Ok, you sign me up. What happens next?
-You get in, you win challenge after challenge and wipe the floor with everyone in Sweden who think they can make better bread than you and you will win and get overloaded with fan mail and marriage offers but you're mine, only mine...
She closed her eyes again and they came to take her away.

Lisa's engagement ring hung in safe keeping in a chain around my neck during the surgery. It felt weird to be at the hospital in my private clothes. Strange to be on the other side, to be family. I walked along the corridors,

trying to look at them from a new perspective.
When I got tired of that, I went to my ward. They had morning fika with knäckebröd, the typical Swedish crispbread.

-Johan, how nice to see you in daylight!

I sat down in the sofa, felt a rare need to talk.

-I was just passing by... or... my fiancé is having surgery, and... it was a bit tough on the nerves, just walking around, waiting.
You know the expression "so quiet that you can hear a needle fall"? This was it. To hear me telling them something about myself was like a sudden rain in the desert. Someone poured me a cup of tea. Blue fruit. Hot perfume. I drank it anyway, grateful for the gesture.
-Is it a big surgery?
I could see their wish in their eyes: "Please, dear patients, don't press the Red Key, we have much more important things to do! We need to hear about this!"
-No, not really, just a laparoscopy. It's still a bit scary though, with the sedation and everything. I don't want her to feel sick when she wakes up. And there's always the possibility that something goes wrong, or that they find anything more that's not as it should be.
My golden ring glimmered in the lamp light. We're not allowed to wear rings or watches when we're on duty, so nobody had seen it until now.
-But, Johan! What's this? Have you got married?
-No, not yet, but we got engaged about a month ago, and we've been trying for some time to have a baby, but...
The whole story flowed out of me, except the small details of exactly how we had tried. I told them that we had been teenage sweethearts, stayed friend all these years and

found that we still loved each other and belonged together.
My colleagues were exalted!
-How romantic! Is it that pretty girl that came to see you one morning? She seemed so sweet! You have to let us know when the wedding is, we would like to give you something!
Never could I have guessed how good it felt to share my worries and joys with people I didn't know outside work! They didn't know me either, but they cared about me and wanted me to be happy. Not that I had thought the opposite, but to hear it aloud gave me a lump in my throat.
My mobile phone vibrated in my back pocket.
-She's about to wake up now. I have to go. Thanks for the tea!
-Thanks to you too! Say hello from us! And we'll keep our fingers crossed!

The surgery had gone well. There shouldn't be any more obstacles. So, buy some champagne and get to work, nudge nudge!
Lisa giggled, still a bit dizzy but relieved beyond belief that this was over. Get to work, you bet! But maybe we should skip the champagne, might be difficult to find the right hole with too much party bubbles in your veins!
I shushed her but couldn't hide a smile.

A couple of weeks later, someone called and introduced themselves but I didn't listen properly. Test filming? No, sorry, you must have got the wrong person, you want to talk to Lisa. No? What was that again? A TV show about baking? They had got my application and thought I might be suitable? If I could come to Stockholm for test filming and an interview, preferably sometime this week?

-I have to check my calendar and get back to you.

Slowly I shut the phone down.
I didn't think she had been serious.
One year ago, I would have declined without hesitating. Now, I wasn't so sure. Yes, the thought of standing in front of a camera was terrifying, especially with my speech defect. But if I looked into the future, I wanted to be able to say to my child that it was ok to claim space even if you weren't so called perfect. My preschool teachers would cheer if they heard me now. Yay, Johan wants to claim space! Finally!
When Lisa got home, I asked her:
-Whatever did you write in your application letter?
She tried to look innocent but she didn't fool me for a second.
-Just told them about you.
-They never let mediocrities be in a show like that.
-You're no mediocrity.
-Of course I am!
-No, you're not! You're special and wonderful in every way!
(Hey, Lisa, don't ruin the title of my book now!)
-Just tell me what you wrote?
-Do you want to do the test film? You don't have to. I just wanted you to have the choice.
-Seriously. Why did you send it?
She took my face between her hands.
-Because you have a lot to say. And you're very good at baking, especially the gluten free. TV has a great impact. You could inspire people.
-To do what?

-To relax. To try new things. I don't know. It was just a vision I got while listening to your voice when I waited for the surgery.

I don't approve of these shows where the one who is considered the weakest has to leave in each episode. Especially not when young people are involved. They put their heart and soul into a performance, just to be told by bored celebrities in the jury that they suck and would be better off flipping burgers somewhere.

King of the Hill is not my kind of game.

Is that the kind of community we want? Where only the best, the strongest, the quickest, the most popular gets to stay? If we don't, why are there so many TV shows about it? The Japanese show from the farm is so much better. Nothing about being best, everything about cooperating and learning new things. Why can't our shows be more like that?

-Another reason for you to join. You're not desperate, you wouldn't do anything to win. You would be in it for the sheer joy of baking. If you manage to bring that about, you have contributed a lot to the turning of these victimization shows!

I called Pontus.

-Bring Pont-du-John. He's got a gigantic task in front of him.

-What?

-He's about to become a TV star!

With the knight in my pocket, I went to the casting. Reality TV, the mediocrity's chance for his fifteen minutes in the limelight.

Apparently, I filled some demographic hole. After testing my basic knowledge and making a camera test, they accepted me. Oh yes, I heard them mumble – his speech defect? Wouldn't this be too much of blemish comedy?

No no, people like that, it's folksy, and someone has to leave in the first episode, right? Someone like him can never handle the pressure.
No? Well, bring it on! I'm ready to prove you wrong!

Maybe you've seen these types of cooking or baking shows. They're more or less the same. Some elements we're allowed to practice at home and choose the ingredients in advance, but there are also some difficult moments where our skills are put to the test and we were supposed to know about everything. The stranger pastries, the better. The more we sweat in agony, the more entertainment for the viewers!
My friends and some colleagues were the only ones who knew that I was going to participate, and they gave me one challenge after the other. Strudels! Bagels! Filled donuts with homemade raspberry jam! Naan! Brandy wreaths! We went through tant Frida's ancient cooking book, searched the internet and asked the local Italian restaurant for recipes. I got the strangest challenges, like how to incorporate beetroots into cinnamon buns, or a sugar free wedding cake, or potato waffles. I had so much fun! Of course I could take some time off during the filming weeks, don't worry, we will all cheer for you!

The only thing I didn't like was when they wanted to film me in my home, to introduce me to the viewers. My private home? I know I signed the contract, but I don't have to like everything in it! I was in a foul mood. Lisa saved me by talking to the Japanese, asking to borrow the farm for a day. Yes, she could, if she would be in the picture wearing these particular clothes and they could buy the rights to send the show in Japan. A win-win situation!
Secretly, I was pleased. Childish of me, I know, but I liked

the idea of showing the world that the mediocrity Johan
had a cool girlfriend. She looked so bizarre in the
Japanese street outfit with purple lipstick on just the
middle part of her mouth, and a hairdo that made me
think of birds in the rainforest. The cows mooed and I
laughed. She pretended to be offended and tripped away
with tiny steps. Then she turned around and shouted:

-Black Forest cake! A real black forest cake, with dark
chocolate and cherry jam, you need to practise making
one of those. I'm sure it will be one of the challenges!

I couldn't figure out why I was one of the ten amateur
bakers who stood there in the kitchen that first day!
We filmed in an old, beautiful baroque castle that had
been rebuilt into a conference hotel. The kitchen was
amazing! Apparently, they used it for exclusive cooking
classes. The winner would get a free weekend class.
Like a good cop and a bad cop, there was one very sweet
host who made everyone feel good, and one sadistic who
enjoyed making everyone even more nervous. There were
also three judges with huge egos who couldn't stand each
other in private, but managed to be civilised when the
cameras were rolling. There was a mingle party the night
before the filming started. I stayed in my king size bed in
the luxurious hotel room, faking a headache, not wanting
to admit that I had a panic attack. A knock on my door
almost made me fall out of bed. At first, I didn't want to
open up, but then I thought that it might be the producer,
telling me that sorry, they had made a big mistake and had
to send me home. Hopeful, I got up and opened.
Outside was a very short little tant, with grey curls and a
little worn hand bag.

-Hello dear, I'm Laura, one of the participants. I just
wanted to check on you, they said you had a headache.
Such a shame! How are you feeling?
She didn't look like tant Frida at all, but she gave me the
same feeling of comfort so I relaxed a bit. My stammering
was worse than ever, though.
-Not so good.
-Oh, dear! Have you taken anything for it?
I shook my head, didn't want to lie to this sweet creature.
-Can I offer you some Aspirin?
-No thanks, I just need to sleep.
-I won't bother you, then. Good night, my dear!
-Good night! And... Thanks for checking in on me!
She smiled and I think I saw a gold tooth.
Somehow, this made me feel better and I managed to fall
asleep.

Our first challenge was to make a genuine Black Forest
cake. Without a recipe, we were to choose from a table
with all sorts of ingredients and from them compose a
cake as close to the original as possible. There were
pineapples, butter, eggs, apples, maple syrup, brandy,
marshmallows... You name it.

In German, it's called Schwarzwälder Kirschtorte. But in
Sweden, we have something called just Schwarzwaldtårta,
with meringue, whipped cream and thin square chocolate
decorations. Not a cherry in sight. So when they asked us
to make a genuine Schwarzwaldtårta, I smiled a bit to
myself and went for the black cherries and a small bottle
of Kirschwasser. When I saw the others look at me, I took
some lemon curd, white chocolate and two lemons as
well, just to confuse them.
Hans, the bad cop, came to disturb me when I was making
my cherry jam.

-You're not making any meringue?
-Nope.
-It seems like all your comrades are making meringue.
-Not my problem.
-It might be.
I looked up for a second and saw a pair of vicious eyes.
Something told me that I instantly had managed to rub
him the wrong way. Pont-du-John stood on the bench,
encouraging me to answer where it might have been
better to shut up.
-There's no meringue in a genuine Schwarzwaldtårta.
-Are you sure?
-Positive.
Hans left, with a look on his face that probably was
supposed to make me feel insecure. I just shook it off.
Laura had the bench behind me and I heard her whisper
to me:
-Good! Don't let him get to you!
I smiled a little to her, and looked at her bench. The
ingredients were for the Swedish Schwarzwald with
meringue. Without a word, I gave her the bottle with
what was left of the Kirschwasser, and three cherries that I
could afford to lose.
Startled, she asked:
-What's this?
-Trust me.
At the judging, I was the only one who had made a
genuine Schwarzwaldtårta. Laura came second. A very
clever move, to mix the Swedish and the genuine version
like this! Kirschwasser in the whipped cream, and the
cherries on top, how original!
This gave the production team a big problem though. I
was supposed to be the first one to leave! They couldn't
send me home after this!

I'd signed a contract where I promised to not reveal too much about the recording methods, and of course not what happens in the show before it's aired, but if you check the aftertext you will see a fine print text for about a tenth of a second stating that the judges decide the outcome together with the production team, so it's no secret.

Laura gave me a hug when the cameras had shut down.

-Thanks!

-You're welcome.

I didn't like the time pressure either, so I used Amanda's method. Before each challenge I took a deep breath and made a plan. Hans mocked me for it.

-You always do this, why is that? Will you forget if you don't write it down?

-I want to know how much time I have for each moment. Bread isn't something you're supposed to rush.

He laughed and looked around the room where the other competitors ran around like dizzy chicken.

-So, what's the secret?

-There is no secret. Make the best bread you can, and forget this competition nonsense.

No, no, you can't say that! Cut! This is a competition! Start over!

-So, what's the secret?

I tried to choose my words, but I had to repeat:

-Just make the best bread you can.

-So, what would you do if you've miscalculated? If there's only five minutes left and you know your bread needs at least another six minutes in the oven?

I put down my pencil and looked him straight into the eyes. As you may remember, I don't do that a lot.

-I leave it in the oven.

-Even if that means you're out of the competition?

-Yes.
-But someone else might have a bread worse than yours?
Steel in my eyes.
-I would never present an underbaked bread. No matter
what!

Famous Last Words.

Challenge after challenge I did well enough to hang in
there, to the producers' discontent. Laura was a sweet
little tant. There was an ex-con with tattoos to his chin
who had started baking in prison and scared the hell out
of me when he was kneading his dough, treating it like an
enemy. One woman from Somalia who came to Sweden
as a refugee only two years ago. A pair of twins who went
to business school. Big personalities, great TV. Except for
me. When the show was aired, not much was written
about me in the social medias. As far as I'm concerned, no
publicity is good publicity but that's not how producers
think.

In the fourth episode, things took an unexpected turn.
One of the challenges each day, or each week for the
viewers, was that we got all the ingredients in exact
measurements on our bench, but no recipe and no
instructions. We had to figure out for ourselves what we
were supposed to do and how.
Butter. Sugar. Eggs. Wheat flour. Vanilla sugar. Baking
powder. Milk. Lemon zest. Vanilla pod.
I put my pencil down and left the kitchen.
One cameraman was fast on his feet and followed me with
a portable camera. So did the good cop, Amira. This
could be good!

According to Lisa, I had chosen a very picturesque scene, when I sat down on the stone stairs outside the castle with my head in my hands.
Amira sat down beside me.
-What's the matter, Johan?
Her voice was soft as velvet. She's just as nice when the cameras are turned off.
Deprecatingly, I shook my head. Couldn't speak.
-Did you get a blackout?
I pulled myself together and tried to explain. Not the whole truth, but close enough.
-No. But... I haven't made madeleines since... My sister... She died, and I was baking because I didn't know what to do with the pain. It just... struck me now.
A hand on my arm.
-She must have been very special.
I nodded, had to hide my face against my arm because I felt the tears coming.
Amira told the cameraman to turn it off for a minute. Then she said to me:
-Not everyone knows that you're supposed to do madeleine cakes. If you feel strong enough, and if you can increase the tempo just a little bit, then go inside and make them. You won't be leaving us today.
Then she nodded. The camera could roll again.
-Make her proud, Johan. Bake for her!
I dried the tears on my apron and stood up. Looked into the camera with red eyes.
-Sara. This is for you. I love you!
The producers were delighted! Here they could add a picture of me and Sara. Oh, did she have Down syndrome? Even more perfect! Heart-warming! Finally!

The next step on the popularity ladder was my favourite: Gluten free!
Full of joy I went through the different kinds of flour they had presented us with. Laura looked lost, like many others. I tried to whisper some hints, but didn't get any good opportunity to help her. I made an African plate with Somali sorghum bread and Pontus' favourite, the small flat Ethiopian teff bread. Throughout the entire session I was smiling, and I got a lot of camera time. Hans' antipathy against me hadn't decreased one bit.
-You've done this before, I guess. Not much of a challenge then.
I was too happy to come with a sharp reply. I smiled at him and said:
-Nope!
Which of course annoyed him even more.
I won that contest, and those recipes got the most hits of all on the show's website. Winning didn't matter so much to me, but I was delighted to show people that you can do so much without wheat. Unfortunately, the lady from Somalia had left us, but she sent me a thank you note when she had seen the episode.

With five of us left, the contest moved to another part of the castle: The old museum kitchen!
Hans almost looked sadistic when he explained:
-Today, you're going to make a bread... without electricity!
Terrified gasps, agony, protests, what do you mean, how are we supposed to do that! You can't be serious!
I just shrugged and got started. Sure, the five ovens were huge, much bigger than tant Frida's, but the principle should be the same. Put in some wood, let it burn out, shove the ashes further back into the oven, and repeat. That would give the right temperature. To knead by hand

was a matter of technique rather than strength, so even if I wasn't nearly as strong as the thug, I managed alright. Laura looked miserably at the oven. She had no idea what to do. We had kept helping each other since that first day, discreetly, but this time it was impossible to hide the cooperation.

-Do you want me to help you?

Hans meddled.

-You're not trying to cheat now, are you?

Usually, I'm a calm person, but this man was so annoying! He had been out to get me since that very first day. I'd had it!

-If helping your friend is cheating, then you can have this stupid contest to yourself! I'm out!

Short crisis meeting. In a way, this was good TV, but it sort of took the focus off the cool thing with the ancient ovens. Ok, Hans, stay away and we'll take it from where you offer Laura your help!

Yes, please, she would love some help!

The others almost turned themselves inside out to see what we were doing, trying to not let us know they were studying us. I didn't mind. As I said, I think it would have been a much nicer show if we could help each other.

The quick challenge while we were waiting for the breads was to make wafers with an old wafer iron.

I just laughed.

The next day, we were video chatting with our beloveds in front of the camera. Laura's grandchildren waved and showed her a drawing they made of her with a tower of cinnamon buns. Lisa was wearing some fancy designer yukata and an incredible makeup that made her look like a maiko. She had something in her hand. I tried to see what it was. A kind of pen? A thermometer?

Laura, with all her grandchildren, knew exactly what it was.
-Oh, Johan! Congratulations!
-What?
Lisa laughed on the screen.
-Finally! You're going to be a father!
I got up to kiss the screen, but my brains and body were disconnected and I fell on the floor. There I let it all sink in, and I screamed out of pure joy, my feet hammering on the carpet, giving thousands of YouTube watchers a good but friendly laugh.
The challenge that followed these greetings was to make something inspired by someone we loved. I just had to do a chilli cupcake with green sencha frosting and a cherry on top, as a joke. One of the judges loved it, the others hated it but I didn't care. I had made it for Lisa and she would have given me eleven points out of ten. The last point for originality.

This isn't a story about the underdog winning the contest against all odds. It's a story about the mediocrity who knew more than he thought he did, who wanted to teach his future child that it's better to do your best and be happy with that, than to do something sloppy just because someone tells you that time is up. Time is never up. Time is unlimited, and when my bread needed two extra minutes in the oven on that very last challenge before the finale, I left it in the oven. Amira almost had tears in her eyes, please Johan, just take it out, I'm sure it will be ok, please?
I refused, and the judges had an easy job that day. With nothing to show, I was out.
Never has anyone been so happy to leave a contest! I looked into the camera and shouted:
-Lisa, allrakäraste! I'm coming home!

Surprisingly soon, the whole thing seemed like a surreal dream.

Laura and I kept in touch, and I invited her to the wedding. We had changed our mind, and wanted a small picnic wedding in the arbour. The guests sat on blankets on the grass. My family, Lisa's parents and some of her friends, Miriam, Pontus and Camilla. I made the wedding cake, of course. Lime and chilli. Laura knew a judge who was willing to come to the forest and marry us, bribed with the promise of her cinnamon buns. She had got up at dawn to make them, a whole basket! She lived in a suburb north of Stockholm so it wasn't very far.

Our wedding gift to the guests was to tell them about the pregnancy. Laura knew, but nobody else. Mom got tears in her eyes and gave me a hug, the first since I can't even remember. Amanda looked a bit intrigued, and Jörgen... He had something in his eyes that I preferred to ignore. Everyone else was happy for us and cheered.

Lisa's gift to me was a bottle of lavender shampoo.

-You seemed to like this. I found it in a retro shop online.

I opened the bottle, closed my eyes and smelled the familiar scent. I wish my teenage self could have seen me now!

Then I looked up and met Jörgen's eyes.

Maybe I didn't want the innocent Johan to know about this, after all.

Friends. We had chosen to be friends.

And this was my wedding day. The existence of my future child had just been announced.

There are several ways to be happy.

You can't have it all, can you?

In Sweden, there are free classes to prepare you for parenthood, with plenty of time for questions and discussions. Lisa refused to go to any of them. She could ask her friends, she didn't want to sit in a group and practice breathing, or talk about the importance of reading books to your babies, or watch some vintage film with men dressed in velour telling her how important the father was. Shove that! She refused to take part in anything that was so stuck in heteronormality! No, she didn't want to go to a rainbow group, why do we have to be divided, why can't we all simply be humans! Pregnancy didn't become her very well. She had heartburn, swollen limbs, haemorrhoids, nasal congestion, nausea and mood swings. One moment she snapped at me, the next she cried and asked me to hold her and assure her that I still loved her. In my eyes, she was more beautiful than ever!

I went to a class, because I wanted to learn everything I possibly could. However, both the leader and the other participants were so disturbed by me coming alone. That was too suspicious and strange, so I left during the fika. Instead I joined a group on an internet forum, with people expecting their babies the same month as we. There was a special group for fathers, but I agree with Lisa, why separate us into men or women, gay or straight, single or couple? Sometimes it can fill its purpose if you want to discuss something that only people in a similar situation would understand, but mostly, I was no more than a human, trying to prepare myself, wanting to share my worries and thoughts and joys. I didn't hide the fact that I'm a man, and soon, the others in the group got used to it. "Hello girls and Johan", they often started their posts, and I think they even liked having me there. They asked me all sorts of things, and asked me to try to explain to

them why their own men behaved in a certain way. For
the first time ever, I felt the joy of being part of a group!
Sure, the choir had been a group but this was different.
We talked about our days. Our thoughts and dreams. Of
the trouble with finding comfortable clothes. Of pain and
sleeplessness. I keep to my rhythm where I'm awake
during the nights, and spent hours comforting crying
mothers-to-be via internet. When I was away for a few
days, staying with Lisa, they said they missed me. I was
completely hooked and had my laptop on all the time
when I was in my own flat. I saw Lisa almost every day,
but we both needed time to ourselves so moving in
together had never been a part of the deal. Needless to
say, I would be with her and the baby as much as possible
after the birth, but the plan was to give the child two
homes from the beginning. Sometimes he or she would
stay with us both in the cottage or in the flat, sometimes it
would be just me or just Lisa. That was plan A anyway.
But when you work in a children's hospital, you're
uncomfortably aware of the fact that life can change in an
instant. I didn't talk to anyone about it, but I often
thought of all the things that could be wrong with the
baby. I've seen so much. Secretly I made plans for every
eventuality. Filled the freezer, just in case we would have
to stay in the hospital for months and didn't want to buy
readymade food every day. Repeated how to handle an
ostomy, if there was something wrong with the guts or if
the anus was deformed. Practiced cup feeding. To have a
normal, healthy baby was something I didn't consider a
possibility. There must be something wrong, right?

In the fall, there were TV trailers about the baking show.
Mom called and demanded to know why I hadn't told her
about it.

Amanda called and asked if I was out of my mind.
Madeleine called and asked if we could fika.
Most of the moms-to-be on internet watched the show and discussed it vividly. It was a bit awkward. Should I reveal that the cute guy who seemed so insecure was in fact their buddy? They didn't know what I looked like, and didn't connect my avatar of Pont-du-John with the little knight figurine on the workbench that Hans made fun of. If I waited too long and they said more things about me I would embarrass them, but if I told them, perhaps they would look at me in a different way. Fortunately, they focused on the bread more than the participants. It wasn't until that episode where I screamed on the floor that I had to show my hand. "It was so cute, did you react that way, Johan?" followed by a smiley. I thought about what to say, but decided to be honest. Well, actually, that's exactly how I reacted.
My internet friends were startled but excited and asked me a thousand questions that I only partly was allowed to answer. Yes, Amira was just as nice as she seemed. Hans? Sorry, I don't want to get sued for defamation, I can't say anything. Why I helped Laura? She helped me as well, many times. And just look at her, wouldn't you have done the same?
When I was out, they all shouted NOOO with capital letters, which made me feel rather good! And as I told them, I left with my head held high and my integrity intact.

The first quarrel Lisa and I had was about where she would give birth.
She wanted a home birth, I insisted that she should go to the hospital.
-I'm not sick, Johan! People have given birth in their homes for thousands of years!

-Sure, and look at the statistics! How many of them died in childbirth?

-There's always a risk involved! And in the hospital, people are coming in and out of the room all the time, your neighbour might have the flu, and a midwife has to run around trying to help several women at the same time, how safe is that?

-Ask me that when we stand here in the middle of the forest and the baby is stuck!

-Don't you *dare* scare me even more! I'm terrified, Johan! You have no idea! Just... Leave me alone!

-No, I won't! *You* have no idea! And if you're terrified, the more reason to go to a hospital where there are doctors to help you if something goes wrong!

Our fears crashed. She was afraid to go to the hospital, I was afraid to lose them both.

In the end, she gave in when she saw how worried I was. First, I was relieved. Then I saw how bad she felt, and it was my turn to back off. Ok, Lisa. We'll do it your way. But please, let me make all the arrangements with the midwife?

Overwhelmed with relief, Lisa left everything to me.

In Sweden, home births are very rare, only about 100 every year which is 0,1%. In the Netherlands, about a third of the births take place at home, so with my intellect I knew that it could be safe and undramatic. My imagination wouldn't listen, though. I asked if I could go beside a nurse assistant in the maternity ward for a shift or two, claiming that it would be good for me professionally to widen my views. No problem, they liked that attitude! In that way, I had at least a tiny bit more experience than before. I also talked to the midwives in the area that worked with home births, and they gained my trust. And naturally, if anything happened, they would call for an ambulance! While I kept my fingers crossed that they would find their way in the forest.

It was four thirty in the morning when Lisa came out to me in the kitchen where I was doing crosswords. The last two months I'd spent every night off with her, and when I was at work, I insisted that she slept in my flat or had someone else with her. It was quite enough with this home birth, I couldn't bear the thought of her having to walk to the main road to be able to make the necessary phone calls. The last weeks, I took time off from work. I never knew what I should do with my vacation days, so they had piled up.

-I think it's time. Could you please call the midwife? No rush, but the contractions are regular now.
This was light years from the sitcoms. A contraction! Panic and rush to the hospital! Lisa had contractions for several days, but assured me that it was just the pre-contractions. Now it felt like the real thing, so we should make preparations.
You know the stereotype where men have to build things when their women are expecting? If they can't build something with their hands, they start working out or jogging. I didn't have that problem, because there was always something to do with the cottage. But I did prepare. Bought an old car that Pontus helped me fix, so that we wouldn't be stuck in the forest. Filled the outhouse (not the sanitary outhouse though) with water containers. Chopped more wood than ever before. It's one thing to have a baby in your home if it had modern facilities, and something else when you had to go back a hundred years in time.
The midwife on duty was just as calm as Lisa and said that she was on her way.

I can't even begin to describe the magic and the power in the cottage that day!
Lisa was so calm and so beautiful. Sometimes she screamed, not out of fear or unbearable pain, but because it empowered her. Sometimes she wanted to lie down and rest, and the midwife told me to do the same. Difficult to obey, I wanted to *do* something, but I tried. Sometimes Lisa wanted to take a walk around the cottage with me. I gave her a back rub, and when she asked me to bake something, I did.
-I want our baby to be born to the scent of newly baked bread, she whispered with a smile.
Just when I took the rolls out, it was time.
Lisa sat on a horseshoe-shaped stool with me supporting her back, and plastic sheets covering the wooden floor.
Then she arrived, our little girl.
Exhausted, Lisa told the midwife to give her to me while she was catching her breath. I opened my shirt, placed her right over my heart and covered her back and head with a soft towel.
Time stopped.
For that short eternity, there was just us. Her and me.
Her heartbeat against mine.
I've never felt so empty as when I had to hand her over to Lisa a few minutes later. At the same time, I've never felt so rich!

It's three fifteen, pitch dark and little Sara Frida Felicia is sleeping under my chin, satisfied after her night meal. Both she and Lisa are struggling with breastfeeding. It doesn't go very well, so in the night time, I step in and feed her with a special cup. Good thing I thought about practicing!
Yes, night time is our time. She's so content here on my chest. My daughter. My life!

We asked Pontus and Camilla to be godparents. Again, it's got nothing to do with Christianity, it's just an honorary title. They moved in with Pontus' mother in the big stone house, and something in their eyes when they look at Felicia tells me that it might not be long before they start a family themselves.
-I'll let you be the test pilot, Pontus joked and punched me on the arm.
-Speaking of test, the book is nearly done.
-What book?
-My autobiography, remember? You challenged me. You and Camilla. And you only have yourself to blame if you don't like what I wrote about you.
-About me? Wasn't it supposed to be about you?
-Well, I cheated.
He went a bit pale.
-You're not serious?
-I sure am.
-You're not going to publish it?
-I sure am.
-You've got to let me read it first!
-I will, if you're nice.
He punched me again and laughed.
-You sly bastard!

This is not the only book I'm about to write. There might be a combined recipe/art book, with pictures of my bread and of Lisa in Japanese clothes, set in the farmhouse. It's all so new that it hasn't sunk in yet.

Felicia brought a new sparkle in my mom's eyes, and dad looks happier than in a very long time. He has made a beautiful cradle and is working on a rocking horse. Amanda and Jörgen has temporarily moved to Gothenburg to continue their studies. I miss them and I often chat with Amanda. It seems that we needed the distance to get to know each other as individuals rather than siblings.

I'm happier than I thought possible, so I'll leave you here. If I keep on writing, the story might take unwanted turns, leaving me bitter and alone while Lisa has found the true love of her life and moved to Hawaii with Felicia after a violent custody fight. Or, by all means, with me, unleashing hidden passions, destroying everything. Let's not go there. Let's keep this fragile happiness for as long as possible. Right now, everything is perfect.
By the way, I don't feel like a mediocrity anymore. I intend to be the best father in the world to Felicia! And I'll try my very best to be a good husband to Lisa. Even though our marriage is unconventional, our love for one another is sincere and we bring out the best in each other. There are probably much worse wedlocks than ours!

Felicia is grumbling on my chest.
What's the matter, sweetheart?
Maybe she wants to remind me to let go of the past and
not think too much about the future. Maybe I won't end
up bitter and alone, so what's the use worrying about that
now?
Something is said about today being a gift, that's why it's
called "present".

Today is indeed a present.
A present that needs a clean diaper.

I don't know if I've managed to prove Camilla's statement
or not, to make a mediocrity's life interesting to read
about.
That's for you to decide.

Thank you and Good night!

Karin Oswald is born in Västervik in 1972. She lives in Uppsala with her husband and two children, where she's working as a child specialist nurse assistant at Akademiska Barnsjukhuset.

Earlier books:

Gravid, 2009 - a comic book about being pregnant

Lajv, 2010 - a comic book about LARP

Välkommen till Mysteria, 2012 - a true story about autism

En medelmåttas bekännelser, 2015 - the shorter Swedish version of this book, written during National Novel Writing Month

Glimpses from a Children's Hospital/Glimtar från ett barnsjukhus, 2016 - a bilingual prose poem book about her work

Thanks to:

* My dear friend Weronica Fremenius for the beautiful cover photo!

* Magnus Simonsson for the portrait!

* Everyone who has helped me check the prepositions and adverbs! Johan's struggle with the language was also mine.

Karin Oswald, November 7 2016